THE KILLING LOOK

THE KILLING LOOK

J.D. Rhoades

Copyright © 2021 by J.D. Rhoades
Cover and jacket design by 2Faced Design

ISBN 978-1-951709-49-5
eISBN: 978-1-951709-67-9
Library of Congress Control Number:
available upon request

First hardcover edition August 2021 by Polis Books, LLC
44 Brookview Lane
Aberdeen, NJ 07747
www.PolisBooks.com

POLIS BOOKS

To my good friend Terrence McCauley,
who inspired this departure from the usual

CHAPTER ONE

The over-and-under barrels of the little pocket gun were small, but they were pointed directly between Cade's eyes, so he reckoned either one was sufficient for the job. He took a deep breath and willed himself to look behind those dark circles and into the sweating face of the young man who held the pistol. The fellow's eyes were unfocused with the effects of the cheap whiskey Cade could smell—hell, almost see—coming off him. Even a drunk could pull a trigger, if only by accident, so Cade kept his breathing even and his outward manner calm.

The young man had come stumbling backward out of a deadfall, one of the hundreds of unlicensed saloons that infested the Barbary Coast. From the shouted command "and STAY out!" it was clear he hadn't been leaving on his own accord. The ejection was accomplished with such vehemence that the young man crashed into Cade with enough force to nearly send both of them into the street. San Francisco had paved a lot of its streets, but a stumble into one of them would still likely leave a man cursing and scraping horseshit from his boots. Cade barely avoided that aggravation by shoving the drunkard off him, then teetering for a moment on the plank sidewalk before regaining his balance. When he straightened up, he found himself facing the man who'd stumbled into him.

The man wasn't contrite. In fact, he seemed to take Cade impeding his retrograde progress as a personal affront. "Why'n't you

7

look where you're goin', you son of a bitch?"

Cade looked him over. He was a scrawny little cuss, dressed in a frock coat and bowler hat that both looked too fancy for the Coast. A young swell out slumming, no doubt. He looked game enough, but Cade figured, given his own height, weight, and sobriety advantage, he had little to worry about.

All of those calculations had gone out the window when the drunkard produced the derringer.

"Easy, son," Cade said in a calming voice.

"I ain't your son, you fucking…" That was all he had a chance to get out. As he spoke, he stepped forward, as if to press the pistol directly against Cade's forehead. That amateurish attempt at intimidation cost him. Cade stepped in and swept his left arm up, then down, trapping the gun arm with his own. At the same time, he reached beneath his long leather coat with his right hand to draw his pistol from the holster on his hip. That combined movement quickly brought them face to face, with the barrel of Cade's pistol jammed up under the drunk's chin.

"You ever seen one of these, young fella?" Cade said in a conversational tone. The young man just stared at him, blinking in bleary surprise at the sudden reversal of fortune. The alcohol stench was stronger now, combined with the faint odor of puke. The youngster hadn't been having his best night. Cade hoped he wouldn't have to ruin it further.

"Colt Navy revolver," Cade went on, fighting down his impulse to gag. "Funny how they call it that, seein' as how it ain't never been to sea. She's a cap and ball pistol, so she's a slow bitch to load, but six shots is enough to blow your addled brains up into the sky where," he pressed the barrel harder against the man's chin, forcing him to look upward, "you can commune with the angels, who might teach you some fuckin' manners." He smiled, a wolfish baring of teeth that drew a whimper of fear from the young drunk. "But I'll tell you what, young'un. I'm in a generous mood. So, I'll give you another choice, if you're interested. You interested?" The dude nodded as best he could with that pistol barrel thrust against his chin.

"I thought you might. So here it is. You can choose to drop that peashooter, walk away, and don't look back, and we'll both go on livin' long and happy lives. I won't even ask you to say you're sorry for being such a pathetic little pissant." He pressed the revolver a little harder into the yielding flesh. "So, what's your pleasure, *son?*"

Cade's finger tensed on the trigger as he felt the muscles of the young man's gun arm move, then relaxed as he heard the derringer clatter to the street behind him. He released the trapped arm and took a step back, then another, his pistol never wavering from the center of the man's body. The young man looked at the derringer lying on the edge of the street, then back to Cade, as if measuring his chances at scooping it up. Cade just shook his head. The young man dropped his gaze like a whipped dog's, then turned and walked away down the street, adjusting his waistcoat with all the dignity he could muster.

Cade shook his head and looked around. A few passersby had stopped to watch the scene, but the crowd was breaking up and shuffling off. Apparently, someone *not* being killed wasn't much in the way of entertainment as far as the denizens of the Barbary Coast were concerned.

As Cade bent to pick up the derringer, a voice called out. "You there!"

He sighed. He probably should have expected that the confrontation would attract the attention of the local law. He slid his weapon back into its holster and dropped the derringer into one of the leather coat's deep pockets. He turned slowly, hands raised in surrender. But it was no lawman standing there.

He saw a black lacquered carriage with gold trim and an open top. A man was standing up in the seat, gesturing to Cade. A black man in a formal suit and top hat sat in the driver's seat, staring straight ahead. Cade looked around to make sure he was the one being summoned, then strode over to the carriage.

The man who'd waved him over was as short and slight of build as the young man Cade had just faced down, but he looked much better fed, and he carried himself with the demeanor of one used to being obeyed. He was dressed in a black frock coat and matching vest of a cut Cade hadn't seen before. His face was round, and he sported a trim black mustache. The pale eyes that looked Cade up and down from their elevated position were bright and intelligent.

Cade touched the brim of his hat. "Afternoon, sir."

"Good afternoon to you," the man said. "May I have the honor of knowing who I'm addressing?"

"L.D. Cade is my name. And you'd be?"

"Hamrick," the man said. "John C. Hamrick." He seemed to savor the sound of his own name. "You've heard of me, perhaps?"

"Sorry," Cade said, "I'm new in town."

"Indeed. I must say, I'm impressed by the way you handled that young fool. I fully expected you to kill him."

Cade shrugged. "No need. He wasn't no killer. Just young and dumb and drunk."

"Still. He had a gun pointed right at you. You would have been justified in shooting him."

"Sorry to disappoint you."

Hamrick shook his head. "Not disappointed at all. As I said, I'm impressed by your judgment. I'm thinking perhaps this isn't the first such confrontation you've had to navigate."

Cade didn't answer.

Hamrick leaned forward; his eyes fixed on Cade's. "Tell me, Mr. Cade, might you be seeking employment?"

The intensity of the look made Cade uneasy, but he was, in fact, looking for work. "I could use a job, yes, sir. An honest one."

Hamrick chuckled. "Don't worry, Mr. Cade. I run an honest business. One that has room for a man of keen judgment such as yourself. A man with such judgment might go far in my employment."

He drew a gold pocket watch from his vest and peered at it. "I have pressing business at the moment, but I'd like to discuss this with you further. Do you know The Poodle Dog?"

The question startled Cade. "Come again?"

"The Poodle Dog. It's a restaurant. The corner of Bush and Dupont Streets. Meet me there tomorrow at noon. Lunch will be on me, and we can discuss employment. Will you be there?"

Cade figured he could at least hear the man out. He'd expected San Francisco to be expensive, but in the week since he'd been there, his purse was getting light at a rate that worried him. A free meal was hard to turn down, and an offer of employment even harder.

"Yes, sir," he said. "I'll be there."

Hamrick nodded to Cade, then to the driver. "Samuel."

The black man didn't look at Cade. He twitched the reins on the team of matched black horses and set them moving again. Cade watched the coach rattle away until it was lost in the traffic. Then he walked on, through the chaos and noise of the Barbary Coast.

He thought of the man's offer. Clearly Hamrick had money, at least for now. Fortune was a tricky thing here, or so he'd heard. The girl who cleaned his room at the boarding house claimed she'd once made enough in silver shares to buy the place, but before she could close the deal, the vein played out, the share value collapsed, and she was back at work. San Francisco seemed like a good place for a man looking to make his fortune.

He'd drifted across the country since the war, doing this job and that, sometimes using the gun, sometimes using his strong back and hands, always in search of something he couldn't name. Now he'd fetched up here, at the edge of the continent. If he wanted to move any further west, he'd have to hop a boat, and he didn't care much for boats. So, whatever he was looking for, he'd best find it here.

CHAPTER TWO

Cade didn't know what to expect from a restaurant calling itself The Poodle Dog, but what he found was a massive six-story pile of bricks at the corner of Bush and Dupont Streets, towering over the corner like a fortress. The impeccably dressed man at the front door looked Cade up and down with barely disguised contempt; Cade had had to borrow more suitable clothes for this place than the canvas trousers, work shirt, and worn boots he'd come west in. He'd finally prevailed on the Frenchman who had the room next door in his boarding house, a florid old sot who described himself as a "temporarily financially embarrassed aristocrat," for something to wear that wouldn't get him tossed out on his ear. Problem was, the old man was a good two inches taller than Cade, and fatter as well, so the clothes hung off him. He felt like a child putting on his daddy's fancy clothes.

Before the well-dressed man at the door could deliver some cutting remark, Cade spoke up. "I've got an appointment with Mr. Hamrick."

Cade may have never heard of Hamrick before yesterday, but in these parts, his was apparently a name to conjure with. Cade waited patiently as he watched the conflict play out on the man's face between the reflex to pitch the shabby figure before him into the street and the need to placate the name of Hamrick. Finally, in a choked voice, the doorkeeper said, "Follow me." Cade suppressed his smile as he fell in behind the man.

The interior of the place was designed to dazzle. Everything was trimmed in gold, and ornate paintings crowded with figures from myth and legend rose above the floor to the ceilings. He'd been in some saloons that aspired to this level of decorative refinement, but they fell far short of this riot of baroque ornamentation.

The doorkeeper handed Cade off to a short, round man with slicked-back black hair and a skinny mustache, whispering something in the waiter's ear that sounded like "Hamrick." That turned the waiter's frosty demeanor to all smiles as he turned to lead Cade through aisles formed by an endless sea of white-clad tables. A few people turned to look at Cade as they passed. He felt their stares, but kept his eyes fixed straight ahead, concentrating on the shiny back of the waiter's head as they turned out of the main room and down a short hallway. Cade was happy to be out of the public eye, but his tension returned as he was led up a staircase, then down a short corridor lined with doors. They passed a couple in the hallway, a man and a woman. The man looked down, not acknowledging the presence of anyone else. The woman eyed him appraisingly, then looked away, dismissing him and his shabby clothes as not being worth her further notice.

Finally, they reached a door at the end of the hallway. The waiter, still smiling, opened the door and motioned Cade inside. Cade entered, eyes scanning every corner of the room. He'd left the cavalry pistol at the house, but he'd pocketed the young dude's derringer, just in case. His right hand slipped into his pocket to lightly grip the small weapon as he entered.

The room was empty, except for a table set with a white cloth and a glittering array of silverware. Hamrick was sitting behind the table, a crystal carafe at his left hand. He stood up as they entered.

"Mr. Cade," he said. "I'm glad you came."

"I said I would." Cade took the seat that the waiter pulled out for him. Hamrick beamed at him, not seeming to notice the shabby clothing. "Welcome. And what would you like to drink? The wines here are the finest in the city."

Cade didn't know much about wine. "How's the beer?"

"Also capital." He nodded to the waiter, who bowed and moved off so quickly he seemed to disappear. "So," Hamrick said, "how long have you been in San Francisco?"

"About a week." The beer appeared in a hefty glass mug at Cade's right hand. He took a drink. It wasn't watered at all, a solid improvement over what he was used to.

"And what brings you here?" Hamrick peered at him over his wine glass.

"Rode in on the stagecoach." He'd sold his last horse for passage and a stake for when he arrived.

Hamrick chuckled. "I meant, what business? Did you come for some purpose?"

Cade hadn't realized how thirsty he was. He drained the last of the beer. "Not really. I'd heard of the place. Thought I'd give it a look."

Another beer had arrived without Cade seeing the waiter who'd brought it. He decided to take this one a little slower. As he took a sip, the door opened and another waiter entered, pushing a cart upon which rested several dishes covered with gleaming silver domes.

"Since you weren't familiar with the place," Hamrick said, "I took the liberty of ordering for both of us. I think you'll find the cuisine to your liking."

It was. A massive beef roast, seasoned with herbs unfamiliar but savory-smelling, was the main attraction. The roasted potatoes on the side gave off an aroma that made Cade's mouth water. He'd wanted to get right to a discussion of this job that Hamrick was dangling, but he was quickly distracted as he tucked into the feast. It wasn't until he'd eaten over half of what had been set in front of him that he realized Hamrick, while taking a few leisurely bites himself, was regarding him with a benign smile that reminded him uncomfortably of someone watching a prize heifer being fattened for the slaughter. He set down his knife and fork and took the final swallow at the bottom of what he realized was his third mug of beer.

"Do I need to ask if you're enjoying the meal?" Hamrick said.

"I am. Thank you, sir, for your generosity. But you wanted to talk about a job."

Hamrick nodded. "I did. But first I'd like to discuss your provenance."

"My what?"

Hamrick chuckled. "Your previous employment. Let's start with the, ah, late unpleasantness."

"You mean the war." Cade was getting impatient at Hamrick's mealy-mouthedness. The beer had his opinions straining to be released, but he held them tightly behind his teeth.

"Given the weapon you carry, I can't help but ask if you were in the cavalry."

"Yes, sir." Cade said it without inflection. He'd long ago left behind the emotion of those days, the wild sense of adventure, the dreams of glory, the feeling of being part of something legendary. That feeling had died slowly as the bodies of both friends and enemies piled up along the way in places he'd never heard of before the war: Winchester. Cedar Mountain. Gettysburg and Yellow Tavern.

He shook his head to clear it. The past was dead and gone. That's what he told himself. At least once a day.

Hamrick gratified him by not asking for stories of those days. The man did have the gift of forcing gratitude from you, despite your misgivings. "And after? Did you go home to…where is it that you said you were from?"

"I didn't, sir," Cade said. "I'm originally from Michigan. But I didn't go back. Not for long, at least." That sparked a new set of memories, even more vivid in Cade's mind: the sting of a horsewhip across his shoulders, an angry voice raised, a girl's voice pleading,

"Just go, Levi, just go…" He put that memory aside. "I packed up and headed west."

"And there you took up the profession of gunfighter."

Cade looked down and sighed. When he looked up, he kept his expression neutral. "Sorry to disappoint you, Mr. Hamrick, but there really ain't such a profession. Not outside the dime novels and cheap newspapers." Seeing Hamrick's disgruntled expression, he hastened to explain. "I wore a deputy's badge a couple times when I was needed." And when there was a salary to be had, he thought but didn't say. "I rode shotgun on a couple of stagecoaches. I was an outrider on cattle drives…"

"And did you ever have to kill anyone?"

This again. Every time anyone saw the pistol, it came up. Children, men, sometimes even women who pushed him for stories with unsettlingly bright eyes.

"Other than in battle, you mean? I've had to shoot a man. Once. But I want to be clear, Mr. Hamrick. I don't kill for money." He looked up into Hamrick's pale blue eyes. "If an assassin is what you're lookin' to hire, well, I'll be glad to pay you back for the meal."

Hamrick nodded. "I'm not seeking to hire a killer, Mr. Cade." He sighed. "Sadly, such men are easy to find in this city. You'll soon see what I mean if you stay here."

"I already have." Cade was not a cowardly man, but there were men—and a woman or two—to whom he'd instinctively given a wide berth, people who seemed to carry a cloud of menace about them. Real menace, not the drunken bluster of the young man who'd run into him.

Hamrick nodded. "As I said, what I need is a man who knows when to pull the trigger and when *not* to. Such men are exceedingly rare." He looked at Cade intently. "So tell me, Mr. Cade, why didn't you kill that young man who threatened you? What was it about him that made you spare his life?"

Cade suddenly wanted another beer, and was surprised to see

that one had materialized at his left hand while he'd been talking with Hamrick. He resolved to ask the waiter the secret of his stealth. He was as quiet as an Apache. After a moment's hesitation, he took a sip. He thought the question over, then spoke.

"He didn't have the killin' look."

Hamrick looked puzzled. "Yet he still could have killed you."

"Yep. I mean, yes, sir. He was so addled, he might've killed me by accident. Truth be told, that's how a lot of shootings happen."

"But you spared his life," Hamrick insisted. He shook his head. "He didn't have the killing look, but he could have killed you, but you spared him anyway. You see my confusion."

When he put it that way, it did sound confusing. Or maybe it was the beer. Cade shrugged. "Sometimes you just kinda have to figure it out as you go along."

Hamrick nodded, his smile returning. "And that's why I would like to employ you."

"Which brings me back to the question, sir. As what?"

"Bodyguard," Hamrick said. He leaned forward, looking at Cade intently. "You may have discerned, Mr. Cade, I am a man of some means."

"I'd noticed, yes, sir."

"Well, in this time and place, a man who's achieved a certain amount of success can't help but collect some enemies."

"Yes, sir." Cade took a sip, a small one, from his beer, collecting his thoughts. Hamrick spoke before he could respond. "I know what you're thinking. What kind of businessman needs a bodyguard? What kind of legitimate businessman, that is."

Cade nodded. "The thought crossed my mind."

"Mr. Cade, when I came to San Francisco, I quickly noticed that the men who speculated in silver and gold stocks made fortunes very quickly. Then they lost them just as quickly."

"I'd heard that myself."

Hamrick went on as if he hadn't heard. "But some investments remained sound. They never stopped increasing in value. Do you know what those were?"

Cade thought back to the richest men he'd met in his travels across the country. All of them had one thing in common. "Land."

"YES!" Hamrick slammed his hand down on the table so hard that the report had Cade reaching for the derringer in his pocket. "Real property. They call it that for a reason, you know." He settled down a little. "I have property interests all over the city. And quite a few of them are in the Barbary Coast. I'm also acquiring properties in Chinatown. There are certain elements who object to me moving in those markets. The tongs, in particular, have made threats on my life. And the life of my family, which I find particularly upsetting."

"Tongs," Cade said. He'd heard the term mentioned, but didn't know much about it.

"Chinese secret societies," Hamrick said. "They claim to be aid organizations for the poor immigrants, but they're nothing but common criminals with fancy oaths and fearsome reputations."

"And they've threatened you and your family."

"More than once. Then there are the Italians. They've brought their own brand of criminality to these shores. And that is to say nothing of the hoodlums."

"Hoodlums?"

"Gangs of young toughs. Roaming the streets. They've taken the name given to them by the press and wear it as a badge of honor. Why, they actually parade openly, brandishing clubs and brass knuckles, and chanting, 'Look out for the hoodlums.'" Hamrick shook his head and looked sorrowfully at Cade. "The police...well, they're better than the rabble that used to pass for law enforcement in this town. They try to keep order. But they're outnumbered. Sometimes even outgunned." He smiled sadly. "That's why the prohibition on going armed in public was lifted here last year. You're fortunate, really. Not so long ago, you might have been at least fined and had that beautiful pistol of yours taken from you."

"Looks like I came here at the right time," Cade said. He still felt uneasy.

"I can offer you ten dollars a week," Hamrick said. "And room. And board." He appeared to notice Cade's ragtag clothing for the first time. "And a reasonable clothing allowance."

Cade was staggered. "Ten..." it was more than he'd ever made in his life. More than most people he'd known had made in their lives. He still had some misgivings. But ten a week...

"Mr. Hamrick," he said, and extended his hand, "I think I'm your man."

CHAPTER THREE

Hamrick beamed. "Splendid. I've taken the liberty of having some papers drawn up. When you finish your meal, we can go straight to my attorney's office and seal the deal."

Cade's fork stopped halfway to his mouth. "Papers?"

"Your contract of employment," Hamrick said, still smiling. "I find it best to put things in writing. It helps to make sure everyone understands their rights and obligations. Wouldn't you agree?"

"I guess." Cade had been used to deals made and honored on handshakes. If a man was going to go back on his word, no piece of paper was going to stop him. But what the hell, he thought, this was the city. Things were done differently here.

The law office of Lionel M. Tremblay, Esq. took up the entire second floor of a stone building a block away from the Stock Exchange. The offices were richly appointed, with dark paneling and gold fixtures. A junior clerk looked Cade up and down suspiciously, but when Hamrick announced that they were there to see Mr. Tremblay, he became the picture of obsequiousness. Cade took an instant dislike to the oily little bastard. The clerk guided them to a large corner office overlooking the busy streets and inquired if they would like any refreshment while they waited. Cade declined, suppressing a belch. Hamrick shook his head as well.

It wasn't more than a couple of minutes before the lawyer came in. Tremblay was a tall drink of water, with a craggy face and a grave demeanor that reminded Cade somewhat of photographs he'd seen of Mr. Lincoln. He even had the chin whiskers. His voice, when he spoke, was deep and sonorous. Cade could well imagine him filling a courtroom with it. He turned first to Hamrick. "John."

Hamrick smiled, but he didn't get up. "Lionel."

Tremblay turned to Cade. "So. This is the new man."

Cade stood up and extended a hand. "Yes, sir. L.D. Cade."

The lawyer took it. His grip was firm and strong, but he didn't pull the trick some big men liked of trying to crush his hand. "Lionel A. Tremblay." He released the hand and sat down behind a massive oak desk, empty of everything but lamp, blotter, and a pair of leather-bound books. As if by some unheard signal, the clerk bustled in with a sheaf of papers and laid them on the table in front of Cade. He set an expensive-looking fountain pen next to the papers and withdrew. Cade picked them up and began reading.

"I think you'll find everything in order." Tremblay's voice held a note of impatience.

"I'm sure," Cade murmured, and continued to examine the document anyway. He'd learned to read and write and cipher at an early age, but a lot of the words in the document eluded him. He could figure out the ten dollars a week, though. He was reaching for the fountain pen when a paragraph near the bottom caught his eye. He looked up at Tremblay. "Can you explain one part to me?"

Tremblay smiled indulgently. "Of course."

"What's the duty of confident…confident…"

"Confidentiality," Tremblay said. He looked at Hamrick. "John here is a man of business, Mr. Cade. Sometimes his business requires him to keep his intentions and capabilities to himself. I'm sure you understand."

Cade nodded. "Can't let everyone know what cards you're holdin'. I get it."

Tremblay nodded. "Just so."

"And sometimes, you can't let it be known just exactly what you've done," Hamrick added.

Tremblay broke in hastily. "Not that anyone is doing anything unlawful that would need to be concealed."

Hamrick nodded. "Of course not." He fixed Cade with a look. "I may from time to time engage in what some people consider sharp practices." He shrugged. "And in any business, there are winners and there are losers. The losers are often quick to complain that they've been cheated. That's part of the reason I need your services, as I said." He leaned toward Cade. "But I can assure you, Mr. Cade, that everything I do, I do within the bounds of the law."

The intensity of the statement made Cade feel a little uncomfortable. It was as if Hamrick was trying a little too hard to be convincing. But what was he going to do, call the man a liar to his face? He wasn't giving up ten dollars a week because of a vaguely itchy feeling between his shoulder blades.

"Okay, then." Cade picked up the pen.

CHAPTER FOUR

After his visit to the lawyer, Cade returned to his boarding house to collect his belongings. It didn't take long. It felt better to have his own clothes on, including his holstered revolver and his battered Stetson. He returned the traps he'd borrowed to the "aristocrat," giving him one of the gold dollars Hamrick had advanced him at Tremblay's office. The man looked at the coin goggle-eyed for a moment before bursting into tears, throwing his arms around Cade, and babbling thanks in what Cade supposed was his native tongue. After a few moments disentangling himself from the blubbering Frenchman, Cade used another portion of his advance to settle up his outstanding bill with the sharp-tongued landlady. The middle-aged widow was as amazed as the Frenchman, but a good deal less teary, and she didn't embrace him, which suited Cade fine. He picked up his small trunk and carried it to the street to await the arrival of the carriage Hamrick had promised. The ride hadn't yet arrived, so Cade set the trunk down and settled in to wait.

The street was busy and passersby glared at him in annoyance for obstructing the sidewalk, but no one was bold enough to say anything to a heeled man, so he ignored them. He took his last cigar from the trunk. He'd been saving it for a special occasion, and he figured now was as good a time as any. He was flush with cash, with the prospect of a lot more on the near horizon. Hamrick had described threats to him and to his family, but Cade had seen some pretty bad characters in his travels. He didn't put much stock in the fears of some rich city dude. He chuckled at the image of young "toughs," as Hamrick described them, marching in the streets chanting, "Look out for the hoodlums." In his experience, the more some blowhard liked to jaw about how rugged he was, the more pigeon-livered he was likely to be.

"Mr. Cade?" a voice said behind him.

Cade stood up, his hand moving toward the pistol he'd strapped back on. He relaxed slightly when he saw who was addressing him.

The man was tall and thin, dressed in the black high-collared suit and flat-brimmed hat of a country preacher. He looked as out of place on this street in the Barbary Coast as Cade had felt at The Poodle Dog.

"What can I do for you, parson?" Cade said politely. His own father had been a preacher, failing at that profession when he wasn't failing at farming, and while Cade hadn't darkened the door of a church in as long as he could remember, he still had that reflexive respect.

The man drew closer, and Cade saw the slightly unfocused and off-kilter look in his eyes. Respect or not, Cade's hand inched closer to his pistol.

"I understand you'll be working for Mr. Hamrick," the parson said.

Cade blinked in surprise. "Word travels fast. Must be a smaller town than I thought."

The parson smiled. He had squarish gray teeth that reminded Cade uncomfortably of tombstones. "I don't recommend accepting that offer."

Cade's eyes narrowed. "And what exactly is your interest here, sir?"

The smile never wavered. "Why, nothing less than your immortal soul, Mr. Cade. Many have lost their way here over the glitter of gold. I would hate to see you become one of them."

"Mister," Cade said, "I don't know who you are, or what you

claim to know, but..."

The man broke in. "Hamrick is not a good man, Mr. Cade. He is not who he pretends to be."

Well, who the hell is these days? Cade thought, but before he could say it, the parson had turned away and was walking down the street. Cade started after him, but then he caught sight of a familiar carriage approaching. The black servant, Samuel, was driving, dressed in his tail coat and top hat. He pulled the carriage to a stop in front of Cade. He had the look of a man on an errand he'd rather not be carrying out.

"Afternoon," Cade called out. He figured he'd be working around, if not actually with, this fellow, so he might as well be friendly.

Samuel didn't seem to agree. He barely gave Cade a glance before facing back forward. "You ready to go?"

"I guess." He threw his trunk in the back of the carriage and climbed aboard. Samuel twitched the reins. "Gee-YUP." Those were the only words he spoke for the rest of the journey.

The carriage wound its way through narrow streets that gradually widened, climbing as they did, the bustling crowd and the traffic jam of wagons and buckboards thinning to a more sedate parade of carriages and two-person buggies. From time to time, he glanced back, watching the city and the broad glittering reach of the San Francisco Bay spread out behind him as they ascended the hills. A forest of masts rose from the waterfront, and a haze of smoke hung over the place. But the air where they were going seemed fresher.

Finally, they pulled to a stop in front of a huge house set a ways back from the sidewalk, behind an iron fence topped with wicked-looking pointed spikes. A faceted multi-story turret with a dozen high windows protruded from one side of the house, like a tower protecting the long wooden staircase that rose from the street.

"I guess this is it," Cade said. Samuel made no reply. Cade swung himself down from the carriage and looked the place over, then looked back at Samuel. The man didn't move. Sighing, Cade hauled his trunk from the back of the carriage and dragged it to the gate. He heard Samuel start up the horses as he fumbled with the latch. The door opened. A woman stood in the doorway, looking down at him impassively.

Cade let go of the latch and touched the brim of his hat. "Afternoon, ma'am. Would this be the Hamrick residence?"

She didn't smile or change expression. "It would." They looked at each other awkwardly for a moment. "You must be the new man," she said finally. She didn't seem happy at the prospect.

Cade didn't quite know how to answer that. "I must be."

She sighed. "Well, you might as well come in." She turned and walked back inside, leaving Cade by himself on the sidewalk. *Well, it ain't like I expected a brass band*, he thought, *but this is a little cold.* He hauled the trunk up the steps and through the ornate double doors. The woman was standing just inside, waiting. Cade removed his hat. "Are you the lady of the house?"

"Yes." In the ensuing silence, Cade looked her over. She was on the tall side for a woman. Her chin was a bit too strong and her nose too prominent to be considered pretty, but they gave her features a strength Cade found appealing. Her eyes were wide and dark brown, and the hair piled up in a fashionably curled coiffure on top of her head was a golden blond. She looked a good bit younger than her husband, but that wasn't unusual in Cade's experience. The first thing a newly successful man looked for was a young and pretty wife. Still, Cade was more than a little disconcerted at the way she stood and stared at him.

"Ma'am?" he finally said. "I was given to understand I'd have a room here. Can I ask where that might be?"

"You can ask," she said curtly, and turned away to march away down the hall.

Well, hell, Cade said to himself. *What do I do now?* It was then that he noticed the little girl.

She was peeking around the doorway halfway down the hall. She appeared to be eight or nine years old, but her blond hair was done up in an elaborate hairstyle that mirrored the one of the woman who'd just left. Her eyes were the same dark brown, and they regarded him gravely.

"Well, hey there, Little Bit," Cade said.

The girl didn't respond to the friendly tone. "My name is Violet. Not Little Bit."

He bowed. "My apologies. It's a pleasure to meet you, Miss Violet."

"Are you a cowboy?" she asked.

Cade put his hat back on, hoping to make the girl feel a little more comfortable. "Well, ma'am," he began, "I have wrangled some cattle in my time…"

"Is that why you have that big gun?" the girl asked. "If the cattle don't behave, do you shoot them?"

Cade was struck dumb for a moment. Before he could answer, the front door opened and Samuel walked in. He looked at Cade's trunk lying in the foyer. "You haven't been shown your room?"

"No."

Samuel grimaced, then raised his voice. "BRIDGET!"

There was no response. Samuel called out again. "BRIDGET!"

Cade heard the sound of footsteps scurrying down the hallway. A short woman with an unruly mop of red curls beneath a maid's cap appeared in the doorway. She was thin, her face pinched and suspicious. She looked at Samuel with a fierce expression. When she spoke, it was with a pronounced Irish accent.

"You can just lay off the shoutin', Samuel Clayborne," she snapped. "I don't work for you." She regarded Cade as if he was a beggar on the doorstep. "An' who might this ruffian be?"

Cade took the hat back off. "L.D. Cade, ma'am. I just took employment with Mr. Hamrick."

The woman, who Cade assumed was Bridget, snorted as if

offended by the information. "And what are we supposed to do with him, is what I'm askin.'"

"We can start with figuring out where I'm supposed to sleep," Cade offered.

"Well, it won't be with me," Bridget declared. "You can put any thought of that out of yer mind, do you hear?"

"Can't put that thought out of my mind, ma'am. It never entered there."

She scowled at him, clearly turning the words over on her head to sift for an insult. She turned away, that question still open. "He can take the red bedroom," she called back over her shoulder. "It's already made up."

Cade looked at Samuel, who regarded Bridget's retreating back with baleful eyes before turning to Cade. "I guess you can follow me."

CHAPTER FIVE

Cade followed Samuel up the stairs to the second floor, then turned left down a long, dim hallway. A stained-glass window set high in the end of the hall provided the only illumination. He stopped at the last door on the left, swung it open, and walked away, brushing past Cade without speaking further. Cade watched him go for a moment, then entered the room and looked around.

The red bedroom lived up to its name. The deep scarlet flocked wallpaper and the peacock feathers in a large urn by the bed reminded him uncomfortably of a New Orleans cathouse. He walked over to the window, looked down on the street a story below, and wondered what in the ever-living hell he was doing here. There was something about the atmosphere of this house that put him on edge. No one seemed happy, and certainly no one appeared pleased to see him.

The door opened behind him and he turned, instinctively putting a hand on the butt of the Colt pistol. Samuel came in, staggering a little under the weight of the clothing he had slung across his shoulders. He stopped as he noticed Cade. "These belonged to Mr. Hamrick's former manservant. He asked me to see if they'd fit you."

"Thanks," Cade said. "But before I go putting on another man's clothes, I'd kind of like to find out what happened to him."

The black man's face was like stone. "You would have to ask Mr. Hamrick."

"Samuel," Cade said, "I don't want to pry, but I feel like I need

29

to ask. Have I done somethin' in particular to get under your fingernails or are you just this angry all the damn time?"

"I'm sure I don't know what you mean, sir."

Cade shook his head in frustration. "Awright. But we can at least be civil. That too hard?"

"Sir," Samuel said as he went to the door, "I am always civil." With that, he left.

"Prickly bastard," Cade muttered. He briefly considered picking up his trunk, hauling it down to the street, and catching the first ride out of this place. But ten dollars a week... He sighed. *Many men have lost their way here over the glitter of gold*, the parson had said. Cade didn't think he'd ever lost his way, but that was more because there hadn't been that much glitter on offer. This town was all about gold. It has been a sleepy seaside village, he'd heard, before the glitter was found in the nearby hills, and now look at it. If that's what gold could do, Cade thought he might need to give this losing his way thing a try.

CHAPTER SIX

The seawater scent of fish from the front of the shop hung in the air, making McMurphy want to gag. He hated dealing with these yellow heathens, even if their interests did overlap at the moment. He cleared his throat and spoke.

"I'm not pleased with the pace of things," he said to the man behind the curtain, who he could only see in silhouette.

He saw the shadow moving. There was a brief glow, like a match being struck, and a slow intake of breath that let him know the man behind the curtain had lit and was drawing on one of the long clay pipes the Chinese favored. McMurphy scowled. *Was the man smoking opium? While discussing business?* But when the man behind the curtain spoke, his voice was free of the dreamy slurring of the opium smoker.

"You are too impatient," the man behind the curtain said, his voice clear, high pitched, with a heavy accent. "Things are moving at their own pace."

"Hamrick knows something is brewing. He's hired some gunslinger to protect him."

"Yes."

McMurphy heard the man draw on the pipe again. "This doesn't bother you?"

"No." The word hung in the air. The shadow on the curtain didn't move. Just as McMurphy was reaching the end of his patience, the man spoke. "Hamrick has taken a step he thinks will make him safe. Now, he will relax." Another puff on the pipe. "Things are proceeding as they are meant to proceed."

McMurphy wanted to grind his teeth. "I haven't got time for your mystical Chinese bullshit." *And I'm running out of money.*

"Mr. McMurphy." The voice was still soft, but the force behind it drew McMurphy up short. "You would be well advised to remember to whom you are speaking."

McMurphy felt suddenly cold. He'd heard stories of what this man was capable of, of enemies having their limbs chopped off one by one and set up still alive on pedestals to serve as warnings. Of enemies skinned alive and thrown into pits of maggots to be devoured screaming. "I'm sorry," he said. "But Hamrick cheated me. Ruined me. I want some justice." *And a piece of his fortune. A big piece.*

"You will have it," the man said. "And a lesson will be taught that will not be soon forgotten. You have my word on that. Just be patient."

There was nothing else McMurphy could say. He saw himself out, through the long corridor that led to this back room in one of the shops that dotted Chinatown. The bins on the street outside that usually held a variety of fish and shellfish were empty, only the lingering and pervasive scent remaining. The Chinese in the street looked away from him as he walked through the bustling streets lined with shops and businesses that advertised themselves in a riot of colorful Chinese lettering. This may have been their territory, but there was no profit in antagonizing an unknown *gwai loh*. Not in this city. Not at this time.

Lost in angry reverie, McMurphy barely took notice of where he was until he stood before the steps of his boarding house. Like he had a hundred times before, he looked the exterior over with an angry eye: the peeling paint; the missing shutter on a downstairs window; the warped boards. He deserved better. His father deserved better. But the last of his once sizable bank balance was going to grease the wheels of his revenge.

His father. He realized he wasn't sure how long the old man had been left alone. He mounted the steps to the front door two at a time and did the same on the interior stairs. He was relieved when he opened the door and saw his father sitting by the window, looking out on the street. Relief turned to dismay as he saw the clerical collar and parson's hat. He caught the faint whiff of horse manure as he drew closer, then saw the shit caked on his father's black boots.

"Daddy," he said, keeping his voice even, "did you go out?"

His father turned toward him. With rising dread, McMurphy looked into the watery blue eyes, wondering if he'd see recognition there. That had been hit or miss in the past month.

"Patrick," his father said. Well, that was something. The next words, however, filled him with dread. "I tried to talk some sense into that man."

"What man, Daddy?" McMurphy knelt by his father and began pulling off the soiled black boots, nose wrinkling at the smell. Getting the boots off didn't make the aroma any better.

"That man. Hamrick's man. The gunslinger."

McMurphy dropped the boot he was holding and looked up, aghast. "You spoke to him? You let him know who you are?"

His father reached out with a trembling hand and squeezed his shoulder. "Don't worry, son. He doesn't know me from Adam's off ox."

McMurphy wasn't reassured. "What did you say?"

His father smiled beatifically. "I let him know he was following a bad man. That his immortal soul was in danger." He looked at the expression on McMurphy's face and his religious fervor crumpled. "I felt it was my duty to try."

McMurphy stood up, trying to restrain his rage. He reached out and took his father's stubbled chin between ungentle fingers. "Now you listen here, Daddy," he grated, "you leave Hamrick to me. That includes his family, and it especially includes anyone who's working for him. And their immortal souls? Damnation is too good for them."

The old man blinked. "I…I can't…"

"You do as I say," McMurphy said, "or go find your own way. Live in the street for all I goddamn care." He hated himself for the fear he saw in his father's eyes and for the tears he saw there. Still, it was necessary.

"How?" the old man whispered. "How did I raise a child so full of hate?"

"You didn't raise me that way, Daddy," McMurphy said. He released his father's chin. "Life made me this way. Life and Hamrick."

CHAPTER SEVEN

In the back room of the fish shop in Chinatown, a man stood up and pulled aside the curtain he'd been hidden behind. He arched his back, the tendons popping and stretching. A young Chinese girl appeared in the doorway. "He is gone?" she asked in English.

The man nodded. He reached down into a satchel beside where he'd been sitting and drew out a pair of gold dollars. "Yes. Thank your grandparents for the use of the room." He held out the coins. "As always."

She didn't take the coins. Her dark eyes regarded him with a suspicion he'd been expecting for some time.

"They want to know," the girl said, "why a man would pretend to be Chinese when he is not."

"Except they didn't say 'man,' did they?" he asked. "They said *gwai loh*. White devil."

The girl looked away. "It is just an expression."

"I'm sure." The man who was not Chinese looked amused. "Why do you think?"

"I am only a stupid girl," she said. "I wouldn't know."

This time he laughed out loud. "Oh, little flower," he said, using the English rendering of Mei, her given name, "you are far from stupid." His smile vanished and he spoke to her in harsh Mandarin. "Answer my question. What is it that you think I'm up to?"

She looked back at him defiantly and answered in the same language. "I think you're going to do something bad. And blame it on the Chinese. People here hate us anyway."

He regarded her without expression. He really should kill her, he mused. She was far too perceptive to let live. But he found her intelligence intriguing. Most of white San Francisco regarded the Chinese as savage brutes, barely human. This girl, quick-witted and suspicious, made him question that. And she was pretty. It was a combination he found enticing.

"Don't worry." He'd switched back to English. "Whatever else may happen, I assure you. No harm will come to you and your family. You have my word."

The suspicion never left the girl's face, but she reached out her hand. He smiled as he put the coins in it. Everyone had a key, a desire that would unlock them. The key to McMurphy was his hatred and lust for vengeance. The key to Mei, he decided, was not the desire for gold, however her greed might appear on the surface. It was the need for safety. Understandable for someone whose life was so precarious. As he picked up his hat and nodded his farewell, he contemplated what further use he might make of a pretty, smart girl. And when he was done...he flexed his long, strong fingers in anticipation. There would always be the pleasure involved in disposing of her.

CHAPTER EIGHT

Cade had tried several of the suits that Samuel delivered to him. Whoever the previous owner had been, he'd been shorter and skinnier than Cade, and he split two pairs of trousers before he gave up. When Samuel appeared in the door again, Cade was dressed in the clothes he'd arrived in. He looked at the pile of delivered clothing on the bed and back at Cade with a heavy sigh.

"Sorry I ain't littler," Cade said sourly.

Samuel didn't speak or change expression. He walked over, gathered up the pile, and walked out with it. He struggled a bit, but Cade had had enough of trying to be nice to the stiff-necked son of a bitch and didn't offer to help.

His next visitor was the girl, Bridget, carrying an armful of towels. "Mr. Hamrick says you're to have a bath."

Cade looked around. "So, where's the tub?"

Bridget rolled her eyes. "Have ye been so long in the wilderness, then?" She crossed the room to a door Cade had assumed was a closet and flung it wide. "Here."

Cade walked over slowly and took in the room. A large ceramic tub with faucets perched over it took up one side of the space. To the other side was an enclosed space with a half-open door. Cade hadn't seen an indoor jakes in some time, and in his experience, they tended to be unpredictable and inferior in sanitation to the simpler outdoor variety. Bridget noticed his dubious look. "The latest in siphonic water closets, I'll have ya know," she snapped.

Cade had no idea what that meant. "Okay."

Bridget dropped the towels on a table by the door. "Get cleaned up. Mister's tailor will be along directly to fit you for a new suit of clothes." She bustled out without looking back. Cade sighed. He'd paid for a bath a week ago at his boarding house, and he wasn't due for another for some time, but he supposed there was no harm in having one now, especially for free.

It took him a few minutes to figure out the taps, but before long he was soaking luxuriously in the tub, scrubbing the sweat and grime of the last week away. When he finally exited the water closet, rubbing his chest with the towel, he was stunned to see a man perched on the edge of the bed, smiling ingratiatingly. He quickly wrapped the towel around his waist. "Who the hell are you?"

The man jumped off the bed, still smiling, and Cade could see he was truly small, a hair over four feet tall. His suit, however, fit him perfectly. When he spoke, it was in an accent Cade had learned to associate with upper-class Englishmen. "My name is Simonson. Mr. Hamrick asked me to fit you for some new clothes." He bent to a satchel on the floor and pulled out a tape measure.

"Well, sonny, do y'mind if I put on some of my old ones first?"

The smile vanished. "I'm forty-one years old, sir. I would appreciate not being called 'sonny.' If you don't mind."

Jesus, Cade thought, *does everybody in this town have some kind of stick up their ass?* "Okay," he said. "But can I at least put on my drawers?"

The smile had returned, a little less enthusiastic and more professional than before. "That would be fine."

Cade hurriedly pulled his undergarments on, suddenly self-conscious about how ragged and malodorous they'd become. "Guess I'm going to need some of these, too."

"Yes," Simonson said dryly. "I'd say so." He gestured to the middle of the room. "Stand there, please."

Feeling like a man in a bad dream, Cade stood where he was

told, raised his hands when he was told, turned this way and that when he was told, as the tailor measured his chest, his waist, his neck, and his inseam. Cade felt more than a little uncomfortable at that part, so he tried to lighten the moment. "I knew a midget in Tulsa once," he said. "Worked in a bar down on…OW! Goddamn it!"

"I'm sorry, sir," Simonson said with transparently false sincerity. "I'm so clumsy sometimes." He held up the large-headed pin he'd "accidentally" jabbed into Cade's thigh.

"Okay, okay," Cade muttered. He just wanted this ordeal over with. The tailor returned to his work, quickly and silently finishing his measurements. When he was done, he nodded. "I can get you completely kitted out in three days." He looked over to where Cade's old clothes were laid across the bed and made a face. "In this case, I shall endeavor to accomplish it in two."

"Thanks," Cade said. "But don't put yourself out."

"I'm not. I just can't bear the thought of you wandering the city in the company of my other client, by which I mean Mr. Hamrick, dressed like that."

"Now wait a damn minute," Cade began to protest, but the tailor broke in.

"Here, now." He walked over to where Cade's pistol and gun belt lay in the untidy pile of clothes on the bed. "Are you intending to wear that," he gestured at the Colt, "as part of your employment?"

"Well, yeah."

The little man sighed. "No one tells me anything." He gestured at the center of the room again. "We have to do all the measurements over again for proper fit. And I have a leatherworker next door to my shop who can design you a shoulder rig for better concealment."

"That's okay," Cade said. "I'm used to it on my hip."

The tailor nodded. "And thanks to the late influx of," he made that face again, "Celestials, open carry of firearms is not only legal again, but back *en vogue.*"

"Celestials?"

"Chinamen." Simonson said it like a curse. "Do you carry a blade as well? A second firearm?"

"Been known to," Cade said. He thought of the little derringer he'd taken.

"Show them to me."

Bristling a little at the tone, Cade fished the little derringer out of his coat, then rummaged through his trunk for his knife. The tailor took them, looked them over, then nodded as he handed them back. "We can fit you with pockets to conceal those as well. Now, if you'll stand back where you were before."

As he took up his position, Cade reflected on the little man's clear contempt for the Chinese. *Guess we all need someone to look down on.* His own inadvertent joke made him chuckle, but he didn't share it with the tailor. He didn't want to get stabbed again.

CHAPTER NINE

After the tailor had finished his work, Cade found himself with nothing to do. He decided to set out and explore the house. Given the generally uncomfortable feel of the household, he didn't know how well his reconnaissance might be received, but he needed to know the lay of the land here. He left his weapons behind. As he walked out of the room, he caught himself closing the door behind him softly and carefully, so as not to make a sound. *What the hell*, he thought. *They've got me so buffaloed, I'm acting like I got no right to be here.* He reopened the door and closed it a little harder. That made him feel even more foolish. He looked around the hallway. Every door was closed. He'd have to ask who slept where. The stairs he'd climbed to get here were halfway down the hall. Another set led up to what he assumed was the master sleeping quarters. He took the steps down to the hallway where he'd entered earlier. As he reached the bottom of the stairs, a doorway opened onto an opulently furnished parlor on his right. It was empty. There was no sound of voices, no indication that the house was even inhabited. The quiet seemed somehow unnatural for a home where people were supposed to be living. There was a heavy walnut door to his left, slightly ajar. He pushed it and it swung open. Behind it was a large room, with a large bay window facing the street that allowed light in. Luxurious-looking green leather chairs were placed about the room, and bookshelves lined with books dominated the wall. It was a study, or library, where the master of the house could retire, possibly with his cronies, and chew the fat over brandy and cigars.

Cade exited and went into the parlor. He noticed a book on one of the side tables. He picked it up and looked at the cover. A lurid drawing of an Indian in an extravagant headdress and buckskins charging on horseback with lance upraised was splashed across it. The title blared *The Yellow Chief: A Romance of The Rocky Mountains*. Cade smiled. So someone in the house had a taste for cheap dime novels. He put the book back on the table and moved on. Down at the end of the hallway he located the large formal dining room, complete with gaslit chandelier. It was there he heard the murmur of voices coming from behind a door to one side. He heard someone laugh, a deep, masculine laugh in a voice that sounded oddly familiar. He swung the door open and the laughter stopped.

He was looking into a long, narrow kitchen. Standing at the iron stove on the left was Bridget, stirring something in a large pot. Samuel was seated on a stool behind a large, waist-high prep table that ran half the length of the room. He had a cup of something raised to his lips and a smile on his face. Cade hadn't known he was capable of smiling. Both of them turned to look at Cade as he stepped across the corridor and into the kitchen. "Afternoon," he said.

"Good afternoon." Samuel's smile had disappeared without a trace. "Anything I can get for you, sir?"

"No. No," Cade said. "Just gettin' the layout. Figgerin' out where everything is."

"Well," Bridget said, "this here would be the kitchen."

Cade ignored the sarcasm. "I reckon so." He stepped back into the narrow corridor and looked down it to see a door at the end. Daylight came through a small glass pane at the end. "And down that way is a back door to…where?"

"Carriage yard," Samuel answered. "Stables and carriage house across it."

"Behind that?"

Samuel picked up his cup. "A twelve-foot hedge, backing up to the yard of the house the next street over."

"A hedge?"

"Bushes," Bridget supplied. "Tall, thick bushes,"

"I know what a hedge is," Cade snapped. "I want to see it. If there's a back way onto the property, I need to know about it if I'm goin' to guard these folks, and the two of you in the bargain."

Bridget and Samuel looked at each other. Samuel shrugged and put his cup down again. "Follow me." Cade stepped aside and let Samuel lead him down the corridor.

"This door kept locked?" Cade asked as Samuel opened it.

"At night, yes." He stepped out. "During the day, there's deliveries. Most of them come to the kitchen door, though." He pointed to another door, off to the side of the kitchen.

"Two back entrances?" The problem was getting more complicated.

"This way," Samuel said. Cade followed him into a large round space, with the earth packed down by years of feet, hooves, and wheels. On the other side of that yard was the carriage house and stable, a one-story building with huge white doors pulled closed. Behind it, he could see the dark green of the hedge. He walked over, passing by the carriage house, and stood in front of it.

The growth was neatly trimmed and, Cade guessed, closer to ten feet than twelve. He put out a hand and pushed against the tightly bunched growth. It was a formidable obstacle, he had to admit, but it was only bushes. "Any gate through this?" he asked. "Any way to the next property over?"

Samuel shook his head. "Missus likes her privacy."

Cade turned. "Missus?"

"Mrs. Hamrick."

Cade nodded and walked down the length of the hedge, to where it turned and ran down the other edge of the property to the corner of the house. It formed a green wall around three sides of the stable yard, with a long, cobbled driveway running by the other side and connecting the yard to the street. Cade was beginning to feel hemmed in. In fact, this whole house had made him feel claustrophobic since he'd walked through the front door. He looked up at the three stories of the structure, at the windows and turrets that protruded here and there. Without speaking, he walked back to the house, Samuel trailing behind. When he walked back in, Cade looked around the hallway and kitchen again, sucking at his teeth as he thought.

Samuel interrupted his contemplation as he stood in the hallway. "Well?"

Cade looked at him. "Well, what?"

"Can you protect the house?"

"This house? Not without more men. I hate to sound like a croaker, but I'd feel a sight easier with riflemen at the back and the front. Someone up in one of those windows keepin' watch wouldn't hurt, either."

Samuel shook his head. "Missus would never approve. She gave Mr. Hamrick the dickens for bringing *you* home."

Cade looked at him, startled. "So just who is it wears the long pants in this household?"

Samuel didn't answer. He turned away and walked back into the kitchen. Cade wanted to grab him and give him a walloping for his insolence, but he restrained himself. It wouldn't do to get shit-canned for fighting. He shook his head and made his way back upstairs, thinking things over.

Protecting the house was out of the question. It was too big, with too many entrances and exits. He'd need to stick close to Hamrick. Problem was, he didn't even know where his employer was at the moment. He'd have to have a serious talk with Hamrick when he saw him again. In the meantime, he reverted to the remedy of all seasoned soldiers when given nothing to do: he lay down on the bed and went to sleep.

CHAPTER TEN

He was awakened by the clattering of dishes and muttered imprecations in a language he didn't recognize. Instinctively, his heart pounding, Cade sat up in the bed, swinging his legs over, his hand going to the pistol hanging on the bedstead. In a moment, he had it out, pointing at the intruder, pulling the hammer back with his thumb.

He found himself staring over the iron sights at the slight figure of Bridget, frozen with her hand holding a silver platter an inch above a side table. Her eyes widened with terror for a half second, then narrowed to the contemptuous stare to which he'd become accustomed. "Can I at least put yer dinner down before ya shoot me?"

He lowered the gun. "Sorry. You startled me."

She nodded stiffly, then turned back to setting his food out. He could see that she was still shaking.

"I really am sorry," he said. "I didn't mean to scare you."

She turned to face him, raising her chin defiantly. "You think you scare me, big man?"

"Yeah," Cade said. "And that's not doing anyone any good at all." He shook his head. "Everyone in this damn house is on edge. Everyone here acts like they're mad at somethin', but I wonder if they ain't just afraid. And I'm supposed to protect them against whatever it is they're afraid of, but I've got no damn idea what it is." He slid the gun back into its holster. "Maybe you can help me figure it out so I don't end up drawing down on the wrong people. Like I just did on you." He patted the bed next to him. When Bridget gave him those narrowed eyes again, he slid all the way up to the space by the headboard and pointed to the posts at the foot of the bed. Reluctantly, the woman walked over and took a seat as far away on the bed as she could get. She didn't look at Cade.

"So," he said, "who is it that wants to hurt our boss man?"

She shook her head. "I don't know." For once, her prickly facade dropped and she looked at Cade imploringly. "I really don't. He doesn't confide in the servants. Well, maybe Samuel. All I know is he came home one night two weeks ago in a tremendous taking. He told Mrs. Hamrick someone had taken a shot at him."

"Samuel said Mr. Hamrick had another fellow working for him before me. Was he around then?"

She made a face as if he'd mentioned a relative caught in sexual congress with a sheep. "Walker," she said. "He was useless."

"So, this Walker...he skedaddled as soon as there was a threat?"

Bridget nodded. "Useless," she said again. "Like tits on a boar."

Cade ran his hand over his face, trying to keep the frustration out of his voice. "But we still don't know who the threat is. Hamrick... sorry, Mr. Hamrick...mentioned the Chinese. And the hoodlums."

Bridget snorted. "The hoodlums? A bunch of children let run wild, thinking they're so frightenin' with their brass knuckles and clubs. Any real man could send them packin' with a look. Besides, they only pick on the Chinese."

"The Chinese," Cade said. "You think maybe it's them?"

She shook her head. "Who can tell with those people? They don't think like us."

"When it comes to killin'," Cade muttered, "we all got a lot more in common than you might think."

"What?"

He shook his head. "Never mind. I guess we just have to go on and see what comes our way."

"Well," Bridget says. "You'll get your chance, soon enough. I heard Himself tellin' Samuel to have the carriage ready tonight for an excuuuuursion," she drew the word out mockingly.

"Business or pleasure?"

She smiled, that same sardonic expression on her face. "You think they let the likes of us know?"

He nodded. "Good point." As he stood up, Bridget slid over and put her hand on his arm. She looked up at him, her dark brown eyes wide and more vulnerable than he'd ever seen them before. "I'm sorry," she whispered. "I'm as in the dark as you. I wish there was more I could tell you. I just feel there's somethin' terrible about to happen." She looked at the door as if expecting a bogeyman to come through it. "Not just for Mr. Hamrick. But for his wife. And that sweet little girl."

Cade moved to put his own hand on Bridget's, but the maid suddenly seemed to recognize how close they were sitting. She slid quickly to the other end of the bed, then hopped down to the floor.

"Bridget," Cade said, but he stopped when he saw that fierce look was back.

"I told you, big man," she snapped. "I'm not bedding you. Not tonight. Not ever."

"I ain't asked," he snapped back as he stood up, "and I wasn't fixin' to." Their fierce staring contest was interrupted by a knock on the door. "Come," he called out.

The door swung open to reveal Hamrick standing there, dressed in black trousers, another elaborately embroidered waistcoat, and a dark bowler hat. His eyes flickered from Cade to Bridget, then back again. He smiled sardonically. "I need you to accompany me on an outing, Mr. Cade. I trust this is not an inconvenient moment?"

"No, sir," Cade answered. "I am at your disposal."

"I was just makin' up the room," Bridget said, clearly flustered.

Hamrick regarded her coolly. "I'm sure."

Annoyed as he was with Bridget, Cade didn't like the way her face crumpled at the insinuating tone, and he cared even less for the way Hamrick seemed to enjoy the girl's humiliation. He also wasn't pleased at the thought that Hamrick had been listening at the door. He took the gun belt off the bedpost and buckled it on. Then he went to the hat rack in the corner and put on his Stetson.

"Ready when you are, sir," he said.

CHAPTER ELEVEN

The carriage was waiting for them out front, Samuel rigid as always in the driver's seat. He looked straight ahead, not acknowledging Cade or Hamrick until Hamrick spoke. "Evening, Samuel."

"Sir."

"Should I ride shotgun?" Cade asked. "Or with you?"

Hamrick smiled. "You're the bodyguard, Mr. Cade. Which do you recommend?"

Cade pondered a moment. "On a trail, I'd want to be up front. To see what might be comin' at us or at the side. In a city," he shook his head as the complexity of the problem began to impress itself on him, "in the city, I don't know which way a threat might come from. Can I ask where we're going?"

"Why, the Barbary Coast, of course. For business reasons, you understand." Cade thought he might have heard Samuel snort derisively, but he wasn't sure, and Hamrick didn't react.

"Then I best sit close as I can." Cade climbed up as Hamrick slid over. Samuel, impassive as ever, twitched the reins and shouted, "Gee-YUP," and they were off.

"So," Hamrick said after several minutes, "if you do want to bed Bridget, I can give you some advice in that regard."

"I don't know what you mean, sir," Cade answered. Hamrick didn't pursue the issue further, but Cade could still see his smirk. *Ten dollars a week*, Cade told himself. *Ten dollars.* He'd put up with a lot of guff from employers for a lot less money. It still didn't mean he had to like it.

They descended the hill again as darkness crept over the city. The lights were beginning to come on. First a few sparks in the gathering gloom, then the gas lamps began to kindle, creating a constellation, then a galaxy of light that they descended into, the view narrowing as they came down from the heights into the crowded city. Before long, the wide prosperous streets began to narrow, the surroundings becoming more and more shabby, until they were back in the Barbary Coast.

The quarter was in its full chaotic glory. The sidewalks teemed with lurching drunks, shifty-eyed footpads, and half-dressed whores leaning out of doorways and windows, promising all manner of delights, some quite improbable. Wide-eyed farm boys in overalls and weary miners, their clothes still dusty, stumbled through the circus of vice, just itching to be parted from their carefully hoarded money. Music, often tinny and off key, spilled from random doorways. Cade kept his eyes moving and his head on a swivel, looking for threats and finding them everywhere. Nothing was specific enough to make him draw the pistol at his hip, although his hand never strayed far from it. This body-guarding job was harder than he'd thought, especially if Hamrick intended to keep visiting the most crowded and violent quarter of the city.

Eventually, the carriage pulled up before a ramshackle three-story building, not that much different from a hundred others in the quarter. A ragged and unshaven vagrant slouching in a chair by the swinging doors of the street-level entrance raised his bleary eyes, then sprang to his feet and ran inside. In a moment, a black boy of no more than ten or eleven years ran out and took the bridle of the right-hand horse before looking up at the stern-faced Samuel in the driver's seat. The sight of Cade and the gun at his hip made the boy flinch back as if he'd been struck. He recovered his composure in a second, however, and stepped boldly back to stand beside the horse and look up at Samuel. "May we look after your horses, sir?"

Samuel looked down at him, imperious as a graven pharaoh, before giving a curt nod. The boy took hold of the bridle again, leaning over to whisper something in the horse's ear. The animal twitched the ear, whinnied, then allowed himself to be led past the front entrance and down a narrow alley between buildings. Cade tensed. This would be a perfect spot for an ambush.

"Rest easy, Mr. Cade." Hamrick sounded amused. "This is a safe haven."

"In my experience, sir, that's where you're most likely to get jumped."

They passed beneath a wooden arch into a small courtyard lit with torches. Shadowy figures lined the walls, slouched beneath overhanging balconies. Cade drew the pistol, but held it down along his leg.

"Are you frightened, Mr. Cade?" Hamrick's voice still held that tone of wry amusement, but Cade thought he might be hearing a crack in the cool facade.

"No, sir," he said. "Not frightened. Just careful. If you know these folks, you might want to give me an introduction."

Hamrick chuckled, that crack in his languid exterior quickly pasted over as if it had never occurred. "That might be difficult, considering no one here uses their real name. Not even me."

The shadowy figures along the walls were coming into better focus as Cade's eyes accustomed themselves to the gloom. They were all female, or at least a reasonable facsimile, dressed even more revealingly than the women he'd seen accosting strangers on the main street. A couple were actually naked above the waist, breasts sagging and pendulous in a way that was the opposite of erotic.

"This is a whorehouse." Cade didn't holster the pistol, but he did relax and let it dangle by his side.

"Indeed. That doesn't offend you, does it?"

Cade shook his head. "No, sir. But I thought we were on a

business errand. Not pleasure."

Hamrick's voice sharpened. "We are on whatever errand I say we are on. Is that clear?"

Cade kept his voice even. "As clear as day, sir. But with respect, it'd make my job of protecting you a damn sight easier if I knew ahead of time where we were going and why."

Hamrick stared for a moment, working his jaw, pride and the need to dominate fighting an internal war with practicality that played out on his face. Finally, he swung himself down to the dirt floor of the tiny courtyard. "Wait here. I'll be back in a few minutes."

"Sir…" Cade protested, but Hamrick had vanished into a nearby doorway. Cade gritted his teeth.

The whores in the shadows began calling out to him and Samuel.

"Hey, big man."

"Want to come upstairs with Big Molly? I don't mind a little dark meat."

"Want me to ride your pony, cowboy?"

Cade stole a glance at Samuel. The black man sat as rigid and deaf as a statue, ignoring the offers coming out of the gloom. One of the bolder whores swaggered up to the carriage and looked Cade over with one bright blue eye. The other was covered with a leather patch. Her long curly hair was dyed a shade of red Cade was pretty sure wasn't found in nature. "So how about it, cowboy?" she drawled. "Come upstairs with One-eyed Suzie. It'll be the best piece of ass you ever had."

"Sorry, darlin'," Cade answered. "I'm on duty. Maybe later."

Her face tightened as if she was going to say something vicious, but the little black boy who'd first greeted them ran out at that moment, clutching glass mugs filled with pale gold liquid in either hand. He ran up to the carriage and held the mugs out, one reaching toward Samuel, the other toward Cade.

"Compliments of the house," he panted, out of breath from hurrying. "While you wait."

Cade looked at Samuel, who looked back at him without expression before leaning down and taking the mug from the boy's hand. He took a deep draught of the beer before lowering the mug and silently tipping his hat to the boy.

Cade was surprised to see the stolid black driver partaking, but he followed suit, including the hat tip after a long swallow. "Much obliged, young fella." That seemed to provide some signal to the gathered watchers. Their attention wandered away from the carriage and its occupants, and they began walking about, muttering and gossiping amongst themselves.

Cade drank the rest of the mug and turned to Samuel. "How long does this here errand usually..." Before he could finish the sentence, a loud female scream split the air. The group gathered around beneath the balconies fell silent, froze, then every one of them vanished into the nearest doorway, leaving Cade and Samuel alone.

"What the hell?" Cade slid down from the carriage and dropped into a crouch, the Colt up and moving as if searching for targets on its own.

"Not our affair. Leave it." The tightness in Samuel's voice belied the nonchalance of the words. Another scream came from upstairs, but this time it was followed by a peal of hysterical laughter, apparently from the same throat. Cade was on the verge of heading into the warren of buildings surrounding them to seek out whoever was in distress, but that last sound drew him up short in confusion. It was followed by the sound of singing, a group of loud, unmelodious voices belting out "Oh, Susannah."

"Goddamn it," he muttered.

"You don't know what's happening." Samuel spoke down from his perch on the driver's seat, but there was no condescension or amusement in his voice.

Cade looked up. "No, damn it. Do you?"

Samuel shook his head. "No. But I'm used to it."

At that moment, Hamrick walked into the courtyard, his coat over his shoulder and a leather satchel in one hand. He tossed the satchel into the back of the carriage, where it landed with the clank of gold coin inside. Hamrick stopped to pull his coat on before looking at Cade. "I'm ready to go now."

"Yes, sir," Cade said. He holstered the pistol and climbed into the carriage beside his employer.

CHAPTER TWELVE

The quiet inside the carriage on the trip back was a distinct contrast to the noise and chaos they moved through. Inevitably, it was Hamrick who spoke first as they began the climb up the hill. "So, you're wondering what our little errand was."

Cade looked straight ahead. "Haven't looked in that satchel you brought out, but from the clatter, I figure it's a rent payment."

Hamrick nodded. "And why, you are likely asking yourself, could the rent not be collected during the day, when business was not in full swing?"

Cade said nothing. Hamrick chuckled. "Or maybe you didn't ask because you already know. You know that there's more than one form of currency in the Barbary Coast."

Cade said nothing. Hamrick went on. "So, Mr. Cade, I'm sure you were offered some of the local accommodation. But, unless I miss my estimation of time, you didn't avail yourself."

"No, sir. Not while I'm working."

Hamrick nodded. "Indeed. Maybe we'll need to take you back as a reward for your fidelity. I hear One-eyed Susie, in particular, is quite skilled in the French style."

After five years of traveling west, frequenting saloons, stews, and whorehouses, Cade was no Methodist prude. He knew exactly what was being described. Still, Hamrick's prurient interest in his personal arrangements was beginning to make his skin crawl. "Thank you, sir," he said, "but I reckon I can arrange for my own entertainment. In my own free time. Sir." The rebuke was bland but unmistakable, and Cade felt Hamrick stiffen beside him. *Well,* Cade thought. *Maybe I'll be looking for work again tomorrow. Wouldn't be the first job I lost for speaking my mind, but it'll be the best paying.*

They passed the rest of the ride in silence, until they approached the Hamrick residence. Cade saw Samuel grow rigid as the house came into view. He leaned forward. "What is it?" he murmured.

Samuel's voice was tense. "The lights are out."

Cade frowned. "I don't suppose that means everyone's turned in."

Samuel pulled the reins gently to stop the team. "No. The lights stay on 'til Mr. Hamrick returns. I douse them myself."

"Right, then." Cade drew the Colt. "I suppose you're heeled."

"What's going on?" Hamrick demanded.

Samuel produced a small silver pistol from an inside pocket of his waistcoat. "I've got this."

Cade grimaced. The little pistol Samuel had looked more like a decoration than a useful firearm, and the man held it as if he'd never touched a gun before. He turned to Hamrick. "Maybe nothing, sir. The lights are out, and that's not usual. You should wait here until I've checked it out." To Samuel, he whispered, "That lady's gun won't do a damn thing 'less you shoot the son of a bitch right in the eye. Stick with Hamrick and fire it in the air if anyone comes near you don't like the looks of. Better yet, go and fetch the law."

"Wait a minute," Hamrick spoke up, "my wife and daughter are in there."

"Yes, sir," Cade said as he dismounted the carriage. He knew his job was to guard Hamrick, but he'd be damned if he'd leave a woman and child in danger. "Stay here." Before either Hamrick or Samuel could protest, he headed off down the sidewalk, the Navy revolver held out in front of him. His mind raced as he considered his options. A charge up the front steps, even in the dark, would expose him to the fire of anyone in the front of the house. Best to slip around back. He reached the iron gate to the driveway. Sidling up next to the iron slats, he fumbled for the latch, straining his eyes in the dark to look down the shadowed passage. He grimaced. There could be a dozen ambushers waiting in that gloom and he wouldn't know it until the first bullet split his skull. But in a situation like this, with nothing but bad options, the worst thing to do was nothing.

When he lifted the latch, Cade opened the gate just wide enough to slip through. After closing it behind him, he crept as cat-footed as he could manage down the hedge-lined cobblestoned path. At the end of that leafy corridor, he stopped and peered around the end of the lane.

The dim light of a waxing moon barely illuminated the dirt courtyard before the carriage house. At the foot of the back steps, Cade could see a cloaked figure pacing back and forth. He took a deep breath to calm himself. Whoever the sentry was, he was at least as nervous as Cade. When he'd taken enough deep breaths to change that balance, at least in his own estimation, Cade stepped out into the open, the Colt held out in front of him.

"Hey," he called out, "who the fuck are you?"

The figure froze for a moment. Then, with a shrill cry, it charged. Something glinted in its right hand, catching the dim moonlight. Cade fired, the report sounding like cannon fire in the cloistered moonlit silence of the courtyard. The figure staggered, but kept advancing. Cade could make out the weapon in its hand, some kind of short-handled hatchet or tomahawk. He pulled the trigger again, then again. The charging figure slowed, stopped, then fell to its knees before falling forward soundlessly onto its face. Cade heard shouting from inside, male voices raised in a babble he couldn't make out, then a piercing female scream. Cade stepped over the fallen figure and bounded up the steps. He heard more shouting, a mix of male and female voices, then the roar of a heavy firearm, most likely a shotgun. Cade saw the back door hanging halfway open. He kicked it out of his way, then stormed inside.

He was back in the narrow hallway that led past the kitchen. Crouched, pistol at the ready, he crept down the gloomy passage, letting his eyes adjust. He could see a little better when he reached the doorway to the empty kitchen. Pots and pans hanging from racks reflected the moonlight that filtered in through the broad windows over the gleaming sinks. Cade paused, holding his breath, listening for any telltale signs of movement in the kitchen, fervently wishing he had a half dozen more trusted gunmen behind him to guard his flanks and rear. He hoped Samuel had done as he'd been asked and gone to fetch the law.

Another feminine scream from upstairs pulled his attention away. With a last glance behind him, he moved down the hall toward the front of the house. He heard the thunder of footsteps on stairs. They seemed to be coming from behind a door on one end of the kitchen, by the stove. *Servant's stairs*, he thought. There was more than one pair of feet crashing down those steps; it sounded like a stampede. Cade took up a position behind the high table in the middle of the room and turned to face the closed door as the commotion reached the bottom. He was so intent on what was in front of him, it was only by the stroke of good luck that he heard the dry creak of a floorboard behind him, turning at the last second to see a cloaked and hooded figure raising something above its head. The hatchet blade caught a stray beam of light as it came down. *It can't be the same man*, Cade thought as he threw himself backward. *It can't. I shot the son of a bitch.* He felt the hard edge of the table against his back and slid sideways, trying to find room to put between him and that wicked blade. He slid past the end of the table, stumbled, and fell flat on his ass, the vicious stroke burying the hatchet in the wood of the table and missing him so closely it tore a hole in the upper sleeve of his long coat. He raised the pistol again as the door from the stairs burst open. Two more cloaked figures emerged, gasping for breath. One seemed to be holding the other up. He turned back to the figure in front of him, who'd stepped forward, hatchet yanked from the table and raised above his head. Cade pulled the trigger once, twice. The report of the pistol was deafening in the darkened kitchen space. The figure staggered backward, but again didn't fall. *That's five*, he thought. *One shot left. No time to reload. And three men, even if one of them's wounded and the other ought to be dead.* A cold feeling came over him. *I am well and truly fucked now.*

He heard a footstep behind him and instinctively rolled to one side as a pistol shot chewed splinters out of the polished hardwood floor. Cade saw that the man from the stairs was still holding up his compatriot, but the gun in his free hand was pointed right at the center of Cade's face. He'd made the mistake of rolling to his right, putting his pistol arm beneath him, and he knew his luck had run out. There was no way the next shot could miss, and then there was the seemingly unkillable man with the hatchet. He was fighting to get his arm free when the next shot came. But when it did, it came from the hallway.

Cade looked over to see Samuel framed in the door to the kitchen, holding the little pistol he'd produced earlier. He fired again, the report sounding like a weak slap. This shot went wide of the man with the pistol, but it hit the man he was holding up with a sickening wet sound. Something warm and sticky spattered over Cade. The pistoleer screamed something in a high-pitched voice, raised his gun, and fired back at Samuel, but the carriage driver had ducked backward into the hallway. Cade heard another door bang open. *Christ, what now*, he thought as he turned. He saw moonlight through the side door as the figure of the hatchet man disappeared into the night. The remaining man dragged his limp burden around the other side of the table, keeping it between himself and Cade and heading for the door. As Cade began to rise up from behind the table, the man snapped off another shot, unaimed, but sufficient for its purpose of making Cade duck. Then they were gone out the side door. Cade considered following, but he'd used up five bullets without killing any of the mysterious intruders, and his bafflement quickly cooled any ardor for further gunplay. He looked down at himself. There was a dark stain across his front and he picked up the faint but unmistakable scent of blood. He checked to confirm that it wasn't his own. It seemed the only one who'd made a killing shot was Samuel.

"Cade?" Samuel called from the darkened hallway.

"In here. They're gone."

Samuel edged his way into the kitchen, his little gun at the ready. He let it fall to his side as he saw Cade. "You got blood on you."

"I'm not hit. That's from the bastard you shot. Killed him, unless I miss my guess."

Samuel's laugh was strained, with an edge of hysteria in it. "Well, you told me to shoot the son of a bitch in the eye."

"That ain't exactly what I told you. But I'm in no mood to quibble. Much obliged, by the way."

Samuel nodded, took a deep breath, and got hold of himself with a visible effort. He looked at the open stairway. "Mrs. Hamrick? Violet?"

"I heard someone hollerin' upstairs. And a shot." They started for the stairs together, then Cade stepped back and motioned for Samuel to go first. "They know you better. And I think the lady's got a shotgun."

Samuel nodded, then started up the stairs. "Mrs. Hamrick?" he called up. "It's Samuel."

There was no answer. Samuel looked back at Cade, who gestured with his free hand to the stairs. "Go on up. I'll go round to the front stairs and check for stragglers. Just don't shoot me when I get up there, okay?"

"I'll do my best." He started up the stairs again. In the distance, Cade could hear shrill whistles approaching.

CHAPTER THIRTEEN

The lights were back on, the warm glow of the gas lamps casting a mantle of reassurance over the house. Cade and Samuel sat side by side on a lushly upholstered couch in the downstairs parlor, watched over by a large, stone-faced policeman with a bushy, grey-flecked mustache. They'd been relieved of their firearms, which made Cade feel unsettled. After what they'd just been through, he wanted his pistol.

Cade leaned over and murmured to Samuel. "Was Mrs. Hamrick okay? And the little girl?"

"Here, you two," the big policeman said. "No talking."

The tone got Cade's back up. "Says who?" He stood up.

The policeman turned to face Cade, drawing his long baton from beneath his coat. "Says me. And Captain Smith."

"And who the fuck, exactly, is Captain Smith, that I should be fuckin' mindful of him? By the way, friend, you might want to be a bit more circumspect with that there little stick, lest you find it crammed into a place that might cause you embarrassment."

The policeman's face reddened with rage until it was almost purple. He drew back the baton. Cade braced himself to charge to within the swing of the weapon. The man had a few inches of reach and more than a few pounds on Cade, but his blood was still up, and he was never in a mood to be bullied.

They were interrupted by a dry voice that came from the doorway. "That will be enough, Sergeant Dunleavy."

The sound of the voice seemed to freeze the big policeman in mid-swing. He regarded Cade, eyes wide, nearly bulging with barely suppressed rage. Then he took a deep breath and stepped back, letting the baton fall to his side. When he spoke, it was in the tones of a child trying to justify a minor offense. "Captain, I think these two were tryin' to get their stories together."

Cade turned to the man who'd spoken first. He was leaning against the doorjamb, smiling sardonically. He was short and slender, with a pale complexion and skin that seemed loose on the bones of his face, like that of a man recovering from a long illness. His clothing was in an expensive cut that rivaled anything Hamrick might wear. He held a bowler hat in his left hand, tapping the brim against his right. The only element that connected him with Dunleavy was the silver star on his left lapel that matched the one on the burly sergeant's long gray coat.

"Thank you, Sergeant," he said kindly. "I'll take that into consideration. Along with your help in this investigation. I can assure you, these fellows are going to get everything that's coming to them. Now, if you'd ask Lieutenant Webster to step in, so we can have a talk with these witnesses?"

Dunleavy looked at Cade and Samuel with narrowed eyes. He clearly wanted to be present for whatever comeuppance his captain had planned, but he was a man of duty. With one last hard glance at the two men on the couch, he left the room. Smith gave the two of them a smile, then took a seat on a nearby chair.

"Now," he said, "let's talk about what just happened."

"First things first," Cade said. "Is Mrs. Hamrick all right?"

"And her daughter," Samuel burst in.

"Mother and daughter are fine," Smith said. He smiled. "In fact, it was Mrs. Hamrick who helped repel at least one assailant. With a shotgun secreted in her bedchamber, as it happens."

Cade recalled the blasts he'd heard from upstairs. "She shot one of them. I saw another one of them trying to drag a wounded man out of here." He nodded at Samuel. "I think this one finished the wounded man off." He realized too late how that might sound, then lamely finished, "Maybe. I don't know."

Smith just nodded as if it didn't matter. "So. Tell me everything that happened," he looked directly at Cade, "from the time you arrived back at the house."

Cade got the point immediately. Nothing was to be said about where they'd been prior to their return. "When we pulled up, all the lights were off."

Smith nodded. "We've established that. The gas was turned off. Do you have any idea how or why that was done?"

Cade shook his head. "I ain't no engineer, sir. I don't even know how you might do that."

Smith just nodded, his expression patient. "Go on."

Cade did as he was asked. When he got to the confrontation in the carriage yard, he couldn't keep calm any longer. "I shot him, sir. I shot him over and over. But the bastard kept getting back up. I don't know how."

"Body armor," a voice came from the door.

The man who spoke was much taller than Smith, at least six and a half feet, and as broad-shouldered as the sergeant who'd detained them earlier. He wore the same long gray coat and silver star. His face was lean and chiseled, clean-shaven, but scarred as if with an old pox. He held a short-handled hatchet in one hand. He advanced into the room as if making an entrance on a stage before tossing the hatchet onto the floor. In the silence his entrance had created, the hand-axe clattered loudly on the floorboards. *"Boo How Doy,"* the man said.

Cade shook his head as if to clear his ears. "What?"

"Chinese tong assassins," Smith said. "Green Dragon, unless I miss my guess." He nodded to the man who'd just entered. "Lieutenant Webster is the police department's chief authority on the Chinese community. And their crimes."

"Well, I've met a few Chinamen along the way," Cade said. "Smart ones, dumb ones, young ones that was strong as a bull, and old ones you could break in half with a little finger." He looked at Webster. "But I never heard of any of 'em bein' bulletproof."

Webster smiled indulgently. "You're new in town, Mr...Cade, is it?"

Cade nodded.

The smile faded. "You don't know what the good people of San Francisco are up against."

"Well, if it's bulletproof Chinamen, maybe we'd best start talkin' terms of surrender."

"That is not an option," Smith said.

"That was actually a joke, sir," Cade replied.

"This is no joking—" Smith began, but Webster interrupted.

"Some of the *Boo How Doy* wear chainmail jackets under their clothing." He smirked. "It helps spread the superstition among the ignorant rank and file Chinese that they are some kind of supernatural killers. Invincible. Immortal."

"Chain mail isn't supposed to stop bullets," Cade protested.

"It will slow them down, though. You definitely injured the man you shot," Webster said. "We found blood in the courtyard." He looked grim. "But these men are fanatics. They consume wildcat meat before battle, thinking it will give them supernatural strength and ferocity. And, of course, many of them are out of their minds on drugs and potions their heathen herb doctors concoct."

It all seemed too fantastic to be true. Cade shook his head. "Okay." He stood up. "Well, if that's all you fellows want to know, I'm goin' to check on Mr. Hamrick."

"Hold up there a minute, Mr. Cade." Smith stopped him with an upraised hand that came close to pushing against Cade's chest before Cade stopped him with a look. He let the hand drop and smiled ingratiatingly. "I assure you, Mr. Hamrick is fine, as are his wife and daughter. We just have a few more questions. I'm sure you want to help the police in this investigation."

Cade sighed and sat back down.

The "few more questions" turned out to be the same questions asked in different ways to see if Cade would change his story. At one point, Samuel was taken out of the room to be questioned separately. Cade held onto his patience as long as he could and told the story over and over. His answers grew shorter, more snappish, and he was about to stand up again and tell them all to go to hell when Smith stood up. "Thank you, Mr. Cade. I believe that's all we will require. I'm sure you're tired."

I was tired two goddamn hours ago, Cade thought, but he just nodded. As he reached the door, Smith called out, "Don't leave town, Mr. Cade. We may have other inquiries." Cade bit back his response and kept going, merely raising a hand in acknowledgment. He trudged up the stairs. All he wanted was to go to his room and collapse. The excitement of the evening had been turned to dust by the steady grind of Smith's questioning, and Cade was tired enough to want to throw himself on the bed and fall asleep without even taking his boots off. But he wanted a drink first.

He went to his bag and rummaged around until he came up with the pint of whiskey he kept in the bottom, a pair of socks rolled around it for protection. He liked to tell the rubes the whiskey was for snakebite, but the only effect it would have on a bitten man would be to let him die with a smile on his face. He pulled the cork from the bottle and took a drink. The sweet burn of the good whiskey made him smack his lips. He bent down, took off one boot, then another, then took another drink. As he tipped the bottle up for a third, there was a knock at the door.

Jesus, he thought, *What now?* "Come in," he called out.

Samuel opened the door, stepped through, and closed it behind him. He looked as tired and ragged as Cade felt. He stood for a moment, shifting his weight slightly from foot to foot, looking at the floor, then at Cade.

"Some night," Cade said to break the silence.

"Yes."

Cade held out the bottle. "Care for a drink to calm your nerves?"

Samuel hesitated, then walked over and took it. He looked around.

"Ain't got a glass," Cade said, "but I'm pretty sure I ain't got nothin' catchin'."

Samuel looked at him quizzically. "Not a lot of white men would share a bottle with a Negro."

Cade shrugged. "I been travelin' a while. Worked with all sort of people. Blacks, Mexicans, even a Jew one time in the Dakotas. Drank with 'em all in various circumstances. This is about as various as circumstances get, wouldn't you agree?"

Samuel nodded and took a drink. He grimaced slightly as the liquor went down. He still seemed to have something he wanted to say.

Looks as if I'm not gettin' to bed just yet, Cade thought with an inner sigh. "Well, pull up a chair and sit if you like."

"Thank you." Samuel handed the bottle back and pulled the room's one chair over by the bed. Cade noted that the bottle was half empty. Tired as he was, he didn't want to pass out. Still, he took another, shorter drink and handed the bottle back to Samuel. "You got somethin' on your mind?"

Samuel didn't take another swallow. "I owe you my thanks," he said. He didn't look at Cade as he said it. "I believe you saved my life."

Cade shrugged. "I figger you did me the same favor. So, thanks right back at you."

Samuel hesitated, then took another drink, a long one. *Gonna need to talk to Bridget about supplies,* Cade thought. Samuel handed the bottle back and looked straight ahead. He let out a long, shuddering sigh.

It began to dawn on Cade what was troubling him. "First man

you ever killed, I reckon."

Samuel looked at him. He nodded, then looked away. "Not your first."

"No."

"Does it get easier?"

"Pray that it don't," Cade said.

"How many men have you killed?"

"Depends. We partners now?"

Samuel looked shocked. "What? No!"

"And why not, considerin' that we just saved one another's lives and are now sharin' a bottle of middlin' good whiskey?" Samuel remained silent, until Cade lost the miniscule shred of patience he had left. "We ain't partners, then the answer to that question ain't none of your goddamn business."

Samuel got to his feet, still without expression. "I'm sorry to have disturbed you."

"Apology accepted. And you're welcome. For shootin' that Chinaman."

"You're welcome as well." Samuel walked out.

"Exhaustin' son of a bitch," Cade muttered. He blew out the lamp. As he stripped to his drawers and laid himself down, he couldn't seem to close his eyes and sleep. He stared at the ceiling for a long time. How many had it been? Hard to tell how many in the war. The fury of the charge, a figure in the smoke, the quick glimpse of a face contorted in fear or rage, the flash of a pistol...he couldn't rightly say how many of those shots had taken life and how many had maimed or wounded, whether a desperate passing saber slash had killed his opponent or left him with a scar to show the admiring townsfolk and grandchildren in the long years to come. He'd ridden through the aftermath of battles, seen the dead lying grotesque and bloated on the ground, and honestly couldn't say which ones he'd killed. He couldn't even tell who, if anyone, he'd killed this night. The thought weighed on him. It occurred to him that a man should know how many people he'd killed. After thinking about that for a long time, Cade finally fell into a fitful and troubled sleep.

CHAPTER FOURTEEN

The light outside Cade's window was still dim when he awoke, the sun not yet up. He made his way to the "siphonic water closet," as Bridget had called it, the ache in his bladder overcoming his trepidation at the unfamiliar contraption. It seemed to work okay. He pulled trousers, boots, and shirt on and went downstairs. The aroma of fresh coffee tickled his nose as he reached the bottom of the back staircase and he followed it to the kitchen. He saw no one there, but the pot was on the stove. After rummaging around in the cupboards, he found a cup and poured himself a generous serving. He grabbed a rickety chair near the wall and hauled it out the side door to enjoy his coffee out of doors in the dawn. It was only after he set the chair down that he noticed Mrs. Hamrick.

She had her back to him, bent over a raised bed of flowers near the carriage house. He grunted softly in annoyance and picked up the chair to take it back inside. She may or may not have heard the sound, but she turned and saw him. He stopped, chair held in one hand, coffee in the other, frozen as if he'd been caught stealing. She didn't move or speak, just regarded him with that unsettling silent gaze. "Um, good morning, ma'am," he said finally, setting the chair down.

"Good morning." She walked over and stood in front of him.

He gestured to the chair. "Would you like to sit, ma'am?"

She shook her head. "You go ahead. And drink your coffee before it gets cold."

69

He felt the heat of embarrassment rising in his face. "I don't think it would be right to sit down and drink while you're standing there empty-handed, ma'am."

She smiled. "Do you want me to leave?"

"No, ma'am. Maybe I should."

"Nonsense." She was still smiling. "Have a seat and wait here." She brushed past him, so close he caught the scent of lilacs in her hair. He didn't know what to do, so he did as he was told, taking a seat and a sip of the coffee. The taste brought an involuntary smile to his lips. The coffee was strong enough to strip paint, but that was how he liked it. It had been a while since he'd had something besides the belly-wash to be found in the local dives.

He heard the door swing open and turned slightly. Mrs. Hamrick was there, holding a cup in one hand and a wooden folding chair in the other. He was astonished when she brought both over, snapped the chair open, and took a seat beside him. She took her cup in both hands, bent down to take a long sniff of the rich aroma, and closed her eyes before taking the first drink. "Ahhhh," she said in a voice so thick with pleasure he wondered if he should be watching. She opened her eyes and smiled at him again. "I hope the coffee isn't too strong for your liking."

"No, ma'am," he said. "Just the way I like it."

"Would you like sugar? Cream?"

He shook his head. "Never got a taste for those. "

She nodded, as if he'd passed a test. "My father was the captain and owner of a merchant ship. He wasn't home much. But when he was, he always had a pot of strong coffee on the stove. The best beans, brought straight from the Indies. He always said, 'If ye wanted a cuppa cream an' sugar, why'd ye ask for coffee?'" The last part was delivered in a Scots brogue that sounded straight out of Glasgow. The mimicry was so unexpected, Cade laughed. She laughed as well. They drank again. It was a moment before she spoke again. "So. Last night."

He didn't know where to go with that, so he answered, "Yes, ma'am."

"We owe you a debt of gratitude."

He shrugged. "Just doing my job."

"Hm," she murmured. She took another sip and waited before speaking again. "Is it true that Samuel killed a man?"

He tried to puzzle out how to answer, whether to try to comfort or soothe her, or to evade the question. She fixed him with a level stare. "The truth," she said firmly, her dark eyes boring into him.

"I…I believe he may have," Cade said.

"Hmmm," she repeated. She took another sip. "I don't know if he's suited to that."

Cade shrugged. "I don't reckon he had any choice."

"Of course not," she murmured. "Those men meant us harm. Me and my daughter. That's why I shot them as well."

"You, ma'am?"

She nodded. "You heard the shotgun, I imagine. Did you think it was my daughter pulling the trigger?"

"I heard, yes, ma'am."

Her smile was thinner this time, with less humor in it. "You look shocked. Are you surprised I would defend myself and my child?"

He shook his head. "I been around long enough to know you don't get between a mama bear and her cub. But a shotgun ain't usually a lady's weapon."

She snorted. "A lady's weapon is whatever the lady has at hand." That silenced him again. She drained the last of her cup and looked at him. "Why did my husband hire you, Mr. Cade?" The companionable tone of her earlier reminiscence was gone. Her eyes were narrowed, calculating, and her voice was hard.

"He said he had business interests that got some people mad at him. Like those Chinese. So he needed a bodyguard."

"Who he then took with him on one of his whoring expeditions, leaving myself and my daughter to fend for ourselves." She said it matter-of-factly, without malice or bitterness. He was feeling deeply uncomfortable again. He took another drink of the coffee, which was rapidly cooling.

"Don't worry, Mr. Cade." She stood up. "I don't blame you. You and Samuel arrived in the very nick of time, and thus, became the heroes of the hour." She shook the last few drops of coffee out of her cup onto the grass. "But perhaps I will be needing your services as much, if not more, than Mr. Hamrick."

"Maybe," Cade said weakly. "Or, you know, we can hire someone for you…"

"That would be an additional expense I'm not sure I'm willing to incur."

He was nonplussed for a moment. She smiled, and this time all the humor in it was gone. "I don't suppose he told you, did he? This house, these clothes, your salary…it all comes from me. Mr. Hamrick has almost no cash to his name. What real estate he has is mortgaged to the hilt. The bulk of the family fortune is mine, built on what my father left me. A fortune which I myself have grown and cultivated. Have a good day, Mr. Cade. I'll call on you when I need you." She turned and walked back inside, leaving him gaping after her like an addlepated rube.

CHAPTER FIFTEEN

"You failed," McMurphy said.

The man behind the curtain replied in that infuriatingly calm voice. "How so?"

"You didn't take the girl. Or the woman. You lost how many men? And for what?"

"Hamrick is in fear now. His torment is just beginning."

McMurphy shook his head at the sheer blockheadedness of the man. How could someone so dense have risen to head the Green Dragon Tong?

The man behind the curtain chuckled. "You *gwai loh* are all the same. Always in a hurry. Always wanting everything at once."

"The wife and the daughter were going to be the key to getting at Hamrick's money. The money he took from me. How are we going to get our investment back?"

"You told me it wasn't just the money. You want your former partner to suffer. And I guarantee you, he is doing so at this very moment. Is it not more satisfying, more...artistic...to make the suffering last?" There was an undertone of sadistic glee in the voice that shriveled Murphy's anger inside him and left a chill of fear in its place. "Now we've got the police asking questions," he said weakly. "It's going to be harder to get at Hamrick. Or his money. And there's this gunman he hired."

"The police in this city are no worry. All of them are grasping, greedy fools. For sale, like everything in this city. If necessary, I will make arrangements with them. Out of my own funds. As for the gunman, he will be no impediment."

"He seemed to impede a couple of your boys pretty well."

"I have taken his measure. He will not stop us."

McMurphy wasn't convinced, but there was nothing more he could do. "What's your next move?"

"You'll be informed."

McMurphy felt his anger rising again despite the fear. "So, I'm to just sit on my hands until I hear from you?"

"It will not be long. I promise." The man behind the curtain stood, his shadow growing larger on the curtain. The audience was over. McMurphy left, fuming to himself.

***

"He will cause trouble," Mei said as she took the gold coins from the man's hand.

He looked down at her, a frown creasing his brow. "You were eavesdropping."

She shrugged, looking at him defiantly. "This is a small shop. And he was angry. Angry voices carry."

"I don't need to tell you the consequences of telling what you see here. For you, and for your family."

She shook her head. "I won't tell."

"Good. Now go." She left without looking back. His frown deepened as she left. He knew there was nothing McMurphy could attempt that wouldn't actually benefit his real plan. But the girl… she could cause real trouble. He decided she was becoming more of a risk than he felt comfortable with. He reached into his belt and drew out his knife. Walking as silently as he could muster, he followed the girl through the door and into the front of the shop.

She wasn't there. The front of the fish shop was locked, a sign hung on the door. There was no sign of the grandparents, either.

"Clever girl," he whispered. "Too clever by half." His misgivings deepened as he re-sheathed the knife and let himself out the back door.

CHAPTER SIXTEEN

Mei hurried through the streets of Chinatown, the gold coins stashed safely in a leather pouch which she'd then pinned to the inside of her skirt at the waistband. From time to time she stole a glance behind her to see if she was being followed. She'd felt the mysterious white devil's growing mistrust of her and knew their business arrangement was at an end. Her usefulness to him had ended as well.

It had seemed such a simple thing at first: he'd told her he needed a quiet and secluded place, away from prying eyes, to conduct what he called "business meetings." The secrecy was needed, he'd explained, because of the delicacy of the negotiations he was undertaking to merge two great business concerns. If the word got out, then it would affect the white devils' stock market in ways he didn't want. She cursed herself under her breath for her simple-mindedness, as if she was a country bumpkin straight off the ship from China. She'd known from the first meeting, where he'd hidden himself behind the curtain and pretended to be the head of the Green Dragon Tong, that she'd been fooled. But the man's threats, some veiled, some more direct, toward her and her grandparents had bullied her into submission. Now there was talk of women and children being kidnapped and held for ransom, something for which she knew the Chinese would be blamed. She knew then that she'd heard too much. Some knowledge was not safe to have. If she could cut it out of her head to keep herself and her family safe, she would. Failing that, there was only one thing to do. It made her heart clench in her chest to think of it, but there was no other way. She might be punished, even killed, for her part in the charade, but that couldn't be helped. She'd bundled her querulous, baffled grandparents off to stay with an aunt, closed the shop, and set off to find a place she knew only by whispers and a man so terrifying that even the whispers were silenced.

She began to notice that she wasn't the only one nervous. Other denizens of Chinatown were walking quickly, looking around, some hunched over as if waiting for a rainstorm or an earthquake. Here and there small groups were gathered, talking in low, worried whispers. Something bad was about to happen, and she had the sick feeling that it had something to do with what she'd overheard. From down the street she heard shouting, then high-pitched cries of fear. Heads turned as people came into view, running down the street in her direction. People hurried into shops, the doors quickly closed and locked, shades pulled down. In moments, the street was nearly deserted. She turned around and found the nearest shop, a dry goods dealer named Mr. Ji who she knew slightly. As she headed for the door, it slammed shut. She ran to the door and knocked frantically. "Mr. Ji," she called out. "It's Mei. Let me in. Please." There was no answer. Behind her, she heard the shouting grow nearer, to the point where she could make out the words, shouted in slurred English. "Look out for the hoodlums! The hoodlums are coming!" Looking around in a panic, Mei located a narrow alley between two buildings and ducked into it. She crouched behind a rainwater barrel, pressing her back against it, not daring to look around and bring attention to herself. More shouts filled the street, along with drunken laughter. She heard the sound of glass breaking. She closed her eyes, then opened them again, chiding herself inwardly for acting like a child who thought she couldn't be seen if she couldn't see. She stole a glance around the side of the barrel.

There were about twenty *gwai loh* in the group, dressed in

embroidered vests, tight trousers, and ruffled shirts with black string ties. Most had whiskey bottles in one hand, with a variety of clubs, boards, and brickbats in the other. None of them looked more than twenty years old, and every one of them was staggering drunk. As she looked, a beefy redhead wound up and threw the brick he was carrying through a shop window. The crash and tinkling of falling glass sent the group into gales of laughter. "Come on out, ya yellow bastards!" a skinny *gwai loh* called out in a high voice. "Come out here and learn not to molest the white women of San Fran-goddamn-…" The diatribe trailed off into a fit of drunken giggles, and Mei realized with a shock that the person shouting was a young woman, her black hair cut short. A couple of men appeared, dragging someone between them. Mei bit back a sob of fear as she saw that it was old Mr. Lee, who owned the laundry in this block. He was babbling in fear, pleading in Chinese, but the unfamiliar words seemed only to anger the hoodlums. The short-haired girl produced a long-bladed knife and brandished it aloft, to the ragged cheers of the rest of the group. Mei stuck the back of her hand into her mouth to keep from crying out as the blade descended. She heard Mr. Lee's shriek of fear. But when the girl raised her hands again, all she was holding in her off hand was Mr. Lee's long black pigtail. She breathed a sigh of relief, but it was premature. One of the men stepped up to where Mr. Lee knelt in the dirt, sobbing with the humiliation of having his traditional queue severed. The man was carrying a long plank in both hands. As he drew it back, Mei ducked back behind the barrel so she wouldn't have to see any more. She heard the flat *thwack* as the board connected. Mr. Lee howled in agony, and the crowd bayed back mockingly. She heard more blows land, more screams. The screams soon stopped, but the blows didn't. *I hate them*, she thought. *I hate them all. I want them dead. All white devils.*

Eventually, it seemed, the gang tired of its sport and she heard them moving off. She looked into the street. Mr. Lee's body lay still in the center of the roadway, unmoving. People were beginning to peer around the edges of doors and beneath shaded windows. She heard a scream of anguish and saw an older man rush from a building across the street. He fell to his knees beside Mr. Lee's body and wailed in unbridled anguish, his face turned upward to the blank sky. "My brother," he screamed. "My brother! Why? Why?" Others ran out to join him, all the while looking around in fear of the hoodlums' return. Mei left the alley and moved along, the old man's cries ringing in her ears. She was more determined on her errand now than ever. She knew what she had to do, as much as it frightened her.

The only way to stop the false dragon was to awaken the real one.

CHAPTER SEVENTEEN

A few blocks later, Mei ducked down a side street, coming to a stop before a short flight of steps that led to a heavy wooden door. There were no signs or advertisements on that door, but everyone in Chinatown knew the business that went on behind it. Outside, seated on a barrel, sat a hugely fat man, his massive arms crossed on his chest. He looked down at Mei from his perch, his eyes surveying her impassively. Then his broad face broke into the type of grin no young girl could feel safe beholding. "Good morning, girl," he said in Cantonese. "Have you come to apply for a job?" He licked his lips. "How about I try you out first?"

She straightened up and looked him in the eye, hoping her long skirt kept him from seeing how her knees were trembling. "I need to speak with Mr. Kwan."

He laughed out loud at that. "Oh, do you? And what business does some street girl have with Mr. Kwan? "

"That is for me to tell him. And he won't be happy if he finds out some stupid ox of a guard kept him from hearing the news I bring him."

The guard's face clouded with anger. "*Puk gai*," he snarled, and slid off the barrel to advance on her. Standing, he looked as big as the building behind him. He balled his fist as if to strike her. At that moment, the door opened, and a middle-aged man stumbled out into the street, blinking in confusion at the bright sunlight. The reek of alcohol coming off his skin nearly made her retch. He almost stumbled into the guard, but pulled himself back at the last moment, goggling at him as if at some apparition. Then his face broke out in a drunken smile. "There you are!" he mumbled, and opened his arms as if to embrace the startled guard. "My good friend!"

The guard shoved him away in disgust. "Piss off, you old..."

Mei took advantage of the momentary distraction to push her way past the drunk, nudging him in the direction of the guard, before bounding up the short flight of steps and slipping through the slowly closing door.

"HEY!" the guard bellowed. Mei could hear the drunk babbling something about needing "just a few coins to get back in the game" before the door swung shut behind her. She turned and surveyed the room.

It was long and narrow, dimly lit by flickering lanterns. On either side of a long aisle down the center, men sat at low square tables, their attention fixed on the bowls and beads of *fan-tan*, the tiles of *mah-jongg*, or the cards of the more westernized forms of gambling Mr. Kwan had introduced as another method of separating the Chinese laborer from his scant pay. A few looked up at the intrusion, but quickly returned their gaze to the table. No gambler trusted another, or the house for that matter, not to cheat a distracted man. The hubbub of voices that had ceased briefly as she came in resumed.

Mei made her way quickly down the aisle, to the bar at the end of the room where an older man in a traditional quilted jacket and round hat stood wiping down the bar. He inclined his head curiously at her as she ran up to him.

"You seem a bit young for a whiskey, young lady," he said in a mild tone.

"Please," she said in a low, urgent voice. "I need to see Mr. Kwan. It's important."

She heard the front door yanked open, and the outside guard's outraged shout. She turned to see him advancing on her like an enraged bull, holding a short wooden club in his hand. She turned back to the bar. "Please," she begged. Then she screamed in pain as the guard grabbed her by the hair and pulled her off her feet. She fell to the ground at the feet of the guard, who struck down at her with the club. She managed to turn and take the blow on her hip, the pain making her cry out. She began to sob, as much in frustration as in pain. The guard raised the club again, the snarl on his face making him even uglier.

"Stop," the bartender said. His voice was quiet, but it halted the guard in mid swing.

He looked at the bartender, confused. "She came in without… she pushed past…"

"That is your failure," the bartender said. "She won't be the one punished for it."

The guard straightened up, his face contorted with anger. "Someday," he said through clenched teeth, "you're going to go too far."

The bartender smiled. "I am sure. But not today. Go back to your post, and try not to be fooled by little girls next time."

Mei thought the guard might actually go after the bartender, who was still smiling. But he only growled something under his breath, turned, and marched back down the once-again-silent aisle. The men watched him warily until the door closed, then the whole place seemed to breathe a collective sigh of relief. The bartender shook his head, then smiled and extended a hand to help Mei up.

"Thank you, sir," she said, her voice still shaking.

"Are you badly hurt?" the bartender asked.

She shook her head. "A bruise is all. I think. It will get better."

He nodded. He seemed to approve of that. "So. You wish to speak with Mr. Kwan."

"Yes, sir. It's about something…I mean…it's just important." A thought came to her. "Are you Mr. Kwan?"

He smiled. "I am. But not, I expect, the one to whom you wish to speak. Perhaps you should tell me what it is you wish to speak to my brother about."

His brother. Mei considered. She'd made up her mind to speak only with the head of the Green Dragon Tong. But there was something about this man that she wanted to trust. She leaned over the bar and whispered. "Someone, a white devil, is doing terrible things. And trying to make sure the Chinese are blamed."

He shrugged and went back to wiping the bar. "This is not new."

"But this time is different. People have been hurt. I saw a group beat poor Mr. Lee. They...they may have killed him." At that her carefully maintained composure broke. She crossed her arms on the bar, put her head down, and wept. She was dimly aware that the hubbub of the gambling house had stopped. *They're all staring*, she thought, but she couldn't stop herself. She was so afraid, and so very, very tired of being afraid. After a moment, she felt a gentle but insistent tapping on the top of her head. When she held up, Kwan was holding out a rag to her. "Here," he said. "Wipe your face. And blow your nose. You're upsetting the customers."

Mei took the rag, glanced at it to make sure it was a clean, fresh one, then wiped her eyes. Kwan looked at her gravely, and there was something in his calmness that steadied her. "Thank you, Uncle," she murmured.

He nodded, pleased at the expression of respect, and placed a glass in front of her before pulling a pitcher from beneath the bar and pouring out a measure of clear liquid. "Water," he assured her, and Mei drank it gratefully.

"Thank you," she said again.

Kwan nodded. "Wait here." He disappeared behind a curtain at the back of the bar. She heard a shouted order, and in a moment, a large young man came through the curtain, looking unsure of what he was supposed to be doing. He blinked at Mei in confusion. An older man came up to the bar, grinning. "Hey, Donkey," he said. "How about a free drink?"

The young man shook his head. "I'm just supposed to watch the bar while Mr. Kwan is gone for a minute."

"Come on, dummy," the man said, reaching across the bar toward a bottle perched there. "Just one. Kwan said it's okay."

The young man's broad shoulders slumped. He looked sick and confused. Mei realized he was simple-minded. The grinning man made as if to come around the bar and seize the whiskey bottle.

"Stop," Mei said.

The man turned to her. "What business is it of yours, little bitch?"

She gave him his scowl right back. "My business is with Mr. Kwan. The older brother. And what do you think he will do to a man who steals from him?"

That stopped him. With a snarl, he turned his back and slunk back to his table.

She looked at the young man. "You are called Donkey?"

He nodded, looking miserable. "I clean up. I'm not supposed to be at the bar."

"But here you are. And you shouldn't let these fools take advantage of you. You're bigger than them." She looked back at the man from the bar and snorted in contempt. "You could break that old man in half if he gave you trouble."

"I know," Donkey said in a small voice. "But I don't like to hurt people. It makes me feel bad."

She nodded. "That makes you a good man."

At that, he smiled. It was a beautiful smile, a child's smile, without guile or artifice. But it faded as quickly as it had appeared and Donkey bowed his head as Mr. Kwan reentered through the curtain.

His eyes narrowed with suspicion as he looked from Donkey to Mei. "What's going on? Was there trouble?"

Mei looked back at the old man, who was staring angrily at her from behind his gaming table. She returned her gaze to Mr. Kwan and smiled. "No. Nothing that my new friend Donkey here couldn't handle."

Kwan looked at Donkey skeptically. "Is this true?"

"Yes," Donkey muttered. "No trouble."

He still looked dubious, but finally turned back to Mei. "Up the stairs. Be quick. My brother is a busy man."

"Thank you." Mei sidled past the two men and through the curtain. The stairs were in front of her, with another curtained-off room to her right. She mounted the steps slowly, her knees beginning to tremble again as she remembered who she was about to confront. At the top of the stairs, she paused, took a deep breath, and knocked.

"Come," a voice said. She turned the knob and entered.

The room was small and cramped, dominated by a large, ornately carved desk. The desktop was bare except for a pair of candles, one at either side. A man sat behind the desk in a large upholstered chair. She couldn't tell how tall he was, but he was slender, with a long face and sunken cheeks. His hands were graceful and long-fingered, resting comfortably on the arms of the chair. He was dressed in a traditional fashion, with an embroidered silk jacket tied up the front despite the heat in the room, but she was surprised to see that his grey-streaked black hair was cut short and parted on one side in the western style. He had no queue. He regarded her with unblinking eyes that reminded her of a hunting hawk's.

"Well?" he said. His voice was dry and raspy, as if he rarely used it.

She bowed her head. "Thank you, Great Sir, for agreeing to see me. I know you are a busy and powerful man."

Kwan snorted. "If I want to be flattered, I can have that any time. My brother says you have something new to tell me."

She straightened up. "Yes. There is a man. A white devil. He is claiming to be Chinese, and stirring up trouble for which he wants the Chinese blamed."

The man in the chair grunted, unimpressed. "The white devils blame the Chinese for all their troubles."

"Yes. But this man is stirring up trouble while claiming to be the head of the Green Dragon Tong."

That brought a flicker of something across the man's face. Surprise. Maybe anger. But it was gone too quickly to tell. His face resumed that blank, unnerving regard. Mei began to speak again, but he raised his hand in a languid yet commanding gesture and she fell silent. He reached into a desk drawer and pulled out a small silver bell. When he rang it, a panel slid open in one side of the room, so unexpectedly as to make Mei jump. A woman was standing there, also robed in traditional fashion. She smiled at Mei. She was stunningly beautiful, her eyes dark and wide, her face perfect in every proportion, as if she'd just stepped out of a painting. The man murmured something, and the woman bowed and stepped back into the darkness behind the panel. In a moment, still smiling, she returned with a chair, which she set behind Mei. It was then that Mei saw the dagger thrust into the belt of the woman's robe. The woman caught Mei's gaze and bowed, still smiling, before stepping back to stand behind the chair.

"Now," Kwan said. "Sit down. Tell me everything." He gestured at the woman standing behind Mei. "And if you lie to me, The White Orchid there will cut your throat."

CHAPTER EIGHTEEN

Cade shook his head. Mrs. Hamrick's revelation, if true, would turn everything he thought he knew about this job on its head. If she was really the one footing the bill, shouldn't she be the one being guarded? "This place is too deep for me," he muttered. He briefly considered heading back down to the Barbary Coast, using the gold in his pocket to buy a good horse and enough supplies for a few weeks, and seeing what there was to see that he hadn't seen already back east. Something in him, though, rebelled against the idea of going back. It felt like retreat. He'd fetched up here, at the edge of the continent, and here it was he'd resolved to make his fortune. In the meantime, he'd set himself the task of protecting this family. The next thing was to get to work planning how he was going to do that.

He walked to the back of the property, to where the high hedge obscured the house behind. The thick greenery formed a solid wall. But as he drew closer, Cade saw something that wasn't there yesterday. A portal had been cut through the vegetation, a ragged hole through which a man, or a few men, might pass.

"Son of a bitch," a voice came from behind him. Cade turned, his hand going to his weapon. Samuel was standing there, looking disgusted. "I finally got that hedge looking the way I wanted it."

"That's too bad," Cade said. "But we've got bigger problems than damage to the greenery. I figure those Chinamen snuck through here to attack the house." He started to push through the few branches that barely obscured the passage cut through the hedge, then thought better of it and stepped back. "What's on the other side of this?"

Samuel rubbed his chin. "I think that's the Sumner house."

"You know them?"

Samuel shook his head. "They weren't here more than a month or two. Then I heard they lost everything on railroad stocks. I think the bank owns the place now."

Cade drew his pistol. "Well, what the bank doesn't know won't cause it any disturbance." He pushed through the hedge.

He found himself looking at the back of a house about half the size of the Hamrick mansion, but with peeling paint across the expanse of the back and the odd board hanging askew. None of the grimy windows had shades or drapery, and they looked down on him like the dead and empty eyes of a corpse, a line of gallery windows on the lower level gaping at him like a skull's grin.

A rustling behind him made him turn to see Samuel forcing his own way through the ragged hole in the vegetation. "You say no one lives here?" Cade asked.

"Not that I know of."

Cade nodded at the house. "Then I wonder why that back door's hanging open."

Samuel regarded the half-opened red door at the corner of the house with alarm. "We should fetch the police."

"Yep. Probably should." Cade walked slowly toward the door. As he reached the short flight of steps leading up to it, he drew his pistol.

"You don't think they're still there?" Samuel's voice came from behind.

"Hush," was Cade's only reply. He advanced up the stairs as cat-footed as his size would allow, his ears straining for any sound or sign of habitation. When he reached the door, he nudged it open with the long barrel of the Navy revolver. It swung open with the slightest of creaks.

"We can't go in there," Samuel whispered, even though there was no one else within earshot. "It's trespassing."

"Yep," Cade answered without turning around. "You'd best go back if you don't want trouble." He moved forward, the gun moving back and forth like a hound seeking a scent. The door opened onto a gallery that stretched across the back of the house, the windows he'd seen earlier letting the morning light in. A hallway on his left led toward the front. A light film of dust covered everything, except for a trail along the gallery by the windows, where an undetermined number of feet had disturbed the grime. A pair of chairs sat by the windows, in the middle of the trail. Cade stopped and listened. Nothing stirred. He lowered the pistol, but didn't holster it before walking down the gallery. There were several objects scattered on the floor beside and between the chairs. He bent down and picked up a metal can with his free hand. "Canned peaches," he read the label out loud. He let the can drop to the floor with a clang and picked another object off the sill of one of the windows. It was a rolled tube of tobacco. He heard footsteps and turned to see Samuel standing there. "You ever heard of Chinamen eating canned peaches and smoking cigars?"

Samuel looked annoyed. "Why shouldn't they?"

"I don't know," Cade said. He looked through the windows. Over the top of the hedge, he could see the tops of the first-floor windows of the Hamrick house. The second- and third-floor windows were clearly visible. He saw a glimpse of someone moving in a third-floor window, caught a flash of red hair. Bridget, at some household chore.

He turned to Samuel. "They laid up here. Watched the house until it was time for them to make their move."

Samuel stood behind him, arms folded tightly across his chest. "It's enough to give a man chills."

"It is." Cade put the cheroot back on the sill.

"We should tell the police." Samuel looked at him. "Don't you think?"

Cade grunted. "Not sure. Something here doesn't feel right."

"Why?" Samuel demanded. "Because you don't believe a Chinese would eat canned fruit?"

Cade looked at him. "There must have been half a dozen policemen crawling all over the house last night. And not a one of them looked back here. Not one of them found what it took us five minutes to find. All they seemed to be interested in was grilling me and you. Don't that seem a mite odd?"

"Do I think it's odd that the police spend all their effort at the scene of a crime questioning the one black man present? No, Mr. Cade, I do not find that odd at all."

"Well, they took a fair amount of interest in me as well. But I take your point. Do you see mine?"

Samuel looked at the Hamrick house through the dirty windows. "You don't trust the police in this."

Cade shook his head. "Lawmen...I don't know. I've worked for some that were decent. I've met some who I learned not to trust at all. Some men wear that badge for all the wrong reasons. So, then I come here and...well, something here is way off plumb. So, no. I don't know who to trust."

Samuel gave him a thin smile. "Welcome to San Francisco, Mr. Cade."

Cade grimaced. "You say that like you're thinking maybe I shouldn't have come. I will allow as how the thought has crossed my own mind." He sighed. "But here I am, and I've taken on a job, and I mean to see it through."

"Well," Samuel said, the sardonic smile fading to be replaced by his familiar look of blank hostility. "That would be a refreshing change."

Cade's bafflement was making him frustrated, his frustration was making him angry, and Samuel's apparently random antagonism gave his anger a focus. "God damn it, man," he erupted. "We never met till yesterday, and yet you still act like I ate your last piece of fucking birthday cake. So tell me, what the everlasting hell is your problem with me?"

Samuel's eyes narrowed and he spoke through gritted teeth. "You really want to know?"

"I'm goddamn askin', ain't I?"

Samuel glared for a minute, then his gaze broke and he looked away. "You're proud of your time in the Union Army, I take it."

Cade was baffled by the sudden tangent. "I did my part, I guess. Didn't dishonor myself. I got no regrets. And, you don't mind my saying so, we did help set your people—"

Samuel flared up. "Don't say it. Don't you DARE say it."

Cade stepped back, more baffled than ever. Before he could speak again, Samuel began in a low, flat voice, leached of emotion. "You want to tell me the United States Army freed us? Then tell me, Mr. Cade...or what was your rank? Lieutenant? Colonel?"

"Hell, no. I wasn't an officer. I worked for my damn living." He saw that the old soldier's joke didn't register with Samuel. "I was a corporal. Mostly. Made it to sergeant a couple of times, but it didn't take."

"So, Corporal, what exactly did the Union Army do once they moved through and, as you were about to remind me, set my people free?"

"We..." Cade closed his mouth and thought for a moment. "We moved on. We were cavalry. We had to go fast."

"And what, *Corporal*," Samuel delivered the word with a bitter grimace, "did you think became of us once you moved on?"

Cade couldn't answer. Samuel went on. "Someday, Mr. Cade, I will tell you exactly what horrors my family suffered when your glorious army *moved on*." He took a deep, shuddering breath, closed his eyes, then opened them again and looked at Cade. "But you haven't earned that. Not yet."

Cade thought it over. "Okay," he finally spoke. "You feel that you and yours were mighty ill-used. Abandoned, even. I allow as how you've probably got a legitimate grievance." He took a deep breath. "But do you see how this is goddamn similar? It's not about what anybody's earned. These people here need help. *I* need help. I been running through my head how I'm gonna keep this here family safe from whoever it is that means them harm, whether it's these boo-hoo-doo Chinamen or someone else. And so far, the only conclusion I can draw is, I can't do it alone. I know you have some affection for them. The little girl, at least. So, can you lay aside this grudge you've got against me and my former profession and help me do this job?"

Samuel looked away. "I don't know what I can do. I'm…I'm not a brave man. As you now know."

"Seems like you kept your head pretty well last night. And you shot straight when it counted, which is pretty damn important."

Samuel shook his head. "That was sheer luck. It was the first time I've ever fired a pistol."

"Well, I can teach you. If you're willin' to learn."

The black man was silent. Then, "For them. For her, I'll do it."

"Okay, then." Cade put his hand on Samuel's shoulder. "Well, then, let's get to work."

Samuel looked at the hand until Cade pulled it away, embarrassed. "Mr. Cade," Samuel said, "please don't do that again."

Cade sighed. "Have I mentioned lately that you are one aggravating son of a…one aggravatin' so-and-so?"

"No," Samuel said. "Not to me. But I make no apologies for it."

Cade had to laugh at that. "Fair enough. Let's get you fitted for some iron."

CHAPTER NINETEEN

When Mei finished, Mr. Kwan neither spoke nor changed expression. He'd spent her entire recitation looking off into the distance, as if he was thinking of something else. They sat in silence for a moment, Mei acutely conscious of the White Orchid sitting silently behind her. She had heard of the woman—who in Chinatown hadn't?—but she'd always dismissed tales of the Green Dragon's merciless female assassin as so much moonshine, lurid fairytales like the ones in the magazines the white devils read. But it seemed as if there was such a person, sitting right behind her. She tried to suppress her trembling, terrified that Mr. Kwan would take it as a sign she was lying and signal the apparition behind her to slash that razor-sharp dagger across her throat. *But I'm so tired*, she thought. *At least then I could sleep.* The rush of the past few hours had worn off, and she felt ready to slide off the chair to the polished wooden floor and slumber for a thousand years.

When Mr. Kwan finally moved, it was merely to nod, but it still made Mei jump as if he'd leaped across the table at her. "You are tired," he said, his flinty expression and his voice suddenly kind. "You will have something to eat. And you will be my guest here while I consider this." It was expressed as an invitation, but the order was clear. Mr. Kwan stood, and Mei heard the rustling of silk as the woman behind her moved. She tensed, wondering if the sudden solicitousness was a trick to lure her off her guard while The White Orchid killed her. But to Mei's astonishment, Mr. Kwan actually bowed slightly and gestured behind her. "She will see to your needs." Only then did Mei dare to turn.

The White Orchid stood there, still with that enigmatic smile, but the dagger was still at her waist, undrawn. She gestured to the door, still silent. Mei turned back long enough to acknowledge Mr. Kwan's bow with a deep one of her own, and followed the graceful assassin out the door.

They went down a long, dark hallway, lit only by a few candles in wall sconces. At a door on the left, the woman produced a key from the folds of her robe and let herself in, beckoning Mei to follow.

The room was small, but opulently furnished, with cushioned chairs, a beautifully carved and joined black lacquer table, and a curtained bed that caused Mei to yearn for sleep.

The woman gestured to a chair beside one of the tables, bidding her to sit. "First you will have something to eat," she said. Her voice was gentle and mellifluous, instantly soothing to Mei despite her tension and misgivings. "Then you may sleep, Little Sister."

The kindness in the woman's voice and the familiar endearment, after all she'd seen that day, nearly made Mei weep. She wanted to kiss the woman's hand in gratitude. But she merely nodded. "Thank you." She gave a tired chuckle. "I don't know if I'm more tired or hungry."

The White Orchid nodded. "I know. But you will rest better when you've eaten." She slipped out the door.

Mei could see the logic in that. Still, she'd nodded off in the chair by the time The White Orchid returned with a bowl of dumplings in broth and a pot of tea. Mei later wished she'd been more awake while she wolfed the dumplings down. All she could recollect was that they were excellent. When she was done, The White Orchid gently led her to the bed and pulled a blanket over her. She was asleep before her head hit the pillow.

CHAPTER TWENTY

As Cade and Samuel pushed their way through the hole in the hedge, back into the rear courtyard, Cade heard the insistent tinkling of a bell being rung as if the ringer intended to wear it out.

"Damn it," Samuel muttered. He rushed to the path that led to the street. In a moment, he was back. A wagon drawn by a single worn-looking horse followed slowly. Simonson, the little man who'd fitted Cade for his new clothes and stabbed him with a pin, was seated in the driver's seat, looking mightily put out.

Cade took a deep breath and pasted a smile on his face. As he approached the wagon, the tailor spoke first. "I am not accustomed to being kept waiting."

Cade knew this man's type. He'd sneer and smirk and lord it over the other people whose job it was to serve, while licking the boots of the bosses and masters. He felt like taking his boot to the little fucker's backside, but he knew how that would look. And he knew the obnoxious little tailor would most likely be checking the fit of his new clothes, a few inches away from Cade's groin with his pins and his scissors. Cade figured it was a good time to exercise what few diplomatic skills he had.

"Sorry," he said with what he hoped was an ingratiating smile. "We were otherwise employed. A matter of some delicacy." He nodded wisely at the tailor. "I'm sure you know what I mean."

Cade could swear he saw the man's ears perk up. Gossip was no doubt as much a part of his stock-in-trade as clothing. "Indeed."

He looked around, taking in the hole in the hedge. His dark eyes widened. "Indeed," he said more thoughtfully.

Cade wasn't going to give him the opportunity to snoop further. "I'm guessing you have my new clothes."

The man tore his eyes away from the hole. "Yes. Certainly. Is there a place where we can check the final fit?"

Cade nodded. "Front room."

The tailor gestured to the back of the wagon. "Your new suits are in the trunks in the back."

Cade was tempted to tell him to bring them in himself until he saw the size of the leather trunks. There was no way the little man could manage them. He considered making the supercilious bastard try, but decided that would just be mean. "Come on," he told Samuel. "Let's do this."

They manhandled the trunks into the front parlor. In a trice, they had them open and Cade was putting on one outfit after another while the tailor buzzed around him, *hmm*-ing and tugging and stepping back to admire his handiwork. Cade had to admit, there was a lot to admire. There was a little bit more fancy trim and filigree than he was used to, but when he looked in the mirror, the fellow that looked back at him looked well-turned out and prosperous. The trousers, vest, jacket, shirts—all fit him as if he'd been born wearing them. There was one exception. The jacket seemed a little baggy on the left side. Cade hesitated about mentioning it, then the tailor reached into one of the trunks. "This is the last bit." He pulled out a complicated leather belt and holster. Cade stripped off the jacket he'd been wearing and let Simonson show him how to fit the shoulder rig around him. With the jacket back on and the Navy revolver nestled into the holster, the lines of the jacket were perfect. He'd told Simonson he'd gotten used to wearing his weapon on his hip, but he was glad the tailor had chosen to ignore him. A gun belt would look as out of place with these duds as a whore in church.

"Sir," Cade said, "you do excellent work."

"Yes," the tailor said absently as he stepped back to examine his work on its living model, "I do."

"Now," Cade nodded at Samuel across the room, "I need you to do the same for my partner here."

The tailor's face froze. "Him?"

"Yeah. Him."

"I…have already fitted this gentleman for his clothes."

"Yeah, and you've turned him out nicely, I have to admit." Cade smiled thinly. "Almost as fancy as me. But we need to get him kitted out for weapons, like you just did for me. And if you know where we might find the pistols to fit the holsters, that would save us all some time and effort."

"Arm…him."

"Yes. Arm. Him. I need him."

The tailor's face was blank. "That would be, let me just say, unusual."

"I think we'd all agree these are unusual times. Wouldn't you say, Samuel?"

"Yes," Samuel said, his voice dry, "most unusual."

"We'll need the iron, at least, by tomorrow."

The tailor's studied composure was beginning to crack. "Tomorrow."

"Tomorrow, yes. And I'd be obliged if you'd quit repeating everything I say. Now, I reckon that will be all, Mr. Simonson. But I hope we'll see you tomorrow."

"Yes," Simonson said, a bemused expression on his face. "Tomorrow." He turned toward the door, then turned back. "Hold out your hands," he said, looking at Samuel.

Samuel blinked. "My hands?"

"Yes. Hold out your hands."

Samuel did so. Simonson looked at the extended hands for a moment, then nodded. "I will see you tomorrow. Same time. And I assume this goes on Mr. Hamrick's account."

"Sure," Cade said. "Let's just leave it that way for now."

Simonson nodded again and left.

When the door closed behind him, Samuel hesitated for a moment, then, to Cade's amazement, he started to laugh. Shortly, Cade was laughing with him.

"Lord above," Samuel said as his guffaws subsided into chuckles. "Did you see his face?"

Cade took out his handkerchief and wiped his eyes. "Little bastard didn't know whether to shit or go blind." That drew another laugh from them both.

Gradually, the laughter wound down again. Samuel looked over at Cade, his face abruptly serious. "When you were talking to Mr. Simonson, you referred to me as your partner."

Cade nodded. "I suppose I did."

"And are we partners, then?"

Cade shrugged. "Well, we do seem to be two men engaged in a common enterprise. So, I'd say yeah."

"And my color doesn't bother you?"

"Frankly, Samuel, your goddamn prickly attitude bothers me a lot more than the shade of your skin, but it seems you got your reasons, so I'm willin' to make allowances."

Samuel nodded. "Very well. I'll make allowances as well."

Cade blinked in surprise. "Allowances? For what?"

"Never mind." Cade was beginning to get his own back up, but when he saw the ghost of a smile on Samuel's face, he nodded and smiled back.

"Okay," Cade said. "Fair enough." He held out his hand. Samuel took it and the two men shook.

"By the way," Samuel said, "is there any of that good whiskey left?"

Cade nodded. "I think there may be a couple of swallows left. Would you care for a little snort to seal the deal?"

"That would seem appropriate, Mr. Cade."

Cade gestured toward the door. "After you, Mr..." He stopped, suddenly embarrassed. "Well, shit. I apologize. I seem to recall Miss Bridget yelling your last name at you, but it's gone out of my head."

Samuel smiled. "It's Clayborne."

"Mr. Clayborne, then. Can I stand you to a drink?"

"I would be honored, Mr. Cade."

CHAPTER TWENTY-ONE

Mei startled awake, gasping as if she was coming up from underwater. She looked around in panic for a moment, disoriented and confused. In the dimness of the candle-lit room, she saw the figure of a woman seated in a nearby rocking chair. As the sleep burned swiftly from her brain, she recognized the slender figure of The White Orchid. Her hands were busy with something in her lap. Mei could hear a clicking sound, like insects in the wall. She rubbed her eyes and looked more closely.

"You're...knitting?" she croaked.

The White Orchid smiled and held up one pale, long-nailed hand. "Keeps the fingers nimble. And improves concentration." She picked up the bundle of yarn and knitting needles in her lap and set it on a nearby table. "How are you? Did you sleep well?"

"Yes, thank you," Mei said, suddenly shy and unsettled. All of the stories bandied about The White Orchid portrayed her as some kind of cold, merciless goddess of death. It was disconcerting to see the legend sitting in a chair and knitting like an old grandmother.

The White Orchid stood. "Would you like something more to eat?"

There was a gold clock sitting on a nearby table, and Mei gasped as she noticed the time. She leaped up out of the bed. "Oh. No. I have to get back. My grandparents will be worried sick."

The White Orchid shook her head. "No need to worry. They've been informed that you're safe. And that they, and you, are under the protection of Mr. Kwan."

Mei blinked in surprise. "We are?"

"Of course. You've done him a great service, letting him know of a threat to him and his interests. And you've done it at risk to yourself. Mr. Kwan does not let service go unrewarded." That perpetual smile changed subtly in a way that sent a chill down Mei's spine. "Or threats go unanswered."

"So, I'm to stay here, then?"

The White Orchid nodded. "For a short time. I'm sorry to say you can't have the run of the establishment, but I can have anything you need brought to you."

Mei looked down at her clothing and grimaced. "I don't want to trouble anyone, but I could use a bath."

"And some clean clothes." She went to the door. "It will be no trouble. Wait here. I'll be right back."

"And...um..." Mei didn't know how to ask what she needed next.

The White Orchid raised an eyebrow. "Yes?"

Mei tried not to blush. "I'm about to start my monthly time."

"Ah. No worries. We'll tend to that right away, then."

"Thank you so much..." Mei paused. "I'm not sure what you call you. Miss Orchid?"

She laughed. "You may call me Lin."

"Thank you, Lin. Is that your real name?"

The woman didn't answer, just closed the door. Mei heard the click of the lock.

She sat back down on the bed. Despite the reassurances, she still felt a cold knot of fear at the pit of her stomach. She was, after all, still in the house of one of Chinatown's most notorious criminals, a man who reputedly trafficked not only in opium and gambling, but in human flesh. She was in his good graces for now, and she still couldn't believe how kind his notorious right-hand woman was being, but she feared what might happen if things changed. There had been a lot of changes in her young life lately, and none of them had been good up till now.

CHAPTER TWENTY-TWO

"Squeeze the trigger, don't pull," Cade said. "And put the front sight on the—" He was interrupted by the report of the gun. Samuel's shot kicked up a fountain of mud at the foot of the rotting post they'd set a bottle on as a target.

Cade sighed. "Don't worry about quick drawin'. The man who lives to walk away is the man who takes the time to put the lead where it needs to go."

It was early morning, and the weak rays of the rising sun made beams through the slowly dissolving fog that hung over the mud flat Cade had picked for target practice. The waters of the bay lapped gently at the shore a few feet away. The sharp, rich smell of salt water and sea life hung over the place. The spot was as isolated as he could find, a good quarter mile away from the nearest buildings. Something, he couldn't tell what, had once stood here. A set of posts extending in a line out into the water showed where a small dock had once stood. The foundation stones of some razed building waited to trip up the unwary in the tall grass behind a stone seawall that created a short drop to the beach.

Samuel raised the pistol, more slowly this time, and sighted down the barrel, one eye closed.

"Keep both eyes open," Cade said.

Samuel made an annoyed sound, deep in his throat, but opened both eyes. His next shot went low, but it struck the post and knocked the bottle to the ground.

"Better." Cade walked over, picked up the still-whole bottle, and placed it back on the post. He turned back to see Samuel taking aim, with Cade still in the line of fire.

"Whoa! Whoa!" Cade held up his hands and leaped to one side as Samuel pulled the trigger. The bottle shattered, bits of glass spraying to every side, a couple landing on Cade's sleeve.

"Damn it, man," Cade sputtered, advancing on Samuel, "watch out!" Samuel was standing there, wide-eyed with shock, looking at the Navy revolver as if it had suddenly turned into a cobra. Cade resisted the impulse to yank it from his hand. He took a deep breath and spoke as calmly as he could. "Don't shoot at somethin' I'm that goddamn close to, okay?" He saw that Samuel's hands were trembling and held out his own. "Okay, give it here."

"I'm sorry." Samuel handed the gun over. "I'm sorry," he said again. The man looked ready to faint.

"It's okay." He looked back at the post and the remnants of the shattered bottle. "It was a good shot, though."

"Thanks," Samuel said. He looked soberly at Cade. "I don't know if I'm cut out for this."

"It ain't a matter of what you're cut out for," Cade said. "It's a matter of what we've got to do. If we're going to be of any use, we've got to get you at least comfortable with a pistol."

"Hey!" a loud voice called to them from out of the fog. "You two!"

Cade looked. The man standing on the wall above the beach was short and stout, with a round, clean-shaven face and a sour expression. He wore the long coat and silver star of a policeman. His wood truncheon was out, held loosely by his side.

"Ah, Christ," Cade growled in a low voice. "These bastards again." Slowly, so as not to cause suspicion, he slid the pistol into its holster. He hadn't wanted to get his new clothes all muddy, so he was back in his old accustomed dungarees, work shirt, and hip holster.

The officer was scowling at them. He gestured imperiously with his billy club. "Come here."

The tone got Cade's back up, especially after his recent encounter with the San Francisco law, but he didn't need any more trouble. "Stay here," he muttered to Samuel as he started over to the policeman.

"No," the man snapped. "Both of you."

The tone made Cade grit his teeth, but he kept going as Samuel fell in beside him. He pasted the best smile he could muster on his face as they reached the wall. "Mornin', constable," he said. "What can we help you with?"

The stout officer's position on the high ground had him looking down at them, a position he seemed to enjoy way too much for Cade's taste. "What are you two doing out here?" he demanded.

Cade kept smiling. "Just a little target practice."

The officer gestured at Samuel with his club. "Did you let this boy have a gun?"

Cade heard Samuel's quick intake of breath and tried to will him to stay calm. "I did. I'm teaching my partner here how to defend our employer and his family. We were attacked by the Chinese the other night."

The officer's scowl deepened. "I don't approve of a coon havin' a gun."

Cade felt Samuel stiffen next to him, but at this point, even he had had enough. "Well, sir," he said in a tight voice, "last I heard, a man's got a right to carry a firearm in this city. An' if I have that right, seems to me I also have the right to hand that firearm to anyone I want without any other son of a bitch's approval."

The officer's face began to redden. "I ought to take you both in." He raised the billy club.

Cade reached down and put his hand on his pistol. "You can try, I reckon."

The man got even redder. He switched the billy club to his off

105

hand and began to reach for the pistol on his own hip. But before he could draw, something in Cade's eyes stopped him. He let his hand fall to his side. "You two get out of here," he said, trying to sound commanding but unable to keep the tremor from his voice.

"Yes, sir." He turned to Samuel. "Mr. Clayborne, we'll continue the lesson elsewhere, if you like."

Samuel nodded, his face grave. "That would please me very much, Mr. Cade."

Together, they stepped up on the wall, which set both of them a good head taller than the officer. The man stepped back. They didn't look back as they walked to the carriage they'd left at the edge of the vacant lot. Neither spoke as Samuel untied the horse and they climbed in. As they pulled away, Samuel spoke up. "Thank you," he said in a voice barely audible over the rattle of the wheels.

Cade waved dismissively. "Trust me, standin' up to a little pissant like that was pure pleasure."

"Still, you could have gotten in trouble. And on my account."

Cade shrugged. "Got to have your back if I expect you to have mine, right?"

"Right." Samuel actually cracked a smile.

Well, that's something, Cade thought.

CHAPTER TWENTY-THREE

Bathed, dressed in fresh clothes, and fed again on a delicious meal of jellied eels and ginger noodles, Mei felt like a new woman. She was getting a little restless, though. Lin hadn't returned, and neither had Mr. Kwan. She walked to the door and rattled the knob. Still locked from the outside. She was still a prisoner. That put a dent in her feeling of well-being. In a moment, the door opened, and an old woman stuck her gray head in. "What do you want?" she said irritably.

"Do you know how much longer I'll be here, Auntie?" Mei kept her voice polite. She was not one to forget her manners.

"You'll be here 'til Boss Kwan says you can go." The door slammed shut.

Mei sighed and sat on the bed. In a few moments, the door opened again and The White Orchid entered, smiling and elegant as always. "I'm sorry we've kept you waiting," she said. "Mr. Kwan has had several meetings to discuss the news you've brought. There is much to be considered."

"Has he decided what to do?"

"Not yet. Mr. Kwan and his brother are in his office now. He does not make a decision without consulting his brother."

"His brother was very kind to me," Mei said. "I'd like to thank him for that."

Lin, as always, was smiling, but Mei was learning to read the subtle variations in that look. This smile was the type one gave to indulge a naive child who's said something foolish. Perhaps the younger Mr. Kwan was not always as kind. "I'll let him know," was all Lin said. "In the meantime, is there anything you need?"

"I'm kind of bored," Mei confessed. "Is there anything I could read?"

"Ah? You like to read?"

"When I have the time, yes."

"And how, if I may ask with no offense, did you learn to read?"

Mei looked down. "When my grandfather's sight began to fail, he and my grandmother taught me."

Lin nodded. "Your devotion to your family speaks well of you." There was a strange tone in her voice that Mei had trouble interpreting.

"They're the reason I'm here," Mei said. "They took me in when my parents died, and smuggled me in when they came here by disguising me and my grandmother as boys."

Lin looked thoughtful. "I don't suppose there'd be any harm in showing you the library."

"The library?"

"Oh, yes. Mr. Kwan's library is quite extensive."

She was right. Up a flight of stairs and behind a pair of locked double doors was an enormous room with more bookshelves than Mei had ever seen. The shelves reached from floor to ceiling, with a rolling ladder providing access to the upper ones. The room had no windows, but a stained-glass skylight above provided some illumination. Mei noted that the design of the stained glass depicted an enormous green dragon that spread across a starry sky. It must have cost a fortune. Mei ran her fingers along the nearest shelf of books. The titles were mostly in Chinese, but a few English titles were interspersed amongst the volumes. She was disappointed to see that most of the titles were dry-looking books of history, philosophy, and science.

Seeing her expression, Lin pointed to another shelf across the room. "Perhaps the books over there would be more to your liking."

Mei looked. The first thing she saw was a slender volume bound in red, lying on a nearby table. She picked it up. "*The Celebrated Jumping Frog of Calaveras County, and Other Sketches,*" she read out loud. She looked at Lin. "Mr. Kwan reads books by the white devils?"

The White Orchid shrugged. "He says he is trying to understand their minds. But they are a mystery."

Mei laughed. "I hear they say the same thing about us." She took the book over to a well-stuffed armchair in one corner of the room and sat down. A nearby gas light fixture provided illumination.

"I'll leave you to it, then," Lin said as Mei opened the book.

When she returned a half hour later, Mei was frowning. She looked up as The White Orchid entered the room. "This story is stupid," she blurted out. "One white devil goes looking for another one, then runs into someone with a similar name who tells him a pointless story about other white devils cheating one another in a frog race. It's ridiculous."

Lin shrugged. "As I say, who can figure them out? But Mr. Kwan has made his decision."

Mei closed the book and stood up, trying to will her knees to stop shaking. "Yes?"

"He has a job for you to do."

"A…a job?" Mei couldn't imagine what it could be. She had never harmed anyone in her life.

"Yes," Lin said. "He needs you to deliver an invitation."

CHAPTER TWENTY-FOUR

Cade and Samuel arrived back at the house to find an enraged Hamrick waiting for them at the back door. "Where the hell have you two been?" he demanded.

Cade swung down from the passenger seat of the carriage. "Early morning target practice, sir," he said. "Getting Mr. Clayborne here accustomed to the use of the pistol."

Hamrick scowled. "Clayborne? Who…?" He looked at Samuel as comprehension dawned.

Cade realized Hamrick had never bothered to learn Samuel's last name. "Yes, sir," Cade said. "Last night, Mr. Clayborne…Samuel… gave a good account of himself. I decided another gun hand would be useful." He paused. "Actually, sir, not just useful. Necessary."

Hamrick looked over at Samuel, who was busy putting the horse away and acting as if he wasn't listening. "*You* decided." He didn't look happy as he said it.

"Yes, sir," Cade said. "You put me in charge of your safety here. So, I reckoned I had some leeway to make decisions."

"I suppose," Hamrick said. Then his shoulders stiffened, as if he was remembering he was supposed to be angry. "And was one of your decisions to leave us completely unguarded while you went off on your target practice?" His lip curled on the last two words, turning them into a sneer.

At that point, Cade once again considered abandoning this whole mess, leaving this unhappy house and its puffed-up little lord and master behind. He'd dealt with strutting tyrants before, in the Army, because he'd had no choice. This was different. He could tell this one to go to hell and walk away without the fear of a court martial or a hanging. Somehow, he couldn't bring himself to do it. He wasn't sure why. The ten dollars a week was surely part of it. But he felt a deeper sense of commitment than just that. He'd taken on a job, recruited another man into it, and something in him rebelled at the thought of just walking away. He straightened his back and looked Hamrick in the eye. He had to look down to do it. "Yes, sir," he said quietly. "I made a calculated risk. The Chinese seem to be fond of attacking at night. Early morning seemed a good time to train."

"Train," Hamrick said with the same derision. "Do you fancy yourself—?"

"John," a female voice said. Cade looked to the back door. Mrs. Hamrick was standing there, holding the kitchen door open. "Come to breakfast," she said. She looked at Cade and nodded. "Mr. Cade."

Cade touched the brim of his hat. "Ma'am."

"I will in a moment, my love," Hamrick said. "I'm just having a word with Mr. Cade here."

She smiled sweetly. "It's getting cold. You should come now."

Hamrick looked at her, then back to Cade. He clearly wanted to say something else, but his wife's words, mild as they seemed, were imperative. He turned and followed her into the house.

Samuel had come up to stand beside Cade. "I see you're getting some idea of the lay of the land around here."

Cade shook his head. "I guess." He turned to Samuel. "I had a talk with Mrs. Hamrick yesterday morning. She said she was the one who has the money here. Is that true?"

Samuel nodded. "Pretty much."

"I don't get it," Cade said. "Why does she let him act the big man? Can't a woman do business in her own name here?"

Samuel shrugged. "She can. But like most places, it's not easy.

Maybe Hamrick greases the wheels for her."

"Well, the son of a bitch is oily enough, that's for sure."

At that moment, Bridget appeared at the back door. "Are the two of ye goin' ta stand there jawin' all day, or are you gonna come in for your breakfast?"

Cade smiled. "Now, how can I refuse such a gracious invitation?"

Their breakfast was laid out on the long high table in the kitchen, a large silver bowl of scrambled eggs was flanked by a silver dish of fat sausages still popping and sizzling from the griddle and a plate of hot buttered toast. A large pot of hot coffee completed the feast. Considering Bridget's apparent contempt for them both, it was a surprisingly generous meal, but if the Army had taught Cade anything, it was to never refuse a good meal, because there was no telling when you'd get another. Samuel seemed to share the same sentiment; when the two were done, there was nothing left but toast crumbs and the thin sheen of grease on the platter where the sausages had once been. They leaned back on their high stools, sighing contentedly.

"Well, if you two layabouts are done stuffing your faces," Bridget's voice cut through their replete serenity, "I'll be needin' to clean up. Have the two of ye not got work to be about?"

Too satiated to be annoyed, they slid down from the chairs. Cade turned to Samuel. "We do need to talk about how we're going to handle things," Cade said, then burped.

Samuel hid a belch of his own behind his hand. "Like how we're going to guard this house twenty-four hours a day while our employer wants to go rambling about the Coast at all hours?"

"Yeah," Cade said. "It's a mystery, ain't it?"

"You might call it a conundrum, Mr. Cade."

Cade blinked. "A what?"

Samuel flashed his teeth. "A confusing and difficult problem or question."

Cade laughed. "What the hell did you do, swallow a dictionary?"

The smile faded. "Mr. Cade, I suspect you and I are alike in one thing."

"Oh yeah? What's that?"

"When someone forbids you from doing something, does it make you more determined than ever to do that thing?"

Cade chuckled ruefully. "I guess so."

Samuel was deadly serious now. "I was forbidden to read."

Cade paused a minute, then nodded. "Okay. I get it." He inclined his head. "Say, was that your dime novel I found in the parlor? The one about the...let me think...*Yellow Chief*?"

Samuel looked away, clearly embarrassed.

Cade laughed. He slapped Samuel lightly on the shoulder. "Don't worry, Mr. High Brows. Your secret's safe with me."

"Mr. Cade?" a voice came from the kitchen door. Mrs. Hamrick was standing there. "May I have a moment?"

"Of course, ma'am," Cade said. He glanced at Samuel with a raised eyebrow. Samuel responded with the slightest shrug. Cade picked up his hat and started to put it on, then remembered his manners and let it dangle by his side as he followed Mrs. Hamrick out of the kitchen.

***

He followed her into the front parlor. The sun was well up now, shining through the big bay windows facing the street as Mrs. Hamrick settled into the largest and most comfortable of the leather armchairs, pausing to arrange her skirts just so, like a queen preparing to address a petitioning subject. Cade stood, hat in hand, wanting very much to be somewhere else.

Mrs. Hamrick waited a moment before beginning. "I understand you're training Samuel in the use of weapons."

So that's what this is about, Cade thought. He straightened his spine and looked her in the eye. "Yes, ma'am."

"And you think that's wise?"

"Why wouldn't it be, ma'am?" Cade asked. Despite the excellent breakfast, he was still a little raw with exhaustion from too little sleep and too much worry, so his next words weren't as measured as they might have been. "It wouldn't have to do with the color of his skin, would it, ma'am?"

She regarded him coolly. "Not in the slightest, Mr. Cade. Do you think so little of me?"

"Ma'am," Cade said, still too tired to dissemble, "I am frankly perplexed as to what to think of you at all."

The words hung in the air for a moment like the dust motes in the sunlight coming through the windows. Then Mrs. Hamrick chuckled.

"Mr. Cade," she said, "that is something I am not unhappy about."

He nodded. "I get it. You like being underestimated."

"I do." She looked down and smoothed her skirts again. When she looked up, her eyes were serious. "In fact, I rely on it."

"Understood, ma'am. But you can see as how it might lead to things being a bit muddled. And this ain't a time when things can really afford to be muddled. If you take my meaning."

"I'm not sure that I do."

Cade sighed. "Ma'am, may I sit down?"

Her cold facade flickered for a moment. "Yes. Of course. I'm being rude."

"Thank you." Cade took a seat in one of the fabric-covered chairs, his hat on his lap. "When I joined up to the Army," he said, "the cavalry troop I was part of was put together by a fellow from my hometown. Well-to-do. Successful. He had the money to raise a unit, so, of course, he got elected colonel." He looked at Mrs. Hamrick.

"Go on," she said in a tone that let him know her patience wasn't infinite.

Cade went on. "We also had a lieutenant. Had done a couple years at West Point. We never knew why he left, but he had it in his head he was a professional military man." Cade shook his head as he remembered. "Everywhere we rode, they were bickering and arguing about what to do next."

"And in this parable," Mrs. Hamrick said, "I suppose I'm the stupid colonel with the money and no brains."

Cade shook his head. "As parables go, it's not a perfect match. Especially since the colonel wasn't stupid. Neither of them were. That was the problem."

She leaned back in the chair. "Go on."

Cade took a deep breath. "We got ambushed by a detachment of Reb infantry. They opened up on us while we were in column, riding down a dirt road somewhere in that godawful maze of Virginia woods. It was a perfect killin' box. Seemed like we were gettin' hit from everywhere." He swallowed as the memory came flooding back to him. The terror, the screams, the acrid smell of gunpowder on the light breeze they'd so recently welcomed as a respite from the oppressive heat and relentless insects... He shook the memory off and looked at Mrs. Hamrick. Her expression had thawed slightly as she noticed his distress. He pulled himself back together to finish the story. "The colonel and the lieutenant were arguing right up until the same Reb cannonball took off the top of both their heads." Cade stopped, suddenly realizing how inappropriate this story was for this sunlit drawing room in a fancy house in San Francisco. "Sorry, ma'am."

But his audience didn't seem offended or shocked. She was leaning forward, her dark brown eyes riveted on his. "And then?" she said. "Clearly you got out. How?"

"We had a sergeant," Cade said. "Crusty old—" he stopped himself, "—crusty old veteran of the Mexican War. He kicked our— he got us organized. Got us out of there."

She leaned back, her eyes shrewd. "And so, the point of this

115

story is that you…and only you…are the crusty old veteran with the experience to get us out of this mess?"

"No, ma'am," Cade said. "Because I'm not completely sure of what mess exactly we're in. What I'm tryin' to express is that I need to know who I'm supposed to take orders from." He stood up, picking up his hat and slapping it against his thigh in agitation. "I mean, first, I'm supposed to guard Mr. Hamrick. Then I get here and I find there's also a threat to you and your daughter. But I can't look after both, because Mr. Hamrick…well, he goes off on his, ah, business trips. So, if I go with him, I leave you and your little girl alone." He realized how heated up he was getting and sat back down, rubbing his temples. "Ma'am, whichever one of you I have to ask for them, I need more men."

"Hmmm," Mrs. Hamrick said. "And did you have anyone in mind? Men you trust completely?"

Cade thought for a moment. "I got some ideas. Frenchy Terrenoire, maybe. Or Wyoming Andy Grant. Dead shots, both of 'em, and you can depend on 'em to stick in a fight. They're men I'd want backing me…us…up."

"I see," Mrs. Hamrick said. "You have an interesting circle of friends. And are any of these killing gentlemen immediately available here in San Francisco?"

Cade sagged back into his chair. "No, ma'am," he sighed. "I'd have to look for them. And last I heard, Frenchy had gone back to Carolina and Andy married some kind of heiress."

"So, there's no one in San Francisco that you trust?"

Cade shook his head. "I'm a stranger in a strange land, ma'am."

"It seems, then, that you'll have to make do with what you have." She twined her fingers in her lap. "Tell me the rest of your story, Mr. Cade. How did your sergeant get you out of the ambush?"

Cade ran his fingers through his hair. "Only way to get out of an ambush, ma'am, is to attack into it." She inclined her head quizzically. "Charge straight at it," he explained.

116

She nodded. "Perhaps that's your best strategy, then."

"Ma'am?"

"If you sit back and wait for our enemy to come, they'll always have the advantage. Maybe you should take the fight to them."

Cade chewed that over for a moment. "Only problem," he said, "is that I'm not completely sure who the enemy is. Other than someone called the Green Dragon Tong. But I don't know anything about them."

"That's your first task, then, Mr. Cade. Find out as much about our enemy as you can. Then, perhaps, you can see your strategy more clearly."

"Yes, ma'am." He stood up. "I guess I better get to work, then."

She nodded. "Yes."

He started to leave, then turned. "Pity the Army doesn't take women, ma'am. You'd have made a fine colonel. Maybe even a general."

She smiled that enigmatic smile. "Thank you, Mr. Cade. But let me let you in on a little secret." She leaned forward. "A woman in this world has to learn strategy more quickly than any military man. Unless she wants to be little better than a slave."

He nodded. "I see your point."

CHAPTER TWENTY-FIVE

Cade encountered Samuel in the hallway. The first thing he noticed was the smile on his face. Then he noticed the reason for it. He nodded. "I see the little tailor's arrived." Samuel was dressed in a suit so new it still had chalk marks from where Simonson had made final adjustments.

"Yes, he has," a sour voice said from behind Samuel. Simonson stepped out from where he'd been standing, concealed by Samuel.

Cade nodded to him, his face reddening with embarrassment. "Morning, Mr. Simonson." He looked back at Samuel. "Got Mr. Clayborne kitted out real fine." He lowered his voice. "Includin' the other thing we talked about?"

Simonson nodded. "Show him," he said.

Samuel reached beneath his coat and withdrew a revolver with a short barrel.

"Colt Pocket Police Model," Simonson said, still looking unhappy about it. "I chose it because it makes a better fit for this... gentleman's smaller hands."

Samuel frowned. "What exactly do you mean by that?"

"Leave it," Cade said. He addressed Simonson. "You seem to know your shooting tackle pretty well."

Simonson didn't lose his scowl, but he nodded. "Since you intimated that your duties involved personal protection, I've provided you with a pair of coach guns." He went down the hallway to the open trunk Cade could see a few feet behind and returned with a pair of stubby-barreled shotguns. Cade took one and looked it over.

"Mr. Simonson," Cade said, "you are a wonder."

Simonson smiled. "Let's just say that it pays to have a diverse inventory."

"How diverse are we talkin' about?" Cade asked.

Simonson looked at him, his eyes narrowed slightly. "I don't know you that well, sir. Therefore, I pray you'll forgive me if I'm a little vague. Let me just say that I can obtain just about anything you might require for your current occupation, or any other. And if not, it's likely I can direct you to someone who can."

"Good to know," Cade said. "And by the way, I'm sorry about the 'little tailor' crack. You do good work, sir, and I regret insultin' you on account of your size." He extended a hand. "I hope we're square."

Simonson looked at the hand expressionlessly, then extended his own hand and took it. "Apology accepted," he said stiffly. He let the hand go, rolled his shoulders as if shaking something off, and grimaced. "I'm a man of business. A man of business can't afford to hold grudges."

"Understood. Hope we can continue to do business together," Cade said.

Simonson nodded. "Until then. I'll see myself out." He walked off down the hall toward the tradesman's entrance in the back.

When he was gone, Samuel looked at Cade without expression. "It takes a big man to accept an apology like that."

"Amusin' as that is," Cade said, "we should probably stop pickin' on the little fella. We may need him."

Samuel nodded. "Understood."

There was a knock at the front door.

Samuel and Cade looked at one another. "You want me to get that?" Cade said. Before he could answer, Mrs. Hamrick came out of the front parlor and went to the door herself. A sudden apprehension came over Cade, and he strode down the hallway toward the door. "Ma'am," he called out, "you need to let me…" But she had already opened it. Cade drew his pistol from beneath his coat when he caught a glimpse of the person standing there. "Ma'am," he said in a tight voice. "You need to step back."

Mrs. Hamrick looked back over her shoulder, frowning. "Don't be silly. It's just a young girl."

"A young Chinese girl," Cade corrected. "Please, ma'am. Step back."

"Oh, for goodness sakes," Mrs. Hamrick said, but she stepped back.

The young woman did seem harmless enough. Cade wasn't good at judging the age of the Chinese, but she looked to be in her mid-teens. She was slender, with a pretty oval face and serious eyes. She was dressed in a plain gray skirt and white blouse. Cade lowered the gun to his side. "Can we help you, Miss?" he asked gruffly.

The girl bowed. "Excuse me," she said in a voice only slightly accented. "Is Mr. Hamrick at home?"

Cade stepped forward and gently moved Mrs. Hamrick aside with his left hand. "And who would like to know?"

The girl didn't seem rattled by the gun still in Cade's hand, but then it was hard to tell. "My name is Mei. I have a message to deliver."

Cade tensed. "A message? What kind of message?"

"It is an invitation. From Mr. Kwan."

"And who, may I ask, is Mr. Kwan?"

"Mr. Kwan," she said, "is the leader of the Green Dragon Society."

"Mr. Cade," Mrs. Hamrick murmured, "I believe some of the information you seek has come to you." She just as gently moved Cade from in front of her and gestured to the girl. "Come in, young lady," she said. "And have a seat in the parlor. I'll fetch my husband."

It was a tense and uncomfortable trio who waited in the parlor. The Chinese girl, Mei, sat rigidly on the edge of one of the luxurious chairs, hands in her lap, staring straight ahead without expression.

Cade sat across the room, with Samuel standing guard by the door—for what, neither of them knew, but after the events of the other night, a Chinese in the house, even a young and apparently harmless girl, had them on edge. Cade watched the girl closely, and it was then he noticed that her hands in her lap were trembling. She grabbed one in the other to try to stop the shaking, but it only made it slightly less noticeable. *The kid's terrified*, he thought. *And she's just a little bitty thing. What the hell are we so jumpy about?* That made him relax a bit, and he looked around the room. He caught sight of Bridget peeking around the corner of the doorjamb. She noticed him looking at her, gave a little squeak of alarm, and pulled back.

"Bridget," Cade called out. There was no response. "Mr. Clayborne," Cade said, "would you be so kind as to fetch Miz Bridget back in here?" Samuel nodded and walked out. Cade turned his attention to the girl. "Miss," he said, "would you care for some refreshment while we wait? Some tea, maybe?"

For the first time, the girl showed some expression as she blinked in surprise. "Tea?"

"Sure." He put on a teasing smile. "Unless you'd prefer something stronger."

The girl ducked her head shyly. "No. Tea would be nice," she said, and smiled slightly. "Thank you."

Samuel had returned, with Bridget trailing sullenly behind him looking as if she was being towed. "Miz Bridget," Cade said. "Mr. and Mrs. Hamrick will be down in a bit. Why don't you brew up a pot of tea for them and our guest here?"

Bridget looked as outraged as if he'd asked her to disrobe. "*Guest!*?" She looked at Mei. "*Guest*, ya say?"

"And for the rest of us," Cade said firmly. "Get along now." Bridget exited, muttering under her breath. The three of them sat in silence until they heard footsteps on the stairs. The girl stood up. That prompted Cade to do the same.

Hamrick came into the room, dressed in his shirtsleeves with no jacket. He had a scowl on his face that reminded Cade of a bare-knuckle boxer stepping into the ring. "What the devil is all this?" he demanded.

Mrs. Hamrick walked in behind him, composed as usual. "This young lady is called Mei," she began.

Hamrick interrupted. "I don't give a damn if she calls herself President Grant. What the hell is she doing in my house?"

Mrs. Hamrick's voice could have caused frost to form on the windows. "She's come to deliver a message."

Mei bowed slightly. "Excuse me. An invitation."

"I think you should hear what she has to say, dear," Mrs. Hamrick said.

"I don't…" he began, but she put a hand on his arm, gently, and he closed his mouth. After a moment, he spoke through clenched teeth. "All right. Say your piece."

The girl bowed again, more deeply this time. She spoke as if reciting a lesson. "Mr. Kwan, leader and Father of the Lu Long Society, sends his greetings. He was sorry to hear of the recent attack on your house, and to hear that none of your family was injured brings him great joy." She took a breath, as if trying to remember the next part, before going on. "He assures you that neither he nor anyone in his employment had anything to do with this cowardly and vicious attack. To endanger families and children is a disgrace he would never bring on his house or his name. All he wishes is that the white man and the Chinese live side by side in peace."

Hamrick stood with arms crossed across his chest, clearly not impressed with what he was hearing. "And who does this Mr. Kwan claim is responsible for the attack on my family?"

"He does not know." The next words flowed more naturally, clearly Mei's own this time. "I do know, sir, that a man, a white man, has been trying to create bad feeling against the Chinese. He's done it by—"

Hamrick cut her off. "Okay, that's enough of this balderdash."

"Mr. Hamrick," Cade said, "maybe we should hear her—"

"Shut up." Hamrick turned to the girl, who was visibly trembling at the display of anger. "You tell your Mr. Kwan that I see through his Oriental tricks. He's not going to escape justice for what he tried to do to my family. I am going to destroy him. Tell him that. Just that."

Mei's face had gone expressionless again. She didn't speak, just bowed.

Hamrick turned to Cade. "Throw this urchin into the street." He turned to his wife. "Marjorie, come with me." He turned and left the room, his footfalls heavy on the floorboards.

She followed, but not before giving Cade a nod. "Mr. Cade." It was all the instruction he needed. She left as Bridget came in, carrying a silver tea service.

Cade turned to Mei. "This way, Miss," he said kindly. They passed Bridget on the way out of the room.

"Is no one goin' to drink this tea, then?" she complained.

"Sorry." Cade led the girl to the front door and accompanied her onto the stairs leading to the street.

"So," Mei said, her voice bitter, "are you really going to toss me into the street?"

"No, Miss. I don't assault children, either." He looked to the street, where a cab, its passenger compartment hidden behind a black curtain, waited. The driver was dressed in a cloak far too heavy for a day so warm, and a slouch hat was pulled down over his face. Probably another Chinese, trying not to draw attention. "That your ride home?" he said.

Mei nodded.

"And would Mr. Kwan be in that cab, by chance?"

"No. He sent me as his emissary." She sighed. "Thank you for your kindness." She looked back at the closed door. "If only he'd listen."

"Maybe he will. I know I would have liked to hear more. If you can tell me the rest of the message, I'll deliver it myself."

She regarded him appraisingly for a moment, then nodded. "What I did not get a chance to say was that two men have been meeting at my house. One of them hid himself behind a screen and pretended to be Mr. Kwan. The other..." she looked at the door, "...the other seemed to have some sort of..." she searched for the word, "...feud with Mr. Hamrick."

Cade gaped at her for a second before finding his voice. "So, this other fella, the one with the grudge against Hamrick, he's tryin' to get the Chinese to do him dirty?"

The girl nodded. "That is why Mr. Kwan wished to have a meeting with Mr. Hamrick. To discuss that they have a mutual enemy. One they could maybe fight together."

Cade shook his head. "I don't see Hamrick meetin' with any Chinaman, let alone joinin' up with one. No offense intended."

She continued to look at him as if she was cataloging him for a menagerie. "No," she said finally, "I do not believe you mean any offense. So, I will tell you something you might wish to know."

"Oh? What's that?"

"Chinese people find that word, 'Chinaman,' insulting."

"Do you now?" Cade said, smiling at her. "Well, my apologies, Little Miss. Seems I have a lot to learn."

She smiled. "The scholar says that real knowledge is to know how ignorant one is."

"Well," Cade said. "That is indeed a deep sayin'. You know this scholar fellow personally?"

"Yes. In a way." She hesitated and looked toward the waiting cab. "Perhaps a meeting could be arranged between Mr. Kwan and yourself."

He was beginning to like this spunky little girl, but that idea set his hackles rising. "Maybe," he said cautiously.

"Maybe." She set off down the steps to the street, not looking back. Cade glanced at the cab, to see that the driver was peering at him. With a shock, he realized the face peering at him from under the hat was a woman's. The perfection of her face nearly took his breath away. Before he could recover from his surprise, Mei had hiked herself up into the cab. The driver gave Cade a wink and an impish grin, then pulled her hat down, shook the reins, and turned away as the cab departed.

CHAPTER TWENTY-SIX

Mei had lied about one thing. Mr. Kwan sat in the other seat of the shrouded cab, dressed in a suit like the white men wore. He saw from the look on her face how the meeting had gone. "Tell me," he demanded.

"I'm sorry, Honored Sir," Mei said. "He didn't wish to meet."

Kwan grunted with irritation. "What were his words?"

"Honored Sir, I...I don't think you would—"

"Don't tell me what I want and do not want, girl! Tell me."

She bowed her head. "He said he wasn't going to be tricked. And that you..." she took a deep breath, "...that you were not going to escape justice. He promised to destroy you."

Kwan was silent for a moment, looking at nothing, thinking. Mei spoke up.

"There is something, sir."

He focused on her. "What?"

"The man who guards him. A man named Cade. He seemed willing to listen."

Kwan's eyebrows knit together. "I am to meet with some sort of underling?"

Mei bowed more deeply. "No, sir. It was just an observation."

When she raised her head again, he seemed to have forgotten her. He was looking away, still deep in thought. When the cab stopped, Kwan got out without speaking. Mei hesitated, then followed.

The cab was parked in a large indoor garage. Kwan was nowhere to be seen. Lin was handing the horse's reins to a groom, giving him instructions in a low voice. She was dressed in long trousers and shirt, with a man's slouch hat pushed back on her head. She turned to Mei. "I see from Mr. Kwan's expression that the talk didn't go well."

Mei shook her head. "That's putting it mildly."

Lin sighed. "Walk with me." Mei followed her up a rickety wooden staircase, through the door at the top of the stairs, and into the labyrinth of corridors that made up Mr. Kwan's headquarters. Eventually, they made their way back to the library. Lin pulled up a chair and motioned for Mei to sit on another. "Tell me what happened. What was said. As exactly as you can."

Mei did her best, sometimes closing her eyes to better recall the exact words. When she was done, The White Orchid was nodding. "And this man. This Cade. You think he will listen to reason?"

"Maybe. But Mr. Kwan thinks it will be a loss of face to meet with 'an underling.'"

Lin snorted. "Men are ruled by their pride when they're not being ruled by their lust." She smiled. "That makes them easy to control."

"You think Mr. Kwan is easy to control?"

"Harder than most. But in the end, he is only a man." She stood up. "Stay here. I'll be back. Are you hungry?"

Mei shook her head. "No, thank you." She felt tears forming in the corners of her eyes. "I'm just scared. I don't know what's going to happen to me. And I'm so tired of being scared."

The White Orchid put a hand on her shoulder. "Don't worry, Little Sister. I won't let anything bad happen to you."

Mei put her hand over Lin's, and the tears came more freely then. She felt the soft caress of one long-nailed hand in her hair, then The White Orchid was gone.

***

Cade could hear the ruckus from upstairs as he went back inside the house. Samuel was at the foot of the stairs, one hand on the carved newel post, looking up. His brow was furrowed with worry.

Cade grimaced. "Really goin' at it, aren't they?"

"Do you think we need to go up there?" Samuel asked.

"Not unless it sounds like someone's gettin' a beatin'," Cade said. "You're better off stickin' your hand into a beehive than gettin' between a husband and wife arguin'. And it sounds like Missus is more than holding her own." There was an enraged male bellow, then a crash of crockery. Samuel started up the stairs. Cade put a hand on his arm. "Hold up a second." The next thing they heard was the heavy tread of shoes on the second-floor stairs, then Hamrick appeared at the top of the stairway, his coat and hat in his hands. His face was flushed with rage as he pulled on his coat.

"Cade," he snapped. "You're with me. Samuel, get the carriage ready."

"Beggin' your pardon, sir," Cade said, "but one of us ought to stay behind. To guard the house."

Hamrick stopped halfway down, his eyes narrowing. "Are you contradicting me, Cade?"

Cade kept his voice as reasonable as he could. "No, sir. But the Chinese…they might come back."

Hamrick looked back up the stairs. At that moment, Mrs. Hamrick appeared at the top. Her eyes were wild, her face red, and her hair had come loose and hung about her shoulders.

"Answer the damn question, John!" she shouted down. "Where *were you*?"

"Marjorie," he called back up, but she hadn't waited for an answer. She'd vanished up the third-floor stairs. They could hear a door slam, a sound like a gunshot that had Cade reaching for his pistol.

Hamrick looked as if he was about to stay something, then

turned back to Cade. Before he could say anything else, Cade spoke up. "I can handle a team, sir. And Samuel's heeled." Hamrick still seemed unconvinced, so Cade played his ace. "There's the little one to think of, sir."

Bridget had joined them at the foot of the stairs, looking up at Hamrick accusingly.

Finally, outnumbered, he broke. "Fine. Be ready to go in five minutes."

"Yes, sir." Cade nodded to Samuel, who stood aside to let Hamrick down before bounding up the steps two at a time. "If you'll wait here, sir," Cade said, indicating the parlor. "Is there still tea, Bridget?"

"Aye," she said. "But it's gettin' cold."

"I'll be around front in two shakes, Mr. Hamrick," Cade promised.

A few minutes later, Cade had the carriage and team ready. As Hamrick trudged toward it, Cade looked up at the house. Mrs. Hamrick was standing at a second-story window, looking down at them. She held her daughter in her arms. Her hair was still down, hanging loosely about her shoulders. He liked the way it looked. Cade touched his hand to the brim of his hat. She responded with a wave and pulled the curtain shut.

"You're sure you can handle this team, Cade?" Hamrick said as he clambered into the carriage.

"Yes, sir," Cade said as he set the team in motion. "Where to?"

"Chinatown."

CHAPTER TWENTY-SEVEN

Cade didn't like the idea, not one bit. But if it would get Hamrick and his wife apart long enough to cool down, he supposed they'd go to Chinatown. The carriage was the fanciest rig he'd ever driven, but the team was first rate, sprightly in step but quick to respond to the reins or his voice. Hamrick sat behind him, silent. "Anywhere in particular, sir?" Cade ventured.

A brief silence, and then, "Sacramento Street."

"Yessir. But I'll need directions."

Hamrick gave him instructions in a tight, tense voice, then sat back. Cade steered the team, trying not to think of blonde curls, loosed and tumbled and wild around the face of his employer's wife.

They made their way down, the streets growing more and more crowded, first with exclusively white faces, then a few black and brown faces mixed in, then a hodgepodge of all races making their way along the streets. The smells of the city became stronger and more mixed as well—the rich aroma of horse manure, the mouthwatering scents of cooking meat coming from the restaurants and smaller eating houses, the smell of sawdust from a nearby mill. It wasn't unpleasant, Cade decided, but on the whole, he preferred the smaller western towns he'd encountered on the way here. They were less complicated, both in terms of navigation and of aroma. But he was here now, and he had a job to do.

Eventually, they reached the top of Sacramento Street. The

crowds became even thicker, but by now nearly all the faces were Chinese. None of them were what could be called friendly.

"Sir," Cade said, "not meanin' to question your instructions, but it might aid me in my job if I knew exactly what we're doin' here. It looks like we're about as welcome as a rattlesnake at a prayer meetin.'"

"That's exactly the point," Hamrick said. "I mean to show these people that I'm not to be intimidated." To Cade's horror, he stood up. "Here I am!" he shouted. "John C. Hamrick! Still here! Come after me, if any of you are man enough to do it in daylight!"

Cade was so shocked, he lost all decorum. "For God's sake, man, have you lost your damn mind? Sit the hell down!"

Hamrick ignored him. "Here I am! Or can your kind only attack women and children in the dead of night?"

Most of the people in the street were looking at Hamrick uncomprehendingly, as if he'd suddenly began cutting flips like a circus acrobat. But a few apparently understood and were scowling at them. One young man moved toward the carriage and made as if to grab the reins. Cade had his Navy revolver halfway out of its shoulder holster before an older man grabbed the younger one by the back of his jacket and pulled him back into the crowd. Finally, Hamrick ran out of wind and sat back down, breathing heavily.

"Well," Cade said as calmly as he could, "did that make you feel better?" He looked back. Apparently, it hadn't. Hamrick was looking vacantly out of the carriage as if he didn't see the crowd. Finally, he spoke, barely loud enough to be heard over the hubbub of the crowd.

"I never thanked you sufficiently for saving my wife and child the other night."

"Part of the job, sir," Cade said.

Hamrick went on as if he hadn't heard. "That gave me time to summon the police." He looked back at Cade. "That's where I was. I went to get help."

"Yes, sir," Cade said. "I understand."

Now he did understand. He recalled Mrs. Hamrick's angry words from the top of the staircase. *Where were you?* she'd shouted. And, Cade imagined, quite a few other things before. Hamrick's wife had made him feel like a coward. Well, he probably *was* a coward, but no man could stand being called out on it, especially in the presence of other men. He'd stormed out, determined to show he wasn't white-livered, and he'd decided to do it in the most reckless way possible. Cade had seen that sort of nonsense in the war, too, from young officers anxious to show they weren't soft.

It was hard to think of a better way to get good men killed.

"You ready to go back, sir?" Cade said. He was looking for a place to turn around. Most of the side streets he could see were little more than narrow alleys, and he had no wish to get bottled up in one of those boxes, as pretty a spot for an ambush as one could pick.

"Yes," Hamrick said. "But not home. The Coast."

Cade gritted his teeth. He didn't much feel like waiting around outside another whorehouse for Hamrick to get his wick dipped, and his mind kept going back to the house on the hill. "Yes, sir," he said. As they reached a wider spot in the street, Cade prepared to turn the team around. That's when he spotted the tall man.

He was a white man, downright pale in fact, dressed all in black, with an unruly mop of gray hair sticking out at odd angles from his head. And he was tall. Freakishly tall, standing over the circle of Chinese surrounding him like a giant. As the carriage drew closer, Cade could see he was standing on a box. He was giving some kind of speech, waving his arms and declaiming something Cade couldn't make out. He held a black hat in one hand that flapped limply as he tried to use it to point with. Suddenly, Cade recognized the parson he'd met on the day he signed up with Hamrick. The words became clearer as he approached.

"The heathen raged," the old man shouted, his voice dry and rusty sounding. "The kingdoms were moved," he raised his arms heavenward, "then the Almighty uttered his voice, and the earth melted."

Cade stole a glance at the crowd to see how they were taking the sermon, particularly the bit about heathens. They didn't seem to mind; most of them were grinning, enjoying the show put on by the crazy old white man. The old parson dropped his arms in a dramatic gesture, looking about him for the *amen*s or applause he clearly expected. They didn't come. The crowd stirred restlessly, waiting for more of the show.

Cade called out. "I don't think they savvy your lingo there, preacher."

The parson turned. His eyes widened in amazement. "You!" He pointed one long, bony finger at the carriage. The crowd turned, interested in this new act in the show. Cade touched his finger to the brim of his hat in respect.

The old man's finger never wavered, and Cade realized he was looking past him at Hamrick seated in the carriage. "John Hamrick!" he yelled in a voice suddenly stronger, given backbone by rage.

"Who the hell is that?" Hamrick said.

"I seen him before," Cade said. "He spoke to me on the street." Before Cade could go on, the parson hopped down off the box and advanced on them. The crowd parted before him, whispering excitedly among themselves. The man didn't seem to be armed, but Cade wasn't taking any chances. He drew the Navy revolver, but held it loosely by his right leg. The crowd pulled back at the sight, but they didn't bolt. They were still too riveted by the drama playing out in front of them. The sight did stop the old man's advance, but he wasn't backing down. He took a stance in the road, the finger still pointed like a rifle barrel.

"John Hamrick!" he bellowed again.

"Preacher," Cade called out, "I'm gonna ask you to step back."

The preacher didn't. "Your day is coming, John Hamrick! A day when your money and gunmen will not avail you!" He raised his eyes to the sky. "The days shall come upon thee, that thine enemies shall cast a *trench* about thee, and *compass* thee round, and keep thee in on *every side.*" He dropped his gaze again to regard Hamrick with baleful, red-rimmed eyes. Flecks of spittle were gathered at the corners of his lips. "They shall lay thee even with the ground, and thy children within thee; and they shall not leave in thee one stone upon another; because thou knewest not the time of thy visitation."

"Shut up, you old fool!" Hamrick shouted back, but he couldn't keep the tremor out of his voice.

"Easy, sir," Cade urged. "I'll handle this." But the old man seemed to have finished his oration. He'd replaced his hat on his head and was trudging back to his box, which he picked up in one hand. Without looking back, he walked over to the wall of a nearby establishment, the nature of which Cade couldn't tell from the Chinese characters hung on a banner over the nearby door. He placed the box against the wall and sat on it. It was low enough that the old man's bony knees were higher than his waist. He slumped down like that, his arms between his spread legs, his head hanging. He looked like a marionette with the strings cut. The crowd of Chinese looked at him for a second, some of them looking back and forth between the old man and the carriage, waiting to see what else might be going to happen. When nothing did after a few moments, the crowd began to disperse. Cade looked at the preacher. He didn't want to leave the old man here, possibly helpless. But he didn't think Hamrick would take kindly to offering him a ride.

"Cade," Hamrick barked. "Let's go."

Shaking his head, Cade got the carriage turned around and headed back toward the Barbary Coast. He hoped whatever knocking shop Hamrick decided to patronize would offer him a beer. It had been a hell of a day, and it wasn't even lunchtime.

CHAPTER TWENTY-EIGHT

McMurphy was laid out on a moth-eaten chaise longue in a narrow space too small to be called a proper room. A curtain separated his tiny cubicle from a darkened corridor lined with identical spaces, each one housing a man like McMurphy.

A candle flickered on a splintered wooden table next to him. He was staring into the flame, as transfixed by the glow as any moth. The opium was wearing off, and he was starting to feel the craving for another pipe, spurred by the return to reality.

The Chinese had failed him. The raid on Hamrick's home had been a fiasco, thanks to the interference of the gunman Hamrick had in his employ. And he didn't know how to reach the head of the tong to complain. He was almost tapped out, with nothing to show for it. But he had enough for another pipe. McMurphy fumbled in his pockets for the coins that would buy him a little more time when he didn't have to think about his situation.

But when the pinched-faced old Chinese man who ran the "resort" pulled back the curtain, it wasn't to offer him more opium. "You go now," the man snapped.

McMurphy looked up, his eyes bleary. "What?"

"You go now," the man insisted. "Your father."

McMurphy struggled to his feet. "What about my father?"

"He in the street. Acting crazy. You go get." He scowled and shook a finger at McMurphy. "*Your* father. Your *duty*."

McMurphy's face grew hot with shame. The old man's wrinkled

face was full of contempt. Shame turned to anger. He wasn't going to be talked down to by a Chinaman. An opium seller, at that.

"Now listen here, you…" he began.

The old man cut him off by calling out a word he didn't understand. The person who came to the door of the cubicle seemed to, however.

He was the biggest man McMurphy had ever seen, easily seven feet tall, and as broad as an ox-yoke. He was blonde, square-jawed, and carrying a heavy wooden cudgel in one huge hand that he tapped meaningfully into the palm of the other.

"You go *now*," the old man said again, his arms folded across his chest.

"Fine," McMurphy snarled. The old man and his giant blond enforcer stood back as he stumbled, still unsteady on his feet, out into the corridor. They followed him down the hall, up the stairs, and to the front door. As McMurphy stepped out, he saw his father, sitting on a box, head down between his knees. The passing crowd of Chinese paid him no more notice than they did the rain barrel a few feet away.

McMurphy turned back to the old man. "What's the problem here?" he demanded. "He's just sitting there."

"Now. He was out here shouting and fighting with another white man. You take him home."

McMurphy's father raised his head. McMurphy could see he'd been crying. "I saw him, son."

"Saw who?"

"Hamrick. Hamrick and his hired killer."

McMurphy stared at him. "Hamrick? Hamrick was here?"

His father shook his head sadly. "I tried, son. I tried to warn him."

"You two!" the old man called out. "Go now!"

McMurphy's anger boiled over again. "Listen." He stepped toward the old man, but stopped as the big white man came out to stand beside him. "I have a message for your boss."

The man blinked. "Boss?"

"Yes. The head of the Green Dragon Tong."

The old man looked stunned for a moment, then burst out laughing. "Green Dragon Tong?" He shook his head. "I don't know no Green Dragon Tong." He made a shooing motion with both hands. "You crazy. You go and don't come back." As if to emphasize the point, the big guard started for McMurphy.

McMurphy's father put his hand on his shoulder. "Come on, son," he said quietly.

McMurphy looked him in the eye and saw that, for the moment, the madness had subsided. It would be back, he knew, but he wasn't going to let one of these increasingly rare interludes go to waste. He put his hand on his father's. "Okay. Okay." But he couldn't resist one last parting shot. He looked at the old Chinese. "Tell him now. McMurphy paid him. Paid him well. And he wants what he paid for. Tell him."

The old man merely shook his head in disgust and bafflement, turned away, and went back inside, the blond guard following. The door slammed shut decisively as McMurphy and his father trudged away.

***

This particular opium den was not, as McMurphy assumed, under Kwan's control. But in the crowded environs of Chinatown, word traveled fast. The old man told the story of the two mad *gwai loh* to the woman who swept up. She told her cousin who worked in the noodle shop where she fetched lunch for herself and the other workers. They were overheard by a carpenter who was on his way to place his daily bets at one of the gambling halls that were controlled by the Green Dragon. And so it was that, before McMurphy and his father had made the long walk to their boarding house, word had reached Fang, the younger Kwan brother, who went upstairs to tell his brother Lee.

"So," the elder brother said, "now we have a name."

The White Orchid spoke up from a chair across the room. "But not the name of the real enemy."

Fang looked at her with irritation. He could never understand why Lee took so much stock in this woman's counsel. Of course, she had a fearsome reputation, but there were plenty of people who could wield a knife. He wondered, not for the first time, if his older brother was sleeping with her, and that's what had softened his head. He turned back to his older brother. "Say the word," he said, "and this McMurphy is a dead white devil."

Lee shook his head. "He's a loose thread. We need to pull on him and see what comes loose."

The White Orchid stood. "I'll fetch him."

"No," Lee said. "Whatever we find out from this McMurphy won't be believed by Hamrick." He tapped his fingers on the desktop for a moment. "Bring me this man Cade."

CHAPTER TWENTY-NINE

Fang scowled. "Cade? What good will he do?"

But it was The White Orchid who answered, nodding. "If we take Cade, and return him unharmed, it will show Hamrick both that he cannot stop us and that we mean him no harm. And we can set Cade to finding out what we need to know." She bowed deeply. "Very clever, Great One." With a contemptuous smile at Fang, she left the room.

Fang's face was hot with rage. "She flatters you. Is that why you let her speak as if she was an equal?" He leered at his elder brother. "Or does she do other things for you?"

Lee's face was like stone. "She does as she's ordered, *Younger Brother,*" he said, placing extra emphasis on the last two words. "And her counsel has never failed me."

Fang looked as if he'd been slapped in the face. "There was a time when you said the same thing of me."

"Your advice has always been wise as well. But lately, I think it's been clouded by greed."

"Money is power, Elder Brother. And power is safety. The proposition..." He stopped at a raised hand from Lee.

"We're not going over that again, Younger Brother. We grow richer every day on gambling and opium. To expand into the importation of women is unnecessary, and would bring us into conflict with the Hip Yee Tong."

"We can beat the Hip Yee," Fang said. "Easily. The white

policemen we pay could be persuaded to wipe them out for just a little more money."

Lee shook his head. "No doubt. But war is bad for business." He stood. "The white devils have a fable about a tortoise racing a hare. The tortoise wins because the hare becomes overconfident and wastes his time and energy, while the tortoise concentrates on his task."

Fang rolled his eyes. "That's a stupid story. Even the Americans don't believe that anymore. Growth is everything here. Growth and gold."

Lee nodded. "And that is their weakness. Let's not let it become ours."

Fang bowed. "I have to get back to work."

His brother nodded. "Slow and steady, Younger Brother."

As Fang left, he couldn't help feeling sad about what he had to do. He did truly love and respect his elder brother. But he was becoming an old man before his time, hidebound and sluggish. And in America, the slow and steady didn't just lose the race. They got devoured whole.

***

Samuel met them at the back door as Cade brought the carriage around. Cade answered his questioning look with a shake of his head that said *not just yet*.

Hamrick strode into the house without speaking. Samuel began helping Cade unhook the horses from the carriage. "What happened?"

Cade shook his head. "Damn fool wanted to prove a point to the Chinese, I guess. Took us down to Chinatown and started hollering and puffing out his chest like he was daring someone to put a bullet in it."

Samuel blew out his breath. "That's not really what I'd call sane."

"Me either."

They put the horses away, rubbed them down, and fed them. Cade gave each one an extra pat on the muzzle. They really were some of the finest animals he'd seen.

Inside the house, Bridget had left them a late lunch, a half each of cold baked chicken with sides of spuds and green beans, the plates covered to await their arrival. A basket of rolls sat on the center of the table next to a pair of pitchers, one of water and one of beer.

As they took their seats, Cade said, "I guess with just the two of us, we need to set a watch schedule."

Samuel tried to speak through a mouthful of chicken, then swallowed and began again. "I could take nights, and you days?"

Cade shook his head. "A sentry on duty too long is gonna lose his concentration. Especially at night." He sighed. "Supposed to relieve a sentry every couple of hours, actually. But neither one of us will get any damn sleep that way. Let's try four on and four off."

Samuel looked dubious, but nodded.

They finished the meal in silence. By the end, they were stuffed and contented, and platters, bowls, and pitchers were empty. They were collecting dishes when Mrs. Hamrick appeared in the kitchen door. "Mr. Cade," she said, "may I have a word?"

Cade looked at Samuel, who nodded. "I got these."

Cade followed Mrs. Hamrick down the hallway, wondering what was up now. He was surprised to see her turn left at the foot of the stairs and go into the study. He'd thought that was Mr. Hamrick's preserve. Maybe she was trying to make a point as well.

She took a seat in one of the leather chairs. He stood there, a little uncomfortably, until she motioned him to another chair nearby. She studied him a moment before speaking. "What does L.D. stand for?"

He wasn't sure he'd heard right. "Pardon?"

"Your initials. What do they stand for?"

"Um. Well, my daddy was a preacher. Part time, at least. So he

141

named me out of the Good Book." He took a deep breath. "My full name is Leviticus Deuteronomy Cade."

Some people greeted that news with amusement, which was why Cade didn't share it often. Mrs. Hamrick didn't laugh. She did say, "A rather unusual name."

He smiled. "You should meet my older brother Genesis."

At that, she did chuckle. "I can see why you go by the initials."

"Yes, ma'am. Or folks just call me Levi."

Her face grew serious. "So, tell me, Levi, what did you think of our visitor today?"

He rubbed his chin. "The little Chinese girl? Frankly, ma'am, I don't know what to think."

"My husband didn't seem to believe her. He's obsessed with the idea that the Chinese are behind the attempt to kidnap me and my daughter."

"Yes, ma'am. But why? Why would the Chinese have such a mad on for Mr. Hamrick?"

"Or for me."

"For..." He stopped. "Ma'am, have you yourself done anything in particular to get on the wrong side of the Chinese?" Something occurred to him. "You said your daddy was a sea captain. Did he maybe offend someone over there? I hear those folks hold long grudges."

She shook her head. "Nothing that I know of."

"Then, ma'am, I confess, I am purely baffled." He grimaced. "I admire your suggestion of taking the fight to our enemy, but I got no idea who our enemy actually is."

She stood up. He did the same. "I have faith, Mr. Cade," she said. "I believe you will find out."

As she breezed past him, he caught a whiff of her perfume. His body's reaction had him sitting back down for a moment after she left.

CHAPTER THIRTY

The rest of the day passed uneventfully. Cade decided to prepare for the night ahead with a nap. He awoke to Bridget tapping impatiently on his door to call him down to dinner, which he and Samuel ate in the kitchen. When he was done, Cade stood up from the long table and put his napkin down. "You get some shut-eye. I'll take the first shift."

Samuel nodded, then frowned. "What if Mister wants to go out?"

Cade shrugged. "We'll deal with that as it comes."

Shotgun in hand, Cade patrolled the darkened grounds, eyes and ears open. The night was clear, but the air was damp and chilly. It always seemed to be chilly here. From time to time, he looked up at the lighted windows. He could see Mrs. Hamrick moving about on the second floor. From the little he could tell from his vantage point on the ground, she seemed as cheerful as he'd ever seen her, so he assumed she was tending to her daughter. He couldn't see where Mr. Hamrick was. He tore his eyes away and went back to treading through the darkness. All he could hear was the call of the night birds and what sounded like a piano, somewhere in a house nearby, playing a sedate melody. He thought of the noise and tumult he knew was going on down in the Barbary Coast and felt a sudden absurd surge of nostalgia. As crazy as the place was, it was easier for Cade to find his way there than it was in this unhappy household, with its push and pull of competing powers and secrets. He clenched his jaw in frustration. There was an enemy out there he couldn't see, couldn't hear, couldn't get his hands on, and the knowledge was a like an itch he couldn't scratch. He knew there was something one or both of the Hamricks weren't telling him.

Eventually, the lights went out, save for one dim lamp in the upper story, where he knew the Hamricks' private rooms were. After a short pause, even that went out, leaving the house in darkness. The moon had finally risen above the trees and houses surrounding the property, and Cade pulled out his watch to check the time. As he did, the back door opened and Samuel came out, carrying his own shotgun.

"You're a mite early," Cade said.

Samuel nodded. "Couldn't sleep."

"Well, you'll learn soon enough to grab sleep when you can. But thanks. Nothin' goin' on down here. Looks like everyone's bedded down inside."

"Looks like."

Back in his room, Cade found himself unable to take his own advice. He tossed and turned, sleep eluding him. He couldn't get the image of Marjorie Hamrick out of his mind. That cool gaze. The way she'd looked with her hair down. The sound of his name in her mouth.

Finally, he got up and took a fresh bottle of whiskey out of the dresser. He sat on the edge of the bed and took a swig, and shook his head. He'd done some damn fool things in his life, but making any kind of advance to his employer's wife would be the dumbest. There was no way a lady like that would take a broke saddle tramp into her bed, and even if she did, there was no way that could end well. After a couple more swigs, he felt the whiskey take hold. He'd probably regret that when Samuel came to wake him up, but that couldn't be helped. He blew out the lamp, lay back down, and fell into a restless sleep.

He awoke suddenly to see a figure standing in the darkness by his bed. "Samuel?" he said groggily.

"Shhhh..." The figure moved toward him and he saw it was the wrong shape and size to be Samuel. It was an unmistakably female body, dressed in what looked like black pajamas.

"Marjorie?" he said, dumbfounded. Was he dreaming?

"Shhhh..."

Cade started to sit up, and suddenly the figure was on him, pouncing with the speed and brutal grace of a big cat. The impact caught Cade by surprise and knocked him back flat on the bed. She threw a leg over him until she was straddling his chest. *Well, that's bold*, Cade thought, then he looked up into the face of the woman pinning him down. It was a beautiful face, with deep brown eyes and perfect features, but it wasn't Marjorie Hamrick. With a shock, Cade recognized the Chinese woman who'd been driving the coach that brought Mei earlier.

"What the...?" he began, and struggled to throw her off. The woman whipped a black cloth out and held it over Cade's nose and mouth. The cloth was damp, soaked with some sort of liquid with a cloyingly sweet smell. Cade gagged on the scent and clawed at the cloth.

"Shhhh..." The woman's smile was pure delight as she pressed the cloth harder over Cade's face. "Shhhh..."

It was the last thing Cade heard before darkness boiled up and swallowed him.

***

He came to slowly, the world coming into focus, then receding again into blackness. The moments of focus came closer together, then blended into one, finally snapping into clarity.

He was in a dimly lit room, candles in sconces on the wall and one on the desk in front of him providing the only illumination. His mouth felt as dry as if he'd taken a long ride in the desert, and his head was pounding. Cade tried to get out of the chair in which he was sitting, then realized he was tied down, thick hemp rope binding his wrists and ankles to the arms and legs of the chair. He pulled against the ropes to test them, but whoever had tied him down had done a more than competent job. He settled back down into the chair and regarded the man behind the desk.

He was Chinese, middle-aged judging from the gray streaks in his black hair. He was dressed in what looked like a black silk jacket with long sleeves loose at the wrist. He was regarding Cade with a curious expression, as if he'd never seen the likes of Cade before. He was seated in a high-backed chair with some kind of fancy carving on it. The girl, Mei, was sitting in a plainer wooden chair beside him. Cade nodded at her, wincing as the motion started the pain in his head throbbing even harder.

"Howdy, Miss," he said, his voice a dry croak. "To what do I owe the pleasure?"

The man behind the desk rattled off a string of Chinese to the girl. She replied to him deferentially. He replied with something peremptory. She nodded, then turned back to Cade.

"Mr. Kwan would like to apologize for the inconvenience of bringing you here this way. He feels it was necessary."

"Uh-huh." Cade licked his lips. "Well, he could start makin' it up to me by lettin' me have a drink of water. I seem to be a little parched."

Mei spoke to the man, who nodded. Cade heard a rustling behind him and turned his head. The woman who'd bushwhacked him in his own bedroom was standing there, dressed in a white robe decorated with delicately embroidered flowers. She was holding a ceramic tumbler of water. Cade was struck all over again by how beautiful she was. She bent to put the tumbler to his lips, smiling. She wore no perfume that he could detect, but the fresh scent of her filled his senses. He drank the water gratefully, feeling the heat of her slender body against his. By all rights, he should have been randy as a goat, but there was something about her that quashed any lust he might have felt. Maybe it was the way she looked at him. The man behind the desk looked at him as if he was a new species of bug, but her smile made him think she'd take great pleasure in pulling the wings off that bug. Or maybe it was the long, wicked-looking knife he saw in the belt of her robe that put him off.

"Thanks." His voice was a lot less rusty-sounding now. "So. Mind tellin' me why all this," he nodded down at the ropes, "is necessary?"

The man said something to the girl, a long string of Chinese that Cade couldn't begin to try to decipher, so Cade watched his mood. He seemed brusque and commanding, but not angry. The girl nodded and spoke to Cade. "Mr. Kwan wished to deliver information for you to give to Mr. Hamrick. And to send a message."

"Well, shit," Cade muttered under his breath, "couldn't you have just used Western Union?"

The girl inclined her head quizzically. "I beg your pardon?"

"Nothing," Cade said. "I think I understand the message." He sighed. "That if Mr. Kwan was the one that wanted the Hamricks hurt, there's no way to stop him. Even me. Maybe especially me." He shook his head sadly, then looked across the table at Kwan. "Okay. You made your point."

Kwan spoke to Mei, who nodded. "Mr. Kwan wishes there was some way to accomplish this without causing you to lose face."

Cade felt a cold bolt go through him. "Lose my face? What?" He was beginning to sweat. He thought of the knife in the woman's belt. His mind raced, filled with the stories he'd heard and read about the Chinese and their ingenuity when it came to torture. "Look. Sir. Just tell me what you want me to say. There's no need to get ugly here."

Kwan raised his eyebrows. He said something quizzical to Mei, who answered before turning back to Cade. "No, sir, please don't misunderstand. When a Chinese person talks about 'face,' it does not mean the actual face." She thought a moment, then ventured, "In English, the closest word, I think, is 'respect.' Or perhaps 'reputation.' It means all that in Chinese. And much more."

Cade relaxed a bit. "Oh. Okay, then. I get it." He looked at Kwan. "Tell him no offense taken. Only respect I have to worry about is my own. And I'm fine."

Mei seemed to hesitate, then translated to Kwan. Whatever she said seemed to amaze him. There was a brief back and forth, with Kwan seemingly incredulous and Mei answering diffidently. Finally, Kwan shook his head and muttered something. Mei spoke again to Cade.

"The information I have to give is this. A few weeks ago, a man came to my grandparents' fish shop. He wished to pay to use the back room as a meeting place. Someone was coming there to Chinatown to discuss a matter of great importance. But the man was not Chinese."

"Okay," Cade said. "Was the other fella a China—a Chinese man?"

Mei shook her head. "That was the odd thing. Neither man was Chinese. But the man who made the arrangements wanted the other to think that he was."

"And how'd he do that?"

Mei grimaced at the memory. "He sat behind a screen. He talked in what he thought was a Chinese accent." She snorted. "Only a fool would have thought him Chinese."

"But apparently this other party did."

"Yes. He wished to pay the man behind the screen to…to kidnap the wife and daughter of Mr. Hamrick. To hold them for ransom. He seemed to feel that Mr. Hamrick owed him a great debt."

Cade nodded. "This is what you were saying at Hamrick's house. That some enemy of his was trying to get the Chinese to do Hamrick dirty."

"That is right. But again, the man he wanted to pay was not Chinese."

Cade whistled. "This man behind the screen wanted to take the money, pull off this kidnapping, and pin the whole thing on," he nodded at the man behind the desk, "Mr. Kwan here."

Kwan may not have understood the words, but he caught the gist. He nodded back.

Cade went on. "And Mr. Kwan ain't happy about it."

Mei smiled wryly. "That would be a mild way of putting it."

"I reckon. So, who were these two?"

Mei shook her head and sighed. "I don't know the man who came to me first. But the other man, the man who was trying to pay to hurt the Hamricks, his name was McMurphy."

"McMurphy. You get a first name by any chance?"

"No. But he has a place to live in what you white d—what white men call the Barbary Coast. He lives there with his father." Mei looked troubled. "The father is old, and his mind is...his mind is not good."

"What does that mean?"

"The father sometimes wanders the streets. He says crazy things."

Cade's eyebrows went up. "Wait...this father of his isn't some kind of parson, is he?"

Mei looked puzzled. "Parson?"

"Yeah. Minister. Preacher." Cade wished his hands were free to gesture. "Stands in church and makes sermons."

Mei nodded. "Yes, yes, he dresses like one of those. And walks around shouting about God in the streets."

Cade shook his head in amazement. "Well, I'll be damned."

"Pardon?" Comprehension dawned on Mei's face. "You know this McMurphy?"

"No," Cade said grimly, "but I've met the daddy. Twice. And now I know why he seems so interested in me."

Kwan interrupted, impatiently questioning Mei. Her answer rocked Kwan back in his chair. He stared at Cade for a long moment, then shook his head in wonder.

Cade decided to address him directly. "Mr. Kwan, I thank you kindly for this information. I expect it'll be a great help to me in getting to the bottom of this situation."

Mei waited till he was finished, then translated. Kwan listened, then acknowledged the thanks with a curt nod.

"Now," Cade said, "if you folks would be kind enough to turn me loose, I'll be on my way."

"I'm sorry." Mei looked as if she meant it. "But we are not finished here." She looked distinctly uncomfortable. "Mr. Kwan would like to employ you to, as you say, get to the bottom of this."

"Thanks," Cade said, "but I already have a job. And I believe it already includes what Mr. Kwan is asking for."

Mei still looked embarrassed. She had trouble meeting Cade's eyes. "So sorry. But he is not asking."

Cade started to get his back up, then swiftly remembered the position he was in. "Look. Tell your boss I'm not turning him down, exactly. I'm just saying it's not necessary."

Mei spoke to Kwan, who replied at length, finishing with a nod in Cade's direction.

"I am afraid Mr. Kwan must insist," Mei said. "It would make him feel more comfortable if you were, how do you say it, on his roll."

Cade was willing to do whatever it took to get out of there, within reason. "All right. Sure. I'm on the payroll. Now, if you could just turn me loose."

Mei looked away, still clearly unhappy. "So sorry," she said again. "Mr. Kwan does not wish anyone to know where he lives. So, you will need to go back the same way you came here."

"What does that me—" He was interrupted by that sweet-smelling black cloth descending over his head from behind and pulled against his nose and mouth.

God damn it, he thought before he passed out again.

CHAPTER THIRTY-ONE

"You owe us more money."

The hoodlum was slouched in a chair across from where the man sat, a pugnacious expression on his unshaven face. He was a broad-shouldered man of about two hundred pounds, handsome in a coarse way, with his thick black hair slicked back. His family name was Shaughnessy, but he was known on the street as Butt due to his signature move in any fight, which was to slam his considerably broad forehead into his opponent's face. It never failed to stun the unlucky opponent into immobility, and Shaughnessy never seemed to take any damage of his own from the technique. Butt Shaughnessy was said to accomplish housebreakings by smashing front doors open with his head, also without noticeable harm to himself. The man behind the desk wondered if that was because of some unnatural thickness of skull or because Butt Shaughnessy had no brains in his head to damage. Brains or not, he'd somehow managed to raise himself at the tender age of twenty-one to become the closest thing to a king as could be found among the loosely affiliated hoodlums of San Francisco. For whatever reason, he was both feared and admired, and he could raise a squad or an army upon request. That made him valuable to the man behind the desk. But that value had its limits.

The man behind the desk answered mildly but firmly. "You were paid the agreed price. And Mrs. Hamrick and her daughter don't seem to be in your custody. Perhaps I should ask for a refund."

Shaughnessy scowled. "How the hell were my people to know the bitch had a shotgun in her damn dressing table? Or that the nigger servant would be heeled, too? Add in that bastard of a cowboy he took on, and I've got one of my boys dead and another who'll be out of action for a month at least."

"If you'd moved a little more quickly, and shot a little straighter..." The man behind the desk shrugged. "Maybe I misjudged you. Maybe the task was too much for you and you should go back to harassing the Chinese instead of impersonating them."

Shaughnessy rose, fists clenched. "Now you look here, you son of a bitch..." He stopped dead at the sight of the sawed-off shotgun the man had produced from beneath the desk.

"Sit down," the man said, his voice still mild.

Shaughnessy didn't flinch. He actually seemed to be trying to judge the distance across the desk, seeing if he could beat the speed of a trigger finger to deploy his singular talent. They remained frozen there for a full twenty seconds before Shaughnessy could complete the calculation. He sat back down, his thick arms folded across his chest, his face sullen. "You ain't always gonna have that scattergun," he muttered.

"Probably not," the man behind the desk said agreeably. "But if you take me out of the picture, that would be the end of the work I throw your way."

Shaughnessy looked away, his jaw tightening. "We'll be fine."

"Of course you will. But not as fine as you could be." The man behind the desk smiled thinly. "Most of what I throw your way is easy work. But it could be made much harder, if you take my meaning."

Shaughnessy didn't answer, just gazed stonily at the wall. The man behind the desk judged he'd had enough putting in his place. Now was the time to offer him a concession. "I'll tell you what. The next job I have for you will bring you in more than enough money to make up for your extra trouble on this last one."

Shaughnessy glared at him. "What makes you think we'll work for you again?"

"Because, like everyone else in this town, you love money." He stood up. "I'll send word for you when I need you."

"Okay, then." Shaughnessy got up again. "Till we meet again." He leaned across the desk to shake hands, but the man behind the desk didn't move.

"What," the hoodlum growled, "you're too good to shake hands with me?"

"No," the man behind the desk said, still smiling. "Too smart to give you a chance to yank me across the desk and smash my head in. Besides, you won't do the job because we shake hands. You'll do it because it'll pay you well."

Shaughnessy pulled the hand back. "Fine, then." He turned to leave.

"One more thing," the man behind the desk said. Shaughnessy turned. "Don't ever come to this office again. I'll let you know when I need to speak with you, and you know how to let me know if you need to do the same, and we can arrange a place to meet."

Shaughnessy grinned. "Too dangerous to be seen with the likes of me, eh?"

"Yes. For both of us."

The grin left the hoodlum's face. He turned and left without another word.

The man behind the desk leaned back and let out the breath he'd been holding. Dealing with Shaughnessy was always a tense affair, like trying to train a Bengal tiger. But he knew how to keep the man under control. He hoped.

He stood and stretched. The past few days had been a tense time all around. He needed some release. And he'd gotten the word just this morning that there was a new acquisition at his favorite house. It was a lesser-known house, and one that catered to men of more exotic tastes. For a price, a man could purchase a girl outright, not just for an hour or a night. And once a girl was his property, a man of his proclivities could rent one of the cellar rooms—for an extra fee, of course. Once down there, he was like God. No, not like God. He *was* God. He could do literally anything.

Cleanup was another extra fee, but he was a man of means, and it was well worth it.

Yes, it was time for some rest and relaxation.

CHAPTER THIRTY-TWO

"Cade," he heard a familiar voice saying. "*Cade.*" Someone was shaking him, and he was trying to wake up, but it was like he was caught in a bad dream. He moaned, shaking his head to try and clear the darkness from it.

"Is he drunk, then?" a female voice said.

"I don't know. Help me get him inside." He felt a pair of hands on his lapels, trying to drag him upward.

"Get him in yourself. I don't need him gettin' sick on me."

Cade opened his eyes. He was in the front of the Hamrick house, sitting on the ground and leaning against the gate at the foot of the steps. Samuel was leaning over him, his face full of concern and his hands tugging at Cade's coat. Cade put a hand on Samuel's and tried to tell him it was all right, he just needed a moment, but finding the words was causing him trouble. He felt a brief moment of panic, wondering if whatever the Chinese woman had drugged him with had permanently scrambled his brains. Then the world came back into focus.

"I'm...okay..." His voice felt and sounded like a rusty gate.

"I won't stand a drunkard in the house," the female voice said, and Cade looked past Samuel to see Bridget standing on the sidewalk, her arms folded across her chest and a scowl of disapproval on her face.

"Not...drunk." He leaned forward and got his feet under him. Samuel moved to his side and helped him up.

Bridget snorted. "Not drunk, he says. Passed out like a common tramp in the streets. And this a respectable—"

"Bridget," Samuel said, "please shut up."

The woman's pale face reddened. "You mind your tongue, Samuel Clayborne! I'll not be spoken to like—"

"I'm not drunk," Cade insisted. "Smell my breath if you doubt it. I've been drugged."

"A likely story," she muttered, but drew near and took a delicate sniff. Her nose wrinkled, then her brow did the same. "You smell, all right, but not of whiskey. And on your clothes, not your breath." She stepped back. "If I didn't know better, I'd swear ye'd been to the dentist."

"The dentist?" Samuel said.

"Aye. He reeks of ether."

"Ether," Cade said. He'd wondered if the woman had used some sort of mysterious oriental herb or potion on him, but plain ether would explain it. He'd been leaning against the iron fence to steady himself, but he felt ready to straighten up. "Let's get inside," he said. "I need water. And I need to talk to Mr. Hamrick."

***

"Let me make sure I understand you, Mr. Cade." Hamrick's face was red with anger. He stood beside the chair in the library in which his wife was seated, one hand on the back of the chair, the other hand resting on his hip. Cade was seated in the same chair he'd spoken to Mrs. Hamrick in earlier. Samuel sat a few feet away on a small couch, with Bridget perched uncomfortably on its arm.

Hamrick went on. "You, whom I've hired for the express purpose of protecting myself and my family against the incursions by the Chinese, were taken unaware from this house by those very Chinese and spirited away to some unknown place where you met with this...Mr. Kwan, is it? Head of the Green Dragon Tong."

Cade nodded glumly. "Yes, sir." When Hamrick put it like that, it did make him seem foolish. "I think he was trying to make a point. If he wanted you, or me, or anyone in this house dead or kidnapped, he'd have done it."

"I see." Hamrick nodded as if in understanding, but he was still clearly furious. "And how many men did it take to overcome your resistance?"

"Ummm, one sir. And…" he took a deep breath, "it was a woman that did it."

Hamrick's eyebrows went skyward in exaggerated amazement. "A woman, you say? And how did she manage to defeat you? Did she have some sort of mystical Chinese spell? Did she entice you with some erotic secret of the Orient?"

Cade was ready to be chastened, but Hamrick's sarcastic tone was starting to get his back up. He kept his voice as even as he could. "No, sir. She jumped me and knocked me out with what we think is ether."

"What an incredible story," Hamrick said. "By which I mean I don't find it in any way credible."

"John," his wife said.

Hamrick ignored her. He leaned forward. "Here's what I think happened. You decided to slip off on some drunken ramble, had a bit too much, and staggered home to collapse on the doorstep of my house, in full view of my neighbors."

Cade could see the way this was going. *Oh well*, he thought, *I knew it was too good to last.* He decided to play his final card. "Sir. Do you remember anything about a man named McMurphy?"

The tirade that Hamrick was building up to end in Cade's dismissal got derailed. He stopped, one accusing finger raised in the air, as if he'd been turned to stone. "McMurphy?" he said.

Cade stole a glance at Mrs. Hamrick. Her hand had gone to her mouth, and her eyes were wide with shock. *Looks like the arrow struck home*, Cade thought. "Yes, sir. It was the name Mr. Kwan gave me. He said McMurphy was the one trying to hire the Chinese to attack you. But the whole thing was a frame-up. A trick to stir up trouble against the Chinese." He looked at Mrs. Hamrick. She'd clearly recognized the name as well. "McMurphy's traveling with his father. An old preacher who's a little wandered in the head. And I was approached by just such an older fella right after you hired me. And then we saw him. Down in Chinatown."

"John," Mrs. Hamrick said, but he'd gotten over his shock and was clearly determined to get command back of the situation.

"McMurphy was an old business associate. We had a falling out. A very public one that anyone could have learned about. Even you." He shook his head. "If you're trying to bolster this absurd tale of Chinese abduction by dropping McMurphy's name, you've made a serious miscalculation." He smiled without humor or warmth. "Patrick McMurphy, Mr. Cade, is dead. He took his own life three years ago. And his father currently resides in a madhouse in Sacramento." He drew himself up to his full height. "Mr. Cade, your services are no longer required. You are dismissed from my employment."

CHAPTER THIRTY-THREE

Everyone sat in awkward silence for a moment, until Cade stood up. "Thank you for the opportunity, sir." He left with what dignity he could muster, stifling the urge to cross the room and lay the stuff-shirted bastard on the floor with one punch. As he trudged up the stairs, the door to the library opened again. Cade heard the tumult of raised voices. It sounded like the Hamricks were at it again.

Bridget exited first, scurrying down the hallway toward the kitchen in the back.

Samuel followed, stopping at the bottom of the stairs, one hand on the rail. "Cade," he called up softly.

Cade paused. He turned back down to look at Samuel. "Well, partner," he said, "it was fun while it lasted."

Samuel gave him a sad smile. "Odd kind of fun," he said, "but yes."

Cade resumed his climb. He encountered the little girl, Violet. She was seated on the floor in the hallway outside the nursery. Her feet were splayed out on the floor and she had one of her dolls seated between them, facing her. The little girl's face was stern, as if she was giving the doll a lecture. She looked up as Cade mounted the stairs.

"Hey, Little Bit," he greeted her.

She regarded him with the grave expression he'd gotten used to from her. "Hello."

He paused before going on to his room. "I guess this is goodbye." Her expression didn't change. "Why?"

"I'm..." He didn't think the little girl needed to hear all the details. "I'm just moving on, is all."

"Are you going back to herding cows?"

He had to smile at that. "Don't rightly know. But I'll find something. It was nice meeting you."

"It was nice meeting you, too," Violet said, and went back to her doll. She didn't speak. It was as if she and the doll were having a stare down.

Strange little thing, Cade thought as he went on to his room. He pulled out his trunk and sighed as he began packing his few belongings. *At least I got some decent meals. And a couple of fancy new suits. Not that I have any place to wear them.* It occurred to him that Hamrick might demand the new clothing back. Well, he could ask. Cade might or might not comply. But he'd taken about all he was going to from John C. Hamrick.

"Mr. Cade," a voice said from the door.

He turned.

Marjorie Hamrick was standing there, regarding him with a direct look that reminded him uncannily of her daughter's. "May I come in?"

"It's your house," he said, then immediately regretted how ungracious that sounded. "Sorry. Come on in."

He was surprised and more than a little unsettled when she closed the door behind her. "I'm sorry things have come to this," she said.

He threw a pair of new socks into the trunk. "Thanks." He stopped and turned to her. "I wanted to protect you. And your little girl. But Mr. Hamrick makes it hard."

"Yes." She looked at the trunk. "Where will you go?"

He shrugged. "Don't know. Haven't been paid yet for the work I did do."

She nodded, her jaw setting firmly in the way he'd come to like. "You will be. I promise you that. And..." she took a deep breath and produced a card from her sleeve, "...you can find lodging here."

He took the card and read it. The words printed on it made him laugh. "The Royal? Ma'am, I couldn't even afford this place if I'd been paid in full. Not for long, at least."

She fixed his gaze with a level one of her own. "Tell them you're the guest of Violet Townsend. Your needs will be met. And once you're settled, I have business to discuss with you."

"Violet...?" He shook his head in confusion.

"Townsend," she said firmly.

He picked up his hat at put it on. "Mind if I ask what kind of business?"

Her gaze never wavered. "Not the sort of business you are probably thinking of. And don't attempt to deny that you're thinking of it. I mean to offer you employment, Mr. Cade. On my own account." She looked back at the closed door. "I am beginning to wonder if my husband truly has my protection in mind. So I want you to look into the matter of this McMurphy."

"Your husband said he's dead."

"So we were told. And so we both believed. But neither of us have seen the body."

Cade pushed his hat back on his head. "You think he might be still alive? And gunning for your husband?"

"Or for me." She went to the door. "I can explain everything later. For now, Samuel is bringing the carriage around. He will take you where you ask. But I suggest you accept my suggestion."

"I don't know how much Mr. Hamrick is going to like me using the carriage. I suspect he's relishing the idea of me leaving on shank's mare."

She smiled a tight, bitter smile. "I doubt he will like it at all." It was clear she didn't give a damn. In fact, she liked that idea better.

As she left, Cade shook his head and went back to packing. There was a part of him insisting that he needed to get out of here and get as far away from this mess as he could. That was the part that had the good sense, the part he too often ignored and regretted it later. But there was the look in Marjorie Hamrick's brown eyes, the set of her jaw, the subtle smell of her perfume. Those were the things his mind kept going to. He knew she and her daughter were in danger. And he had a powerful desire to find out from whom.

He found Samuel waiting out front in the carriage. He was dressed the way he was when cade first met him, in a black suit and top hat. "Mr. Clayborne," Cade greeted him as he slung his trunk into the carriage and climbed in behind it.

"Mr. Cade," Samuel said formally. "Where to?"

"You know a place called The Royal Hotel?"

Samuel nodded. "Yes, sir. I know it quite well."

"Well, let's get goin', then."

"Very good, sir." Samuel twitched the reins and the horses began a slow walk. As they sped up, Cade looked into the window where he'd seen Marjorie Hamrick before. This time, she wasn't there.

CHAPTER THIRTY-FOUR

"So," Cade said as they made their way down the paved streets toward the downtown area, "Mrs. Hamrick keeps a place at this Royal Hotel?"

There was a moment's hesitation, then Samuel answered without looking back. "Yes, sir."

Cade frowned. "What's this 'sir' stuff, partner?"

This time, Samuel did look back. "We're not working at the same place, Mr. Cade. I would say that renders our partnership moot."

"Moot? What in the hell does that mean?"

Samuel turned back to the road. "It means that it's over, sir. Null and void."

"Well, shit, that doesn't mean you have to treat me like we never met."

"If you say so, sir."

Cade sat back, fuming. Getting chucked out of the job was bad enough, but he'd thought he and Clayborne had at least become friends.

They made the rest of the drive in silence until they pulled up in front of a six-story building that took up the best part of a city block. The place had an ornate frontage, with dozens of curtained windows facing the street. A sign out front proclaimed in gold letters that this was the ROYAL HOTEL. Tall, white Corinthian columns held up the roof of a broad front porch behind a set of white marble steps. As Samuel pulled to a stop at the curb, he turned to Cade with a softer expression on his face.

"I'm sorry things worked out the way they did, Cade." He looked away. "I'd gotten to enjoy your company."

Cade swung down from the carriage and held out his hand. "Me too, partner. You look after those folks, now."

Samuel took the hand and gave it a firm shake. "I'll try. But I'm not sure how."

A young boy had run out from the porch and caught hold of the reins. A thin young man dressed in a red jacket and tight black pants stepped to Cade's side. He was wearing a little round red cap that made Cade think of an organ grinder's monkey. "May I take your bags, sir?"

Cade, who'd let go of Samuel's hand to reach for his small trunk, stepped back. "Sure, sonny. But let me help."

The young man took the trunk and hefted it easily. He was apparently stronger than he looked. "I'm fine, sir. If you'll follow me."

Cade touched the brim of his hat to Samuel. "Don't be a stranger. Keep in touch if you can."

Samuel gave him a sad smile. They both knew that wasn't going to happen. "Sure." He gave the reins a shake and set off. Cade sighed and followed the bellboy inside.

The lobby was huge and spacious, with more columns in a row toward a front desk impressively carved with twining vines and flowers. The man behind it was dressed in a black suit with a shirt that looked so heavily starched, the high collar would cut his throat if he didn't keep his chin held high. "Good day, sir. Welcome to The Royal. In what name is your reservation?"

"Townsend," he said. "I'm a guest of Violet Townsend."

The only way Cade could tell that the name was familiar was that the front desk man didn't even bend to look it up in his ledger. He just nodded. "Very good, sir." He took a brass key from beneath the desk and nodded to the bellboy standing to the side. "Room

345."

The bellboy nodded. "This way, sir."

The room was the biggest hotel room Cade had ever seen, with lush carpet on the floor and red striped wallpaper. The bed looked big enough for five people, with a carved headboard that reiterated the vines and flowers theme of the front desk. The bellboy put Cade's trunk down on a nearby stand and stood back. "Is there anything I can bring you, sir? Anything at all?"

Cade had been standing in the middle of the room, turning around and around to take it all in. He realized he was looking like a rube.

"Anything at all?" the bellboy repeated.

"I dunno," Cade said. "Bottle of whiskey?" He'd meant it as a joke, but the bellboy just nodded.

"Very good, sir." He closed the door behind him as he left.

Cade resisted the temptation to take of his boots and wriggle his toes on the carpet. It only took him a few minutes to unpack his things from his trunk and stow them in the dresser on one side of the room. There was a window next to the dresser, with its shade pulled down. Cade walked over, raised the shade, and opened the window. It overlooked a narrow alley between The Royal and the office building next door. The sounds of the nearby street were muffled, so he left the window open to get some fresh air, or what passed for fresh air in this city.

There was a knock on the door. Cade answered to find the bellboy standing there with a fifth of whiskey and a pair of small glasses on a silver tray. He entered silently and placed the tray on top of the dresser. "We also have ice available, if you wish," he said as he turned to Cade.

"Ice? Who the—never mind. That'll be fine."

"Very good, sir." He didn't make any move to leave.

"Ummm...that's all I need right now, sonny."

"Yes, sir." The bellboy cleared his throat, but didn't move.

Cade realized he was waiting for a tip. He grimaced. He hoped Mrs. Hamrick made good soon on her promise to get him his pay, because he was about tapped out. He fished in his pockets and came out with a dime. "More where this came from, soon," he said as he held it out.

The bellboy looked at the offered coin as if Cade was holding out a mouse turd. "One can hope." But he took the dime and left.

Cade took the bottle. It was Jesse Moore. AA quality. Top of the line. He poured a couple of fingers of the rich brown liquid into the glass and took a drink. It went down like smooth fire. He fervently hoped that "Mrs. Townsend" had the bill covered for that as well, else he might find himself sweeping floors in this place to pay his bill. He hung his hat on the bedpost, sat down, and poured another drink.

CHAPTER THIRTY-FIVE

Cade was dozing on the bed when a knock came at the door. He startled awake and reached for the pistol he'd hung in its holster on the bedpost. Then he recollected where he was and reached for his boots instead. As he was getting them on, the person outside knocked again.

"Hold your damn water," Cade grumbled. "I'm comin'." It suddenly occurred to him that his visitor might well be Marjorie Hamrick. "Be there in a second," he called out again in less grouchy tone.

It wasn't Mrs. Hamrick. The man from the front desk stood there, smiling pleasantly. "Sorry for the interruption, sir. I was asked to inform you that your presence is requested for dinner."

"Dinner? Who?"

"The personage who made the request wished to remain anonymous for the moment."

"Well, that's damned mysterious," Cade muttered, more to himself than to the front desk man.

"Yes, sir," was the only reply.

"So, when is this dinner?"

"Now, sir. If you require more time to get ready, I can—"

"No, no…" Cade said. If it really was Marjorie waiting for him, he didn't want to keep her waiting. "Wait," he said. "Is there some kind of fancy dress required for this establishment?"

The desk man's smile became more pained. "No, sir. You'll be in a private dining room."

"Well, lead on, then." He briefly thought of going back for the pistol, but decided against it. He figured he was pretty safe here, especially if it was Marjorie waiting for him.

It wasn't. As the front desk man opened the door of the second-floor dining room, a man Cade didn't know stood up from the other side of the dining table. He was short and wiry, bald on top, but with an impressive set of black sideburns. Cade noted that his skin was deeply tanned, the complexion of a man who spent most of his time outdoors. His eyes were bright blue and fixed on Cade with a steely intensity. He held out his hand.

"Mistah Cade," he said in a somewhat gravelly voice, surprisingly deep for such a small man. He had a pronounced New England accent. "Pleashah to make your acquaintance. My name is Jedidiah Alton. Captain of the *Marjorie Ann*."

Puzzled, Cade took the hand and shook it. "Pleased to meet you, Captain."

Alton gestured to the table. "Please. Sit." It was a voice that sounded used to being obeyed.

Cade was even more puzzled to see that only one place was set, the one he was being pointed to. Alton's place had only a heavy glass mug before it, half full of beer. Whoever this captain was, he wasn't staying for dinner. Cade sat down, never taking his eyes off Alton. He wondered if leaving the gun behind was such a good idea.

Alton sat down and took a drink from his beer. He gestured to Cade with it. "Care for one?"

"I'll wait."

Alton nodded. "I would do the same in your position." He had a clipped, precise way of speaking, as if he was biting the excess off of every word. "No doubt youah wondering who I am and what I'm doin' here."

"No doubt," Cade said.

Alton reached down for something next to his chair. Cade

stiffened, but all the captain came up with was a large envelope. "Mrs. Hamrick apologizes for the mystery." He handed the envelope across the table. "But I believe this will explain everything."

Cade took the envelope. It was heavy. "Do you now?"

Alton smiled thinly. "I figgah it will. I have no idea what's in it."

Cade went to open the envelope, but it was sealed. He decided to wait until this Alton fellow was gone. "So," he said, laying it on the table, "what's your connection with Mrs. Hamrick, if you don't mind my asking?"

A waiter had appeared from wherever the waiters in these places seemed to hide themselves. He looked quizzically at Alton's glass. Alton shook his head. The waiter turned to Cade. "Something to drink, sir?"

"Sure," Cade said. "Beer." The waiter nodded and left.

"No trouble with you asking," Alton said as the waiter left. "I've worked for Mrs. Hamrick's father since befoah Marjorie was born."

Cade remembered that Marjorie told him her father had gotten rich in the shipping business. "Is her father still alive?"

Alton shook his head. "Gone these five year."

"So…she owns the company now?"

Alton stood up. "That, Mr. Cade, is a complicated question. One you'll need to ask her about. What I can tell you is that I've known Marjorie since she was a girl. Mr. Townsend, her father, was one of the best men I've ever known, and he asked me to help look after her. So there's very little I would not do for her." He stood up. "She wanted me to tell you that your room and meals here are on her account." He smiled. "But she asked that you please be moderate with the whiskey."

"Okay." Cade was even more baffled than before. But there was one question uppermost in his mind. As Alton reached the door, he said, "Wait."

Alton turned back to him, one hand still on the door. "Yes?"

"Can you tell me where she is? If she's safe? And the little girl?"

Alton smiled. "Theyah perfectly safe, Mr. Cade. But that's all I can tell you."

"Thanks," Cade said. He wanted to ask if he could see her, but the words stuck in his throat.

As Alton left, the waiter returned with his beer and placed it on the table. "And for dinner, sir?"

"Um, beefsteak, I guess. Rare. And roast potatoes."

"Very good, sir." He left Cade alone with the envelope.

Cade stared at it for a long minute, then picked it up and slit the seal with the butter knife. Inside was a number of gold coins. Cade shook them out on the table. A folded piece of paper fell out as well. Cade picked it up and unfolded it. It was a note, written on fine paper in a strong hand.

Mr. Cade, please forgive the roundabout manner in which this comes to you. I am also ashamed and embarrassed by my husband's beastly and unjust behavior toward you. You are a good man and deserved better.

I would like to employ you on my own account to continue looking into the question of McMurphy and who it is that wishes my family harm. Enclosed I believe you will find sufficient funds to pay the wages owed to you by my husband, as well as an advance on future earnings.

I have faith in your abilities and your judgment. When you believe you have an answer, please contact Captain Alton, on board the clipper ship Marjorie Ann, *at the Gold Wharf.*

I do not believe my husband has my best interest or that of our daughter at heart or that he is being completely truthful. Our safety depends on your finding out the truth. I implore you to do your utmost.

Marjorie Ann Townsend Hamrick

Cade put the note down and counted out the coins. Thirty dollars in gold and silver. He sat back in his chair and stared at the pile in front of him. With that money, he could get out of this town, set himself up nicely somewhere else, away from these rich people and their problems. But he didn't have it in him to run. *You are a good man,* she'd written. He'd not heard that often. He hoped he could live up to it.

The dinner came. It was an excellent meal, but he barely tasted it. He was too intent on planning what to do next.

CHAPTER THIRTY-SIX

"When can I go home?" Mei asked. She was seated in a chair in Mr. Kwan's library. Lin was standing behind her, combing her hair.

"Don't you like it here, Little Sister?" The White Orchid carefully undid a tangle.

"I'm worried about my grandparents. And I know they're worried about me."

"They're fine. They're under Mr. Kwan's protection, and everyone in our community knows it. And I'll make sure that they know you're safe." She put down the comb. "All done."

"Thank you." Mei turned in the chair to face her. "And thank you for all you've done. Please don't think me ungrateful. But this is not my home. And I miss my family."

"Ah." Lin's face lost all expression.

Mei reached out and took her hand. "I've offended you. I'm sorry. But don't you know how it feels to miss your family? Your parents? Your grandparents? "

Lin gave Mei's hand a squeeze, then pulled away. "My parents are back in Guangzhou." She sat down, not looking at Mei. "And no, I don't miss them at all. In fact, I hope they are long dead and buried."

Mei was horrified. A statement like that was close to sacrilege. "Surely you don't mean that!"

Lin's face was like stone. "I do mean it. I would kill them myself if they were here." Her expression softened as she saw the look on

Mei's face. "I'm sorry, Little Sister," she murmured. "I don't mean to shock you."

Mei shook her head. "I'm not…well, I guess I am shocked. Did they hurt you? Is that why you're…" She stopped before she could blurt out the next words.

Lin did it for her, smiling sadly. "A killer? A criminal?" She sighed. "I suppose it is."

Mei got up and walked over to where Lin was sitting. She put her hand on the older woman's shoulder. "Would it help you to share the pain, Elder Sister?"

Lin looked up at her and shook her head. "You are so kind. How can someone like you live in this terrible world?"

"I've found that most people in this world are kind," Mei said, "given a chance. And those who aren't, well, it's because of something that happened to them." She knelt by the chair and looked into Lin's eyes. "What happened to you?"

"You really want to know?"

"If it will help you, my friend, yes."

Lin nodded. "Take a seat, Little Sister."

***

Cade finished his meal and got up from the table. As he did, the door opened and the young waiter came in, so quickly that Cade wondered if he'd been listening at the keyhole.

"How much do I owe you, sonny?" Cade asked.

The waiter smiled unctuously. "Everything is on Mrs. Townsend's account, sir." The smile widened a bit. "Will she be joining you tonight, sir? Perhaps for dessert? A demitasse?"

"Doesn't look like it." Cade took out a quarter and flipped it toward the waiter, who reached out and caught it deftly. "Think you could direct me to the nearest livery stable? I mean to take a drive and I'll need to rent a buggy."

The waiter pocketed the coin. "There's Clawson's down the street. The front desk clerk can make arrangements."

"Thanks. I'll walk down there and do it myself. I feel the need to stretch my legs a bit."

"Very good, sir."

Clawson's was still open, but the only employee in attendance was an elderly black man with a harelip and a severe limp. Cade had meant to rent a carriage with his new-found bankroll, but his eyes lit on a likely-looking gray mare in one of the stalls. A few minutes later, he was saddled up. The tack was old but serviceable, the horse docile and good-natured. Cade hadn't realized how much he'd missed being on horseback. The gentle rhythm of the horse's walk helped settle his mind.

He'd been puzzling over how he was supposed to find this McMurphy. He didn't even have a description, much less a photograph. There was the one thing that set him apart from the mass of humanity in this town: his crazy father, the manic street preacher. Find him, and he'd bet his bottom dollar he'd find McMurphy not far off. And when he did, he could get the skinny on whoever it was trying to frame the Chinese. But where to start? He was still awed by just how big and bustling this city was.

Well, he couldn't be in one of the rich neighborhoods. He'd stick out like a sore thumb. Cade had last seen the old man in Chinatown, but he didn't think he'd be welcome there for long. The old man had looked too shabby and down at the heels to be staying in a place like The Royal. That left one possibility. Cade spurred the horse to a trot and turned toward the Barbary Coast.

CHAPTER THIRTY-SEVEN

"The worst thing that can happen to a poor girl," Lin began, "is to be born pretty."

Mei blinked in surprise. "I'd think the opposite was true."

Lin shook her head. "No. To a poor household, a pretty daughter is a commodity. Something to sell for the money to buy your way out." She'd reverted to that stony expression. Mei could almost feel the rage pent up behind that dam, and she began to feel a little afraid.

Lin must have read her expression, because she smiled. "Do you think I'm being vain, Little Sister, when I talk about being pretty?"

"No," Mei answered sincerely. "There's no sense in denying it. You are beautiful. Truly the most beautiful lady I have ever seen."

The White Orchid acknowledged the compliment with a slight inclination of her head. "Thank you. But my father didn't see me as someone to be cherished. He couldn't wait for me to reach the age when he could peddle me to some rich man. Like a prize heifer." She'd been speaking calmly until then, but the last words were as bitter as gall.

"What about your mother?"

Lin sighed. "She was beaten down before I was born. She had no voice left."

"Beaten...by your father?"

"Yes. And by life. She was no better than my father's slave. When the man came to take me away, she didn't even cry."

Mei felt the tears starting in her own eyes. "I'm sorry," she whispered.

Lin went on as if she hadn't heard. Her eyes were far away. "The man he sold me to was a merchant. A fat, disgusting pig. He actually licked his lips and stared at me while he was counting out the money."

Mei swallowed, not wanting to ask the next question, but needing to know. "How old were you?"

"I was twelve."

"Aiiii…"

"Yes. That night, he took me. He paid no attention to my tears. My pleas. My *blood*. I was in agony. He didn't care. He actually seemed to enjoy it more when I screamed that he was hurting me. When he was done, he fell off me and went to sleep. He lay there, snoring, with a stupid smile on his face." Lin's voice had become almost monotone, her face a mask. "It was the smile that did it for me. There was a vase on a stand near the bed. I picked up the vase, but it didn't seem heavy enough. I picked up the stand instead. And I smashed his head in with it."

Mei's hand had gone to her mouth, her eyes wide with shock.

Lin caught the look, but this time there was no comforting smile. "It took more than one blow. It took several. He tried to fight. But I've always been stronger than I look."

Mei was stunned, but she had to ask. "What happened then? How did you get away?"

"I ran from the house. I didn't know where I was going. It was dark and I was in a part of the city I'd never seen. Finally, I ended up down at the riverside. It was almost dawn, and the light on the Pearl River was earning it its name. I still remember how beautiful it was. How glad I was that so much beauty would be the last thing I saw before I died."

"Before you…died?"

"I knew that if I was caught, I'd be executed. But not until after they tortured me to make an example of me. I wasn't going to be hurt anymore. So, I gathered up rocks, took my torn clothes, and made a bag of them that I hung around my neck. Then I jumped in the river."

"But you didn't die."

The White Orchid chuckled at that. "No, Little Sister, I didn't die. I hadn't done a very good job. The bag came undone, the rocks fell out, and I bobbed to the surface. When I woke up, I was on one of the Red Boats."

Mei's brow furrowed in confusion. "The Red Boats?"

The White Orchid nodded. "You've never heard of the Red Boat Operas of the Pearl River?"

Mei shook her head.

"They were traveling players," Lin explained. "Up and down the river, two boats to each company, putting in at any town that seemed likely to provide an audience. Traditional dramas, mostly, but there were some humorous short plays that the audiences seemed to like." Lin smiled at the memory. "One of the older players, Chee So, took pity on me. Took me in. He was a good man. At first, I was just set to cooking and cleaning up. Only men were allowed as players, dressing up as women. But then, I got lucky in the lottery."

Mei inclined her head curiously. "The lottery?"

"At the beginning of every season, everyone drew lots to see who slept where. The best cabins were the ones up front, of course, away from the kitchen and the toilets. And I got one."

"Didn't they resent that? You were new. And a child."

"Ah, Little Sister, that was the beauty of the lottery system. Even the newest and poorest members of the company could get the best cabins, and then the other, richer ones could buy those cabins from them."

"Ah." Mei nodded. "So the new members could get a start in life."

"Just so. Except when they came to me, I didn't ask for money."

Lin smiled. "I demanded to be part of the company. And to learn to fight."

Mei blinked. "I don't understand."

"The secret of the Red Boats was that they formed part of the resistance to the Quing emperor. The time of the Manchus was done, they believed. And they hoped to bring on a new way."

"But what does that have to do with fighting?"

"Many of the Red Boat plays featured fights and battle scenes. But the stage fighting was a cover for the real art of Wing Chun."

Mei frowned. "Wing Chun is just a story."

"No, Little Sister, it's very real. Hidden for years, but kept alive from generation to generation. And Chee So was a master of the art."

"So, they just let you join?"

Lin shook her head. "They laughed at me at first. Till I challenged the biggest and strongest player, a young man everyone called Ox, to fight me."

"And you defeated him?"

Lin chuckled. "Oh, no. He beat me soundly. I learned that watching an art be practiced, no matter how intensely you observe, doesn't really teach it to you." She sighed in remembrance of the pain. "Oh, yes, I learned that lesson well that day. And for all the days after of nursing my bruises. But what made up Chee So's mind was this: whenever Ox knocked me down or threw me to the ground, I'd get back up. Finally, Chee called an end to the fight. I was limping and bloody, but I was not beaten. So, I became a member of the company."

"But you said only men could be players."

"And soon the word spread on the river about the new boy who could play the female parts so convincingly." Her face became wistful again. "It was a good life. And I learned so much more than fighting."

"But…it came to an end."

"Yes. A man rose up in the south of China. He claimed he was the brother of the white devil's god, the one named Jesus. Totally mad, of course, but he gathered an army of millions to oppose the Qing emperor. Many of the Red Boat troupes saw opportunity and joined him." Her face took on that blank look again, the one that caused Mei to want to draw away from her. "It was the same story as ever. The rebels began to bicker among themselves. The madman died, some say by his own hand. And the rebellion was crushed."

Mei felt her heart fluttering in her throat. "What happened to your troupe?"

The White Orchid's eyes were far away. "I had gone to the market to buy oranges. I loved oranges. I still do. I was on my way back to the docks with my little bag of oranges when I saw the smoke."

"Oh no..."

"The emperor's soldiers had come. There were ten of them. Ten against a hundred on the boats, but they had guns. Even a small cannon. The troupe had rifles too, of course, but they were caught by surprise." She took a deep breath. "When I got to the docks, the boats were on fire. My home was on fire. They had everyone lined up along the wharf. The emperor's soldiers were prodding people into lines with their bayonets to watch their home burn. Then they began shooting." She turned that bleak gaze on Mei. "They shot everyone down. Everyone. Actors, acrobats, even the cook. Some tried to run. Some tried to fight. But everyone was killed. Killed in cold blood." Then The White Orchid did something that chilled Mei to the bone. She smiled. Mei had seen many different smiles from the older woman—friendly, mischievous, affectionate—but this was the most terrifying smile she had ever seen on a human face. It barely looked human at all. Lin's voice was almost crooning as she said the next words. "But I had my vengeance, oh, yes. Yes. I ran away, but not before I memorized every soldier's face. I followed them back to their barracks. And then, over the next few weeks, I lived like an animal in the streets. I stole food. I slept in alleys near the barracks. But I caught up with each of the soldiers. One by one. In the taverns, in the brothels, in the market. And I killed them. Every one of them. And on each body, I left a flower."

"A white orchid," Mei whispered.

The smile went away. Mei was never so happy to see a smile leave a person's face. "Yes. And you know what I felt when it was done? When I stood over the body of the last soldier with his life's blood dripping from my blade?"

Mei shook her head, unable to speak.

"Nothing," Lin said. "I felt nothing. All the fear, the pain, the rage…it was gone. As if it had been poured out onto the alleys and tavern floors with the blood of the soldiers. I was totally empty. And I'm empty to this day." She looked at Mei. Her eyes had lost all expression, her face blank. Mei had seen her face go as solid as a mask before, but now she realized that the bright, vivacious, sometimes affectionate persona of The White Orchid—that was the true mask. And behind it, despite Lin's words, there wasn't total emptiness. There was a deep well of rage and malice that was terrifying to contemplate, embodied in a smile that Mei knew would haunt her dreams.

The White Orchid went on. "The emperor's men were looking everywhere for me. It was only a matter of time before they caught up with me and sent me to the Board of Punishments. You've heard of them?"

Mei nodded.

"For killing the soldiers of the emperor, the Board would see to it that I took days to die," Lin said. "Maybe weeks. But Mr. Kwan heard about me. He thought I was someone he could use. He sent his younger brother Fang to offer me employment and a place to live. And when they came to America, I came with them." She looked at Mei. "And now that you know my story, now that you know what I am, I don't suppose we can be friends anymore."

"I…that's not true." In truth, Mei didn't know what to think.

Part of her wanted to run, the other half wanted to rush over and comfort the shattered woman who she still wanted to believe was her friend.

The door opened and the old woman who seemed to run the household stuck her head in. "Mr. Kwan wants to see you," she snapped. "Now."

CHAPTER THIRTY-EIGHT

The Coast was in its usual state of bedlam. Groups of men lurched about the sidewalks. Cade spotted a few dressed in what looked like naval uniforms, so maybe the U.S. Navy was in town, its bluejackets like sheep looking for a place to get sheared. Barkers called out from the doorways of bars and music halls.

"Pretty waiter girls! Most beautiful in town!"

"Plain talk and beautiful girls!"

"Enough to make a blind man see!"

Cade had seen enough of those "pretty waiter girls" when he'd first hit town to render him permanently skeptical of even the mildest of those claims.

A short, wiry little man in ragged trousers and a frock coat was turning away from a group of young dudes. He was carrying a baseball bat under one arm. He caught sight of Cade and walked purposefully toward him. "Hit me with a bat for four bits? Only four bits to hit me with this bat, sir?"

"Not tonight, Oofty," Cade called back.

The man blinked, looking up at Cade. "Oh, howdy, Mr. Cade. Didn't recognize you on horseback."

Cade beckoned to him. "Come on over. Maybe I have an easier way for you to earn four bits."

The man only known to the Barbary Coast as Oofty Goofty walked over with his distinctive bow-legged stride. His real name was lost to time. He'd come to the city performing "The Wild Man of Borneo," shaking the bars of a cage in a Market Street freak show, screaming, "Oofty Goofty! Oofty Goofty!" at the fascinated crowd, who supposedly figured they were being hectored in the native language of whatever savage land Borneo was. Unfortunately for him, his "wild man" costume, composed as it was of horsehair stuck onto him with road tar, proved bad for his health, landing him in the hospital for a stretch. About that time he discovered his true God-given talent: for whatever reason, he'd become completely insensitive to pain. After that, he began roaming the streets, offering to be kicked, slapped, even hit with his famous bat, for a price. That kind of entertainment had never been to Cade's taste, but apparently enough people found amusement in it to keep Oofty fed and bandaged.

Cade stopped the mare, by the side of the street, where she seemed oblivious to the milling crowds. Oofty patted her on the muzzle, looking up at Cade. "What can I do for you on this fine evening, Mr. Cade?"

"I'm lookin' for a fella named McMurphy." He recalled his last conversation with Hamrick. "Patrick McMurphy."

Oofty rubbed his chin. "Don't recollect the name."

"Stays with his pappy. The old man's a little gone in the head. Wanders around street preaching."

Oofty nodded, his wrinkled face screwed up in concentration. "I've seen the old preacher. He's out sometimes down near Kearney." He shook his head. "Folks is pretty bad to him. They toss mud, sometimes bricks at the poor old fellow."

"Guess they don't come to the Coast to hear the world of the Lord."

Oofty frowned in indignation. "But what I want to know is, how is a man supposed to make an honest livin' gettin' hit when bastards like him is givin' it away for free?"

"Folks'll always prefer the work of a professional, Oofty." Cade handed him a dollar. "Here. Take the rest of the night off. And send word if you see McMurphy or his pa. I'm stayin' at The Royal."

Oofty's bushy eyebrows went up. "The Royal. You're movin' up in the world, Mr. Cade."

"I wish. G'night, Oofty."

"See you around, Mr. Cade." He patted the horse on her muzzle again. "Nice horse."

"Thanks." As Cade urged the horse into a slow walk, he heard Oofty behind him, approaching another group of men. "Hit me with a bat for four bits, gents? Only four bits to hit me with this bat, gents." He sighed. Some people just loved their work too much to take a day off. He headed down to Kearney Street. Maybe he'd get lucky.

***

Kwan was seated behind his desk. He didn't look pleased.

"Cade is no longer employed by Hamrick," he said. "He no longer lives at the house. He is at The Royal Hotel."

Mei wondered at how Mr. Kwan always seemed to know what was going on, even among the white devils.

The White Orchid took a seat without being asked. Her face was grave. "Will he continue to search out the people behind this plot against you?"

Kwan placed his hands flat on the desk in front of him. "I want you to remind him of what I expect."

The White Orchid nodded. "How strong a reminder would you require?"

"There is no need for harsh measures. Not now. Just let him know what his obligation is."

"Sir?" Mei spoke up.

Kwan turned to her, his eyebrows raised in surprise. "What is it?"

Mei swallowed. She couldn't believe herself that she'd been bold enough to speak up. But her hesitation was making him impatient, she could tell. "You speak of obligation. But he isn't family. He isn't even Chinese."

Kwan frowned. "So?"

"I think she means you should pay him," The White Orchid spoke up. "Perhaps some in advance."

Kwan nodded. "Yes. Of course." He grimaced. "They have no loyalty, and they trust no one. They think only of money."

Lin and Mei exchanged glances. "Yes," Lin said.

Kwan reached into his desk drawer and pulled out a beautifully carved wooden box. Without speaking, he counted out a stack of coins and pushed it across the table. "Here. Get this to him. And let him know there is more to be had if he succeeds."

"Your generosity is legendary, sir," The White Orchid murmured. She took the money and tucked it into a fold in her robe. "Come, Little Sister," she said to Mei. "We have a call to pay."

CHAPTER THIRTY-NINE

The Kearney Street area was a bust. He didn't spot the preacher, so he stopped into a few taverns, music halls, and toward the end of the evening, some particularly greasy looking deadfalls, asking if anyone knew McMurphy or his father. The name drew blank looks, but quite a few people recalled the crazy preacher. Cade spread some money around, letting folks know there'd be more coming if anyone could help him find McMurphy. The coins disappeared into pockets and petticoats with a knowing wink and an assurance that yessir, Mr. Cade, I'll let you know. Cade had little faith in any of it, but he figured just one strike at his hook might lead to landing this particular fish.

He turned the horse back in at the stable and gave her a pat on the muzzle, before making his way back to the Royal. This late, the ornate lobby was deserted and dimly lit. There was a different man behind the front desk, a hulking bruiser with a walleye that wandered to the side of whoever the man was looking at. Cade figured he'd been hired more for his size and his ability to intimidate late-night troublemakers than for his good looks.

Cade walked up to the desk and gave the man a nod. "Any messages for Cade?"

One eye squinted at him suspiciously, while the other regarded the lobby. "And who the hell are you?"

Cade replied with as much patience as he could muster. "I'm Cade."

The front desk man looked as if that meant nothing to him, so

Cade added, "I'm a guest of Mrs. Townsend. Room 345."

That got a result. The desk clerk actually got up off his stool and stood reasonably straight.

"Sorry, sir. Yes, sir." He turned to a row of cubbyholes behind the desk, searched for a moment, then pulled out an envelope. "Here you go, sir."

Cade took it and examined the outside. It was made of what seemed to be very expensive paper, and it felt strangely heavy. "Thanks. I'll be turning in."

"Very good, sir." The clerk looked sheepish. "And sorry for the misunderstanding, sir."

"No worries. You look sharp, now."

"Yes, sir."

As Cade mounted the stairs, he hefted the envelope in his hand. On the second-floor landing, curiosity got the better of him. He didn't want to wait until he got to his room, so he took out his pocketknife and slit the envelope open.

It was full of gold coins. Several of them. He took them out and examined them, jingling them in his hands. He frowned. He'd already been paid by Mrs. Hamrick's captain. Now this? He noticed that something else had fallen from the envelope, a small piece of paper. He bent and picked it up. It was a square, about two inches by two inches. There was no writing on it, just a symbol. No, a stamp, embossed on the fine paper in green ink. It took a couple of seconds to register what it was.

A green Chinese dragon.

Cade stuffed the coins back in the envelope and took the steps two at a time going back downstairs. The walleyed desk man looked up in surprise. "Help you, sir?"

Cade shook the envelope at him. "Where did this come from?"

The vehemence of the question took the desk man aback. "Some...someone dropped it off, sir."

"Who?"

"An old man. A Chinaman."

"An old…tell me what he looked like."

"Why, he looked like a Chinaman, is all. Seemed harmless enough. He was blind, after all."

"Blind?"

The desk man nodded. "Led around by his daughter."

"His…" Cade shook his head, remembering the young girl who'd translated for Kwan. "Where did they go?"

The desk man looked baffled. "Wherever those people go, I suppose. Why?"

"Did they say anything? Leave any other kind of message?"

The clerk shook his head. "No." His voice went high and sing-song in a poor imitation of Chinese. "Just 'this for room three four five.'"

"Just for…" How in seven hells did they know which room he was in? He fought down the urge to look behind him. "Is that all?"

"Yes, sir. Is there something wrong, sir?"

There was plenty wrong, but nothing he wanted to discuss with this fellow. "No. But if anyone else comes asking about me, you let me know right away, got that? And keep them here."

The man nodded, still clearly baffled, but obedient. "Yes, sir."

Cade tucked the envelope inside his coat and headed back up to the room. When he got to the door, he stopped.

There was a light coming from beneath the door. Cade tried to remember if he'd left the light on, and couldn't. He drew his pistol and slowly drew the hammer back with his thumb, cursing the sound of the snap as the weapon cocked. He fumbled with his left hand for the key. He slid it into the lock as quietly as he could, then turned it and flung the door open in one motion, the Navy revolver leveled in front of him.

Mei, Kwan's messenger girl, was sitting on the edge of the bed, dressed in her usual plain skirt and blouse. She slid off the bed and bowed. "Please pardon the intrusion, Mr. Cade."

CHAPTER FORTY

Cade didn't move. "Where's your friend?"

Mei nodded to the space beside the door. "She is right here."

"Then tell her to step out. Where I can see her."

"Mr. Cade," Mei said, "we are not here to hurt you."

"Tell her to step out."

Mei said something in Chinese, and the woman who'd kidnapped him earlier stepped into view. She was dressed in the baggy shirt and loose trousers of a Chinese man, her dark hair tucked up beneath a white cap. She held a bamboo cane loosely in one hand and there was what looked like a scarf hanging around her neck. A scarf, or perhaps the eye bandages of a blind man.

"The old blind man and his daughter," Cade said. "Nice trick. How'd you get in here?"

Mei smiled sadly. "To be Chinese in this city is to be invisible. A beggar, a servant, an old blind man...no one likes to see us. So we stay unseen." She nodded toward the woman. "The White Orchid taught me that."

The only way that woman could be unnoticed, Cade thought, was to cover that beautiful face. "I ain't gonna argue the point," he said. He gestured with the gun. "Tell her to put the cane down. And to go over to sit by you."

Mei spoke to the woman, who gave Cade an indulgent smile, as if she was humoring a child. That smile worried Cade. She had some kind of Chinese trick up her sleeve, he just knew it. But she let the cane clatter to the floor, then went and sat on the bed. Those disconcerting eyes never left Cade's face. He tore his own gaze away and stepped inside, pistol still raised. He closed the door with his heel. A slight draft made him glance over at the window, which was still open. *Guess I need to start locking those*, he thought.

"Please lower the gun," Mei said. "We truly do not mean you any harm."

Cade had to admire her coolness, staring down the barrel of a pistol as she was, but it put him in even less of a trusting mood. "Just tell me what you want."

"We are here to make sure you received the money Mr. Kwan sent."

"Oh, I got it." Cade reached into his coat pocket and took out the envelope. He tossed it on the floor at Mei's feet. "Tell him what I told him at his place. I already have a job, doin' pretty much what he wants me to do."

Mei's brow furrowed. "But we know that you have been…" she paused as she searched for the word, "…fired by Mr. Hamrick."

"I have a new employer. So tell Mr. Kwan I don't need his money."

The White Orchid said something to Mei, who answered quickly. There was a brief exchange in Chinese between them that ended with the older woman giggling behind her hand.

Jesus, she even laughs pretty, Cade thought. The big pistol was growing heavy in his hands, but he didn't dare lower it. "What was that all about?"

"Nothing," Mei said. "Nothing important."

Good god, she's blushing, Cade thought. He looked at the woman. She was smiling, dark eyes practically twinkling at him. *Damned if that ain't what I'd call the come-hither look*, he thought. Then he tore his eyes away and recollected himself.

Mei was speaking again. "I'm afraid Mr. Kwan is very firm in his determination that you need to complete this job."

"I'm goin' to," Cade said. "But for my new employer. Not for him."

Mei looked puzzled. "You turn down money?"

Cade hesitated. When she put it that way, it did sound a little squirrelly. But he didn't want to be indebted to any Chinese crime boss. "I do. I don't want there to be any confusion about who I work for."

Mei shook her head. "The obligation is on you either way. So why not take the money?"

"Because..." Cade sighed. "Oh, what the hell." His arms and wrists were screaming with the effort of holding the Navy revolver out. He slid it back into his shoulder holster. "Will there be anything else, ladies?" He nodded to the bottle of whiskey on the dresser. "A drink before you go? Maybe I could have some tea sent up?"

Mei apparently didn't catch the sarcasm. "No, thank you. I am too young to drink whiskey. And we must be going." She stood up. The White Orchid did the same.

"Before you go," Cade said, "I have a question."

Mei sat back down. "Yes?"

"You said someone was talking to McMurphy. The man trying to blame the Chinese for attacking Hamrick. Can you describe him?"

She shrugged. "He was a *gwai*—a white man." She thought. "He was tall. Even for a white man." She ran her hand over her chin. "He had whiskers here." She traced a finger over her upper lip. "Not here."

"Tall, with chin whiskers." Cade grimaced. "That describes a good chunk of the males in this damn town. What about his voice?"

She looked up, as if searching for the memory on the ceiling. "He changed his voice. When he was pretending to be Chinese, he spoke in a high voice." She pitched her own voice almost to a falsetto, mimicking the mystery man's tone. Then her voice dropped dramatically, to a hoarse croak. "When he spoke normally, his voice was deep." Her tone returned to normal.

"Okay, then." He looked at the open window. "You going out the way you come in? Or do you prefer the door?"

"The door, if it would be all right with you."

"Fine." Cade stood aside.

The White Orchid was picking her cane up off the floor. As she straightened up, she seemed to blur for a second, then Cade was stunned to find her pressed up against him, her arms wrapped around his neck. Her beautiful face was inches from his, her eyes dancing with mischief. Her eyes closed, her full lips parted slightly as if for a kiss. Cade made a sound in his throat, bent down to her...

Her eyes snapped open and she nipped him on the nose, not hard, but it was surprising enough to make Cade yelp. She let him go, and he sprang back, hard enough to bump the back of his head on the wall.

He could hear her laughter through the door even after they'd closed it behind them.

CHAPTER FORTY-ONE

"Why did you do that?" Mei asked.

"Do what, Little Sister?" The White Orchid was back in her disguise, the bandages wrapped around her eyes and forehead, her cane tapping on the sidewalk. Her other hand rested lightly on Mei's shoulder. There were few people on the street at this late hour, and none of them took any notice of an old blind man and his young guide.

"You know what!" Mei shook her head. "Embrace the white devil. I thought you were going to...to kiss him!"

"And why not?" Lin's voice was merry. "He's not bad looking, for a white devil."

Mei couldn't repress a shudder. "Ugh! So hairy. Like an ape! And so big!"

"Big all over, perhaps?"

Mei nearly pulled away. "You're shameless."

The White Orchid chuckled. "Perhaps. Or perhaps I enjoy scandalizing you."

Mei shook her head. "That's not kind."

Lin was silent for a moment. Then she said, "You're right. I'm sorry."

"It's all right."

They walked on for another half a block, then Lin said in a small voice, "Are we still friends, Little Sister? Even though I tease you? And...and after what I told you about me?"

Mei thought a moment, then sighed. "Yes. We are. But as a friend, may I be honest?"

"Of course."

"Sometimes, Elder Sister, you frighten me."

There another pause. Then the White Orchid said, "You never need to fear me, Little Sister. I promise you that. Never. Or anything else. Nothing will harm you while I'm alive."

Mei couldn't bring herself to tell her friend that the tone in her voice, rather than the words, frightened her even more.

***

He trudged up the steps from the basement, whistling softly to himself. It had been a special night. Usually, the girls sold to him for what he called his "escapades" were whores who'd been used up, unfit even for the filthy cribs of Chinatown. Emaciated, hollow-eyed, some nearly catatonic, it often took very little time for them to succumb to his particular brand of pleasure. Some even seemed to welcome it. But this one had been younger, more spirited. Not fresh off the boat, and still too worn to ever be called pretty, but she'd provided rare sport for him. Perhaps she'd rebelled and been sent to him as a lesson to the other girls.

He reached the top of the steps and opened the door into the front room. The ancient woman who ran the place sat in her accustomed place behind the front door. The huge Chinese guard who always stood over her was in his usual spot as well, arms crossed over his barrel chest, glowering.

The man smiled. He was in an expansive mood, and not even Chinese insolence could make a ripple in the euphoria his escapades left in him. He took out a gold dollar and flipped it to the old woman. "Cleanup may be a bit more extensive than usual."

She didn't reach out to catch the coin, and it clattered on the table in front of her. She regarded it as if he'd thrown a fresh horse turd on her makeshift desk, then looked back at him. There was no expression on her face, but he knew the old woman and her silent protector hated him with every fiber of their being. They didn't know, or perhaps didn't care, that their hatred just made things sweeter for him. They may have hated him, but money shielded him from the consequences of that hate. For him, that was what money meant: freedom from consequence. Gold had unlocked a whole world for him, a dark paradise where he ruled all.

He was still whistling as he exited the house on the quiet side street. In the light of a gas streetlamp, he reached into his vest pocket and withdrew a cigar. When he went to light it, he noticed something unusual. He puffed the cigar to life, clenched it firmly between his teeth, and examined his hand in the final guttering light of the lucifer match. What he saw made him grimace. There was still fresh blood under his fingernails. He shook his head. He certainly couldn't go home like that. He realized that the sky was beginning to lighten. It would be daylight soon, and a new work day. Well, it wasn't as if he was going to get any sleep anyway. Not in his current state. He'd get to work early, clean his fingernails before anyone else arrived, and be there to greet them. It would be a good example for the slackers in his office.

He picked up his tune again and strolled off into the dawn.

CHAPTER FORTY-TWO

Despite the comfortable bed, Cade slept fitfully. The laughter of the woman Mei had called The White Orchid was still ringing in his ears. She'd reeled him in like a fish with that pretty face and those hypnotic brown eyes, then she'd landed him and thrown him back, just to let him know she could have gutted him and devoured him any time. Cade had faced down armed bullies, road agents, poisonous snakes, and on one occasion a mountain lion, but the only thing that had truly shaken him up to now was a beautiful Chinese woman half his size.

Well, she'd made her point. If she worked for this Kwan fellow, he was going to do his best to make sure they were on the same side. After tossing and turning half the night and getting up several times to make sure the window was locked, Cade finally fell asleep.

***

The euphoria of the night before was beginning to wear off, and the eyes of the man behind the desk were beginning to droop. Taking the day off to nap, however, was not an option. Not for a man in his position. He had no doubts in the force of his will to get him through the day.

He was reading the morning mail when he discovered an envelope with no address and no marking at all on the outside. He frowned. Taking a gold-handled letter opener, he slit the envelope open and shook a folded piece of paper out onto the desktop. When he picked it up and read it, what he saw there gave him a jolt that blew the fatigue away. He got up and snatched his hat and walking stick from the stand by the door.

Ten minutes later, he was seated across from Butt Shaughnessy in a tavern down the street.

"You took your time gettin' here," the hoodlum growled. Despite the early hour, he'd already downed three shots of whiskey, judging from the empty glasses in front of him.

"I came as soon as I got the message," the man said.

Shaughnessy grunted and signaled for another drink. The man frowned. "I hope you don't think all these are going on my tab."

"I don't think it, I know it." Shaughnessy grinned and downed the shot the waiter girl brought him. As she walked away, he gave her a light slap on the rear end that was barely covered by a scandalously short skirt.

The man silently vowed to deal with this impertinence later. "You're sure of your information?"

Shaughnessy nodded. "It's all over the Coast. Cade's looking for McMurphy."

"But why?"

The hoodlum shrugged. "Word is, the Chinese hired him." He grimaced. "No way would I take money from those fuckin' heathens. A man's got to have standards."

The man doubted very seriously that Shaughnessy would hesitate to sell his own mother to the Chinese if the price was right, but he let that pass, too. "He has to be stopped."

"Two ways I can think of to do that. You want one dealt with or both?"

"Use your discretion. Payment will be delivered on completion. As always."

"It is." Shaughnessy burped.

"Mr. Shaughnessy," the man said calmly. "I give you a certain amount of tolerance because you and your people are valuable to me. But that only goes so far. Don't make me give you a reminder of who I am, and what can happen when my patience runs out."

They stared at each other across the table. It was the hoodlum whose gaze broke first. "Okay, okay," he muttered. "Don't get your knickers in a twist."

The man got up. "I want to hear by tomorrow that Cade and McMurphy are no longer a threat to me." He threw a handful of coins on the table. "This should cover your bill. Don't get too drunk to do the job."

Shaughnessy scooped up the coins, his good mood somewhat restored. "Not to worry."

***

Cade awoke to a polite knocking on his door. He rolled over and checked his watch on the bedside table. "Shit," he muttered. It was going on ten o'clock. He never slept this late. He pulled on his trousers and went to the door in his stocking feet.

Cade didn't recognize the short, dark-haired man who stood outside, but his red coat and round cap marked him as hotel staff. He didn't seem to notice Cade's disheveled appearance. "Excuse, sir," he said in an accent Cade didn't recognize. "You have a visitor."

"A visitor?" Cade ran a hand over his stubbled chin. He wasn't really in any shape to receive callers.

The man's bland expression turned to an unctuous smile. "It is a lady, sir. She asked for a private dining room and ordered breakfast for the both of you."

"A lady...?" Damn. There were only two ladies he knew in this town, and one had already paid him a visit. He really didn't want to meet Marjorie Hamrick looking like last week's laundry, but he also didn't want to keep her waiting. "Tell her I'll be down in a minute," he said.

"Very good, sir." The man bowed slightly. "And if sir would care for a shave afterward, I can arrange for the hotel barber."

"Yeah," Cade said. "That'll be good. Thanks."

He'd made himself halfway presentable when he entered the room the front desk had directed him to. Marjorie stood up as he entered. The smell of eggs, bacon, sausages, and coffee wafted to him from covered silver serving dishes arrayed on a large table in the middle of the room. The aroma made his stomach growl, and the sight of her inspired a different hunger. She was dressed in a long red skirt and a white blouse that clung to her in all the right places.

"Mr. Cade," she said. "I took the liberty of ordering breakfast. I hope you don't mind."

"Not a bit, ma'am." Cade gestured her back to her seat. "Have a seat. Please."

She smiled. "You first. I'll serve."

Reluctantly, he took the seat opposite hers. She removed the lids from the silver serving dishes and picked up his plate. He caught a whiff of her perfume as she bent over to spoon a generous helping of eggs, bacon, and sausage onto his plate before setting it in front of him. It was as close as she'd ever been to him, and it took him a couple of seconds to realize she'd said something. "I, ah, beg your pardon, ma'am?"

She smiled and began putting a smaller helping of food on her own plate. "I said, I trust the accommodations are satisfactory?"

"Yes, ma'am," he said. "Very comfy."

She took her seat. "Good. I keep a standing reservation here. For times…well, sometimes I need to get away."

He took a bite of eggs. "Yes, ma'am." He didn't know what else to say.

She regarded him gravely. "And I'm sure you're wondering if my getaways are solitary ones."

He'd been thinking that very thing, but he replied, "It's none of my business, ma'am."

"The answer is, not always. Does that shock you?"

Cade shook his head. "There's not a lot left that shocks me, Mrs. Hamrick."

"Truly?" She stirred at her food with a fork, looking down at the plate. When she looked back up, she spoke again in a flat, dry voice. "My husband goes out and takes his pleasures whenever he wants. Why shouldn't I?"

Cade set his fork down. "What I'm trying to figure out, Mrs. Hamrick, is why you came down here to tell me all this."

She held his eyes with hers. "Because I need to get away. From John. And I don't want to do it alone." She stood up and walked over to him, standing close enough that he could feel the warmth of her body. "I trust I've made my meaning clear, Mr. Cade."

I guess breakfast can wait, Cade thought. He stood up as well, his napkin falling to the floor. "Maybe you ought to call me Levi."

CHAPTER FORTY-THREE

They lay together, the sheets a sweaty tangle at the foot of the bed. Marjorie's thick blonde hair was undone and spread out across Cade's torso as she rested her head on his chest. He took a strand and wrapped it around his finger, toying with it idly. She ran her fingers gently through the dark hair on his chest and sighed with contentment. "Thank you," she murmured. "That was just what I needed." All of her previous reserve was gone, shed like the clothes that lay on the floor.

"Glad to oblige," Cade said.

She smiled and tweaked his nipple, then began kissing his chest. "I bet I know what you're thinking," she murmured.

"Yeah? What's that?"

She looked up at him, amusement in her brown eyes. "You're wondering why."

"Why what?"

"Why I'm here."

"Well," he said, "I don't usually like to question good luck. But this much good luck does leave me a mite puzzled."

She laughed, deep in her throat. "I'll take that 'good luck' as a compliment. But you didn't seem puzzled a few minutes ago." She propped herself up on one elbow. "Is it so hard to believe I saw someone I wanted to be with and decided to make it happen?"

He shrugged. "Now I'm the one that's flattered. But it seems like you're takin' an awful risk."

She snorted. "I'm not afraid of John Hamrick. And you shouldn't be either. He's a weak man."

Her open contempt was making him feel uncomfortable, even as he shared it. "You don't seem to like him very much."

"I don't. I hate him." She looked away. "Shortly after my daughter was born, he came home from one of his whoring expeditions. He brought a disease to our bed." She saw the look on his face and hastened to add, "Don't worry. I'm cured. After months of painful and humiliating treatment, I was cured. But I'm unable to have any more children. And I haven't let him touch me since."

He whistled softly. "Yeah. I can see how that would be. So why are you still with him?"

She was silent for a long time. "I've had to make compromises in my life, Levi. My mother died when I was small, and my father never remarried. Never had any sons. So, he raised me to take over his business. Taught me to be strong. To reach for the things I wanted."

"Seems like you do a good job at that. But why—"

She went on as he she hadn't heard him. "My father hadn't been in the ground a week before the wolves started moving in. People tried to steal from me. People tried to swindle me. They thought I was weak and stupid because I'm a woman, and when I showed them I damn well wasn't, they froze me out."

"Froze you out how?"

She reached down and began picking up her undergarments from the floor. "You may have noticed, Levi, that the most successful men make their fortune with other people's cash." She pulled a stocking on. "The world doesn't just run on money, it runs on borrowed money. To get that, you need credit. And when the shipping business needed capital, I couldn't get any." She pulled the other stocking on and looked at him. "I wasn't a good risk, as far as the banks were concerned. I wasn't respectable, you see. Because I was an unmarried woman."

"So, you got married."

She nodded. "John Hamrick seemed like my solution. He was charming. He was on his way up. Banks were falling over themselves to finance him."

"So, you married him for his prospects?"

"For his *respectability*." She almost spat the word. She shook her head angrily. "I was so stupid."

"No," Cade said. "Never stupid." He sat up next to her and put an arm around her. "Never stupid." He sighed. "Sometimes people do things when they got their back against the wall they wouldn't do otherwise."

"But you see," she said, "I'm not so different from other women. The ones who marry for money, not for love." Her voice caught as she said, "I used to think I was so damned special."

It was the first time he'd seen her vulnerable. "Well," Cade said, "my opinion may not matter for much. But I think you're pretty damned special."

She put her own arm around him and they pulled each other close. The nearness of her body was starting to have an effect on him. She looked over and noticed, then smiled with a raised eyebrow. "Again? Truly?"

He smiled. "Hey, it's been a while. I'm making up for a long drought."

She laughed. "Me, too." She gave him a long, lingering kiss.

"Leave the stockings on," he said.

***

"That was even better," she whispered. She rolled off Cade and stretched out on the bed beside him.

He was still trying to catch his breath. "Yeah," was all he could get out.

She reached up and stroked his chin. He really did need that shave, but the stubble didn't seem to bother her. "What about you, Levi? What do you want?"

He smiled. "I think I just got it."

She smiled back. "You know what I mean."

He lay back and thought about it for a while before speaking. "When I was in the Army, it was tough, sure. But it was someplace I belonged. There was work to do I was good at. It was important."

"But that ended."

"Yeah. When I went home, I thought I'd settle down, inherit my daddy's farm, marry this girl I'd been courting before the war."

She propped her head up on one elbow and looked at him. "I guess it didn't work out."

"No. Her family was rich. We…well, we weren't. I thought coming back havin' done my duty for my country would make up for it. Her daddy didn't agree." He stopped.

She waited for him to go on. When he didn't, she murmured, "I'm sorry, Levi."

He was looking up at the ceiling, his mind far away. "There was no place for me back home, either. So, like a whole lot of other people, I headed west."

"Looking for somewhere to belong." She sat up.

He regarded her soberly. "I was thinking maybe I'd found it."

She sighed. "You know that can't be, Levi. I have a husband and a daughter."

He reached out to hold her. "To hell with him. Stay with me."

She shook her head and began to get dressed. "It's not that simple."

He sat up and sat cross-legged on the bed. "You've got your own money now. You don't need his credit."

She looked at him as she pulled her undergarments on. "No. I don't. But, sad as it is to say, we need each other. As much as we despise each other, our lives are too tangled together now to unsnarl. And I have a daughter." She laughed bitterly. "Even though it's not his."

That rocked him. "Say what?"

"Oh, she's legally his daughter. Even though she has none of his blood, she was born while we were married. So he has certain... rights. And I'll never leave my girl with him. Never." Her eyes were blazing, her expression fierce. He felt something in his heart give way. She saw the look on his face and smiled before leaning over to give him a quick kiss. He reached up and pulled her more tightly to him. She finally broke away from the kiss. "Stop," she gasped. "If we go on, I might never leave." She took a deep breath. "Besides, I need you to get to work. To find out who it is that's working with McMurphy to threaten us."

Her rejection of the idea they could be together felt like a hole blown through him, but if he couldn't have her, he wasn't going to let her come to harm. He put the pain away as best he could. "McMurphy," he said. "Tell me about him."

She explained as she continued to dress. "John and Patrick were business partners. They were heavily invested in silver stocks. They'd made a lot of money in it. But John was getting nervous. He wanted to branch out into other things. 'Can't put all our eggs in one basket,' he kept saying. McMurphy didn't agree. He thought silver was the path to get richer and richer, faster and faster." She was pinning up her hair. "That's the thing about money, Levi. No matter how much it is, or how fast it comes in, it's never enough. Some people go after money to feel safe, but even when they see how easily it can be lost, they don't realize they've been wrong. They just think they need more."

Cade thought of the girl who cleaned the boarding house, how she claimed to have won and lost a fortune in a matter of weeks. He shook his head. The whole town was built on the illusion that money and power were forever, but it was a castle built on the shifting sands of the bay.

Marjorie went on. "So, when they came to a parting of the

ways, John and Patrick divided up the business. They'd just invested heavily in a silver strike in the Monterrey hills. McMurphy took all that stock, John took the growing real estate holdings."

"Don't tell me. The silver strike went bust."

She nodded. "The vein played out the week after the papers were signed. Patrick showed up at the house, raging. He accused John of knowing all along that the strike was about to go bad."

"Did he?"

"I don't know, Levi. But knowing John as I do now, it wouldn't surprise me."

"But you said McMurphy killed himself."

"That's what we thought. Patrick's house burned down. The police said the fire was deliberately set. The bank was foreclosing on the property, so the detectives said Patrick had burned the place down with he and his father in it."

Cade grimaced. "Hell of a way for a man to do himself in."

She was fully clothed again now, smoothing down the front of her skirt. "Truth be told, it didn't make a lot of sense to me, either. But we trusted the police."

"Sure." Cade started to dress as well. "Why wouldn't you? They work for people like you." He pulled his pants on and stood up. "Okay. I'll keep looking for McMurphy."

She walked over and embraced him. "And if you find him?" she said against his naked chest.

"I'll have a word with him."

She looked into his face. "It may take more than a word. I need you to be sure. Sure he'll never try to harm me or my daughter again."

Cade nodded. "I'll make sure. Trust me."

She put her head back against his chest. "I do, Levi. I trust you completely."

At that moment, Cade felt ten feet tall and bulletproof. He squeezed her back, hard. *Maybe she can change her mind*, he thought.

But it was she who broke the embrace and went to the door. She turned, her hand on the doorknob, and looked at him. "Good luck, Mr. Cade," she said, her tone once again formal. He couldn't read the look in her eyes, but the message in her tone was unmistakable.

"Thank you, ma'am," he replied.

CHAPTER FORTY-FOUR

He hit the streets of the Barbary Coast again, buying drinks at saloons, dance-halls, melodeons, and cheap wine shops, all the while inquiring if anyone knew of a fellow named McMurphy with a crazy street preacher for a father. The most common response from the pimps, thugs, gamblers, whores, and various other denizens of the Coast was a shrug and a bland denial of any knowledge. A few of the whores suggested various things they could do to pass Cade's time while waiting for word of McMurphy, which Cade declined as politely as he could. A few of the people he questioned suggested, with various degrees of enthusiasm, that Cade go fuck himself. He declined those invitations as well. On one occasion, he spotted a head above the crowd and caught the characteristic rhythms of a street corner sermon, but when he got closer, the man atop his soap box was not the preacher he was looking for.

Gradually, footsore and weary, he worked his way down toward the docks. If the rest of the Coast was a sinkhole of debauchery and misery, the waterfront area around Front and Battery Streets was the gateway to Hell itself, the saloons dirtier, the boarding houses more ragged-looking, the whores hanging out the windows calling to passersby paler, skinnier, and more broken down. The smells of horse dung, frying food, and unwashed humans filled the air, mixing with the salt-air smell from the bay. A number of second-hand clothing shops dotted the landscape, their soiled and tattered wares flapping on lines outside the doors. Sailors, alone and in groups, staggered through the streets, blind drunk in the middle of the afternoon. Some, particularly the ones walking alone, were tailed by shifty-looking characters following like ravens trail behind a marching army, knowing that there'd be good dining soon. Only once did Cade spot any sign of law and order, and that was in the form of two of the biggest policemen he'd ever seen, walking side by side, their eyes constantly moving over the scene, alert for danger. On his belt, each one carried not only the usual wooden club, but a scabbarded blade at least a foot long. Even Cade hesitated to step into some of the dives in the area, but he steeled himself and continued his search, keeping his eyes moving as if his head was on a gimbal. He spotted a couple of ruffians looking him over with appraising eyes, sizing him up as potential prey, but when he gave them a hard stare back, their gazes skittered away. He was too big, too sober, and almost certainly heeled. Not worth the effort when there were so much easier pickings among the drunk and lonely Jacks off the ships whose masts he could now see towering over some of the buildings. He recalled his conversation with Captain Alton and decided to have a look at this ship he commanded, the *Marjorie Ann*. He stopped a passing sailor and inquired the way to the Gold Wharf. The response was a blank look and a gabble of language he didn't understand. He tipped his hat and moved on toward the masts.

When he reached the dock area, he couldn't help but be impressed by the size and variety of the fleet he saw lined up at the moorings. There were new and glistening steamships, their stacks standing tall. The masts of sailing ships—sloops, barquentines, schooners, and even one ship that looked like the picture of a Chinese junk he'd seen in a dime novel—looked like the spears of a giant's army reaching for the sky. He spotted one of the bigger sailing ships and made his way to it. As he drew nearer, he could make out the carved wooden figurehead, a sculpture of a young woman in a flowing white gossamer dress, trimmed with gold. She stood barefooted on the crest of a wave, arm extended like an admonition toward the shore. Cade drew closer. He didn't know much about ships, but he couldn't help but be impressed by this one. She was a little over two hundred feet long, lean and sleek as a greyhound, her bow jutting aggressively out over the water. She bore three huge masts and a baffling web of rigging. Her name was painted in gold along the bow: MARJORIE ANN. A single gangplank near the bow was guarded by a sailor seated on a wooden crate who stood up as Cade approached. He was huge, at least seven feet tall, with a bald head and a handlebar moustache that curled up at the ends.

Cade raised an open hand in greeting. "How do."

The sailor didn't speak.

"Is Captain Alton around?"

The sailor stared down at him impassively, still not speaking.

"Can you tell him L.D. Cade would like to see him?"

A voice spoke up from behind Cade. "It won't do you any good. He can't talk."

Cade turned. Alton was walking up the dock toward him, a package held in his arms. This time, he wore a long dark blue coat with shiny brass buttons instead of a suit, a captain's gold-braided hat perched on his head.

Cade touched the brim of his own hat. "Captain."

Alton nodded. "Mr. Cade." He called up the gangplank. "It's all right, Sorokin. He may come aboard." The sailor glowered at Cade, but stepped aside. Cade followed Alton up the gangplank. "Sorokin's from Russia," the captain said over his shoulder. "He's a Cossack. Wonderful soldiers. Brilliant horsemen, and fiercely independent. Sorokin apparently spoke out against the tsar one time too many. The secret police imprisoned him and tore his tongue out with red-hot pincers."

"Jesus," Cade muttered.

Alton stopped next to Sorokin and slapped him on the shoulder. "Damned good man in a fight, though." He sounded like a cattleman

210

bragging on a prize steer, but the huge Russian smiled, revealing a mouthful of broken teeth. Alton turned back and kept walking toward the stern. Cade followed. A pair of sailors at work on some complicated web of rigging looked up at him suspiciously as he passed. One had the darkest skin Cade had ever seen, the other was a skinny white man with a livid white scar across his cheek.

At the stern of the boat, behind the rear mast, sat what looked like a wide cottage, complete with a chimney and a skylight. A pair of longboats sat on skids in front of the house. The captain walked between the boats, toward a heavy wooden door in the front of the house, fishing a large key from the pocket of his coat. He unlocked the heavy brass lock and gestured Cade inside. They entered a short, low-ceilinged corridor with doors on either side and one at the end that Alton opened with another key.

The captain's cabin ran the width of the stern house. It was luxuriously appointed, with a carved bedstead along the back wall beneath a row of portholes that let in the daylight. Alton set his package on a low wooden table just inside the door, then took off his coat and hung it on a hook. He began unwrapping the package. "Can I persuade you to join me in a drink, Mr. Cade?"

"I'm persuaded, sir. And thank you."

Alton pulled a bottle of brown liquid from the package. His voice was reverent as he pronounced, "The Glenlivet."

Cade nodded as if he understood. "Okay."

Alton looked annoyed at the obvious incomprehension in Cade's eyes. "This is the finest Scotch whiskey in the world, Mr. Cade. Aged twelve years."

"Lookin' forward to it, then," Cade said.

Alton took a pair of glasses from a cabinet on the wall.

"You have a beautiful boat, sir," Cade said.

Alton stopped with the bottle in hand. "This is a ship, Mr. Cade. A boat is a craft carried on a ship."

Cade thought of the sleek longboats he'd seen outside. "Ship, then. She's still a beauty."

"Ayuh, that she is." A mollified Alton poured two fingers of the rich brown liquor. "Sad to say, she's likely one of the last of her kind. Now that they're near to finishing the canal in Arabia." He picked his glass up and sniffed it delicately. Cade had no idea what a canal in Arabia had to do with anything, but he did the same. It smelled like whiskey to him. But when he followed the captain's lead and downed the Scotch, he had to admit, it was as smooth and warm as any drink he'd ever had. "Good whiskey," he said.

"Indeed."

Alton gestured toward the glasses with the bottle, but Cade didn't relish the prospect of making his way back across the waterfront and the rest of the Coast without his wits about him, and he could sense how this Glenlivet stuff could draw a man in. He shook his head and put his palm over the glass. "You go ahead, though."

Alton poured himself another two fingers. This time, he sipped at the whiskey rather than downing it one gulp. "So, what can I do for you, Mr. Cade?"

"I need to get a message to Mrs. Hamrick. I'm going to need more information if I'm going to find out anything about McMurphy."

Alton raised a startled eyebrow. "McMurphy, you say?"

Cade nodded. "She'll know what it means."

"Hmm." Alton poured another two fingers of the whiskey. "McMurphy," he said thoughtfully, and took a sip. "Second time I've heard that name today."

Cade's heart leaped. "You've heard something about him?"

Alton nodded. "I heard he's dead."

"Well, that's what the Hamricks thought. They thought he'd killed himself years ago."

Alton shook his head. "No. What I heard is that a man named McMurphy was murdered this morning. In a boarding house on Kearney Street."

CHAPTER FORTY-FIVE

Cade pushed his glass across the table. "I think I will have another drink. If you're still offering."

Alton poured. "What is this McMurphy fellah to the Hamricks?"

Cade thought of the agreement he'd signed, about keeping Hamrick's business secret. To hell with it, and with Hamrick too, he decided. "Mr. Hamrick's old partner." He tossed back half the drink. "He accused Hamrick of doing him dirty in a business deal a few years ago. They thought he'd done himself in. But then someone went after Mrs. Hamrick and the little girl. And, well, we got some information that this McMurphy was in town, stirring up trouble for the Hamricks and trying to blame it on the Chinese."

As Cade was speaking, Alton had taken out a big Meerschaum pipe and begun packing it from a pouch in his jacket. "And you were sent aftah him, Mr. Cade, to do what exactly?"

"Figured I'd decide that once I found him." He laughed bitterly and finished his drink. "Guess that plan's gone down the drain."

Alton took out a lucifer and lit the pipe. "Is Marjorie still in danger? From the Chinese, maybe?"

"No. It was never the Chinese. McMurphy had someone he'd been talking to that was going to try to make it look like the Chinese were behind it."

Alton puffed thoughtfully. "Everyone likes to blame John Chinaman for all the ills of the city."

"It wasn't them," Cade insisted. He thought of Kwan's mandate to him. "And I still need to find out who it was."

"Because whoever it was is still a danger to the Hamricks."

Cade nodded. "And to Marjorie." He thought of Alton's earlier words. "You said you told her daddy you'd look after her."

Alton was looking at him shrewdly through the wreath of smoke from his pipe. "And from the way you just said her name, it sounds as if you have a bit of a personal interest in the mattah."

Cade felt the blood rising to his cheeks. Before he could answer, Alton stood up abruptly. "I'll have one of my men take you to your lodgings. Where are you putting up?"

Cade stood as well. "The Royal Hotel."

Alton nodded. "Ah. The Townsend Suite."

Cade was startled. "You know about that?"

"Of course. Mr. Townsend kept a suite of rooms there for when business acquaintances came from out of town, or out of country, as may be. His daughter maintains the account as well."

"Business acquaintances." Cade rolled the words around in his mind.

Alton raised an eyebrow at the tone. "Yes. And if you're about to ask if the rooms have been used for anything else, the ansah is it's none of either of ouah business. Would you agree, Mr. Cade?"

"I guess so."

Alton nodded. "Good. I'll send Mrs. Hamrick your message. And I wish you luck in yoah inquiries."

"Thanks," Cade said. "I'm going to need it."

It was Sorokin, the huge silent Russian, who drove Cade in a wagon called up by Alton from a nearby stable. Cade was glad of the relative quiet. It gave him some time to think.

He had no idea which way to go next. McMurphy was dead. At least that was the rumor, although he'd apparently been dead before. But assuming he was dead for real this time, who had done him in? Life was cheap in the Barbary Coast. People had been killed for pennies or for a sideways look. Or maybe it was the mysterious stranger that Mei had told him was behind the plot.

He also wondered about McMurphy's father. Could the old man have seen something that might help? If he did, would he be too crack-brained to convey it? Most likely, he'd fallen victim to the same killer. These were the thoughts on his mind as the wagon pulled up to The Royal. It was getting dark, and the lights were coming on inside, making the place glitter like a palace.

Cade handed the Russian sailor four bits, which the big man pocketed, still unsmiling. "Don't worry, son," Cade said. "I can see the thank you in your eyes." Sorokin looked stonily at him, then got the team moving.

At the front desk, the man who'd first checked him in waved him over. He spoke in a hushed whisper that Cade had to lean over the desk to hear. "There's a visitor here to see you, Mr. Cade."

"A lady?" Cade said, then realized how that sounded.

The desk man cleared his throat. "No, sir. It's a, um, gentleman of color."

"Samuel?" Cade looked around the lobby. "Where is he?"

"Waiting for you, sir." The man came around the counter. "Follow me."

Cade frowned as the man led him out of the lobby and down a short corridor. The smell of cooking food made his mouth water, so he figured they were headed for the kitchen. They found Samuel seated in a wooden chair, just outside the door marked KITCHEN. He folded the newspaper he was reading and stood up, his face without expression. "Here you are, Mr. Cade," the desk man said, and scurried away.

Samuel looked after him. "Someone needs to let him know that black isn't catching."

"Sorry about that, Samuel." Cade extended his hand.

Samuel took it, his expression softening a little. "Not your fault." He shook Cade's hand and looked around. "We need to talk."

"I know where we can do it," Cade said. "Follow me." He turned and walked back the way he came, with Samuel following. The two of them walked back into the lobby under the startled gaze of the front desk man. Cade found a table by the wall with a pair of chairs on either side. He plopped down in one of the chairs, motioning to the other as he put his hat on the table. Samuel took the seat, smiling, but the smile didn't last long. "It's Missus, Cade."

Cade was instantly alert. "What about her? Is she all right?"

Samuel shook his head. "When she got back in the afternoon, Mr. Hamrick like to have lost his mind. They've had some dust-ups, but this one was the worst we ever heard. Bridget locked herself in the kitchen and wouldn't come out."

"Shit," Cade muttered. Hamrick must have figured where she'd spent her morning.

"It gets worse. He'd already hired some other men to look after the house." Samuel grimaced. "Pinkertons."

"Pinkertons." It was a name of ill omen in the west. The Pinkerton Detective agency had distinguished themselves in the war by providing a private intelligence operation for President Lincoln, even foiling an attempt on the president's life, according to one rumor. But since then, their reputation had grown more sinister. They were turning, it was said, into a private army for the money men. Legbreakers. Enforcers.

Samuel nodded at Cade's expression. "They've got the house locked up tight. Missus and her daughter can't go out. And Bridget says Mr. Hamrick's trying to get Missus to sign over her holdings to him. Says he'll ruin her if she doesn't."

"God damn it." Cade stood up. *This is my fault*, he thought.

Samuel stood up as well. "What are you going to do?"

Cade picked up his hat and put it on. "I'm going to go have a talk with Mr. Hamrick."

Samuel looked alarmed. "A talk, you say?"

"Yeah. Just a talk."

"Mr. Cade?" a voice said.

Cade turned. Smith, the police captain he'd met at the Hamrick place, stood a few feet away, smiling pleasantly. Behind him was Officer Dunleavy. The mustached copper was smiling unpleasantly.

"Mr. L.D. Cade?" Smith repeated.

"You know who I am," Cade growled.

"Mr. Cade," Smith said as Dunleavy took a pair of heavy iron cuffs from his coat pocket, "you're under arrest on suspicion of the murder of Patrick McMurphy and the aggravated assault of Devlin McMurphy."

CHAPTER FORTY-SIX

"Like hell I am," Cade said. He was about to go for the pistol in his shoulder holster, but Dunleavy already had his own pistol out, pointed at the center of Cade's chest.

His smile widened. "Give me a reason, shit-kicker."

Cade turned to Samuel. "Go to Gold's Wharf. Find a ship called the *Marjorie Ann*. Tell Captain Alton what's happened." He turned back to Smith. "This is bullshit. And you know it."

"Be that as it may," Smith said, "you're coming with us. Sergeant, take his weapon."

"He's got his hands full," Cade said. "And going to have them fuller if he takes his own gun off me. You come get it."

Smith hesitated, trying to gauge the expression in Cade's eyes.

Cade bared his teeth in a wolf-like smile. "Come on, I won't bite."

Smith turned to Dunleavy. "I'll be in the way of your shot," he said. "So if Mr. Cade tries anything," he nodded at Samuel, "shoot the Negro."

"Yes, sir," Dunleavy said.

Cade let Smith approach and reach into his coat. The movement brought them face to face. Cade kept his eyes locked on the captain's, which never wavered either. They were close enough that Cade could smell the other man's breath. It carried the faint reek of decay and illness. The eyes looking into his were pale blue and cloudy. Cade didn't know what was wrong with the man, but his prospects didn't look good. Smith stepped back, holding Cade's Navy revolver by the butt.

"Give it to my friend here," Cade said. "To hang on to till I get out."

Smith shook his head. "This could be evidence."

"Why? Was McMurphy shot with a cavalry pistol?"

"No. He was beaten to death."

Cade spread his hands wide. "Now why would I do that, when I have a perfectly good pistol to do the job with?"

"That's one of the questions we mean to have answered." Smith nodded to Dunleavy, who advanced with the cuffs.

As he put them on, the policeman whispered to him, "Still think you can put me nightstick somewhere inconvenient?"

"The night's still young."

Cade turned to Samuel, who answered before he could speak. "Gold's Wharf. Marjorie Ann. Captain Alton."

Cade nodded. "Good man."

The Black Maria was waiting outside, a black box on wheels with a single barred window in the rear. Passersby gaped as Dunleavy and Smith bundled him into the tiny cell on wheels. The metallic click of the lock as the door clanged shut let him know he wasn't going anywhere. He didn't want to press his face against the bars like an animal, but the atmosphere inside was so close and fetid, he quickly found himself needing air. He moved to the back of the wagon as it lurched into motion. He spotted a pair of figures in the buzzing crowd that had gathered.

A blind Chinese beggar and the young girl guiding them.

***

"What do we do now?" Mei asked.

The White Orchid replied from beneath her bandages. "If we

219

hurry, we can intercept them. I can deal with the soldiers."

"You mean...*kill them*?" Mei was aghast. "We can't do that. And they're policemen, not soldiers."

Lin shrugged. "That is no difference to me."

Mei shook her head firmly. "We need to let Mr. Kwan know what's happened. He'll know what to do." She noticed Lin's fingers wrapped around the head of her cane. They were clenching and unclenching, as if she was already imagining them wrapped around a white devil's neck. "Come on," she said. "We need to go."

The White Orchid sighed. "As you wish, Little Sister."

***

The first thing they'd done was take away her shotgun, a beautiful Needham and Company 12 gauge, made in Great Britain, that her father had gifted to her on her eighteenth birthday. The next thing was the documents John—she refused to call him her husband any more, even to herself—had presented to her in the library. After giving them a cursory look, she'd thrown them in his face. "You're out of your damned mind," she'd snarled at him.

"Actually, dear," he'd said with that infuriating calm, "it's your sanity that's in question. You've been unstable for some time. And now this latest...peccadillo."

It took every ounce of her will not to hurl herself at him and slap that smug smile off his face. "As if you haven't been out whoring as lately as this week."

"There's a difference between whoring and playing the whore." The smile vanished. "You've humiliated me for the last time." He picked the papers off the floor and rearranged them. "My god, Marjorie," he said, "at least your other dalliances have been more discreet. With people of our own kind. But this...my god, you'll be fucking Samuel next."

"I'd prefer even that to ever having you touch me again," she spat.

"Can you even hear yourself?" He shook his head. "You're sick, Marjorie. Your judgment is clearly impaired. Oh, and by the way, your cowboy is about to be arrested."

"Arrested?" She sprang to her feet. "For what?"

"The murder of Patrick McMurphy." The smile came back, thin and cruel. "I think we should make plans to attend the hanging."

Her voice was reduced to a stunned whisper. "You told me McMurphy was dead."

"And so I believed. But it seems we were wrong." He pushed the papers back across the table at her. "You need to sign these. I'll take the responsibility of managing the assets you clearly don't have the capacity to manage yourself."

"No. Never." She stormed out of the library and up the stairs. When she turned toward her daughter's room, she nearly collided with one of the burly Pinkertons John had brought into the house. He was standing outside Violet's room, his thick arms crossed across his broad chest. He looked down at her, his face expressionless.

"I want to see my daughter," she said.

"Sorry, ma'am," the man replied. "Mr. Hamrick's orders."

She could hear the little girl singing through the door, some song she didn't recognize. The sound brought tears to her eyes. "Please," she whispered. "I just want to know she's all right."

The Pinkerton man's stony expression never wavered. "She's fine, ma'am. The Irish girl is with her." Sure enough, as the song ended, she heard Bridget's bright clear voice join with Violet's.

Oh, make my grave
Large, wide and deep
Put a marble stone
At my head and feet
And in the middle
A turtle dove
So the world may know

I died of love...

The tears flowed more freely now, and she turned and fled to her own room, pausing only to lock the door behind her. She stood just inside the door, taking deep breaths to calm herself. A rustling sound at her feet made her look down. Someone was shoving the papers under the door. She heard John's voice.

"You have until morning," he said. "After that, I'll have no choice but to have Mr. Tremblay begin the lunacy proceeding." She heard his footsteps fading as he walked away.

CHAPTER FORTY-SEVEN

To Cade's surprise, they didn't take him directly to the cells. Webster, the big lieutenant who'd taken part in the interrogation at Hamrick's, joined them at the doorway of the police station and conducted them to a room furnished with only a desk and two chairs. Dunleavy shackled Cade to one of the chairs. Captain Smith took the other, with Webster leaning against the wall, arms folded across his chest.

Smith smiled at Dunleavy. "That will be all, Sergeant."

Dunleavy's face looked like he was sucking unripe persimmons. He'd already taken out his baton, clearly ready to use it on Cade. As he exited, he leaned over and whispered, "I'll see you later, shit-kicker. Count on it."

Smith sat for a moment, looking at Cade without speaking. Cade stared back silently.

It was Webster who finally broke the silence. "I think we can conduct this interview like civilized people. Don't you agree, Mr. Cade?"

"I reckon," Cade said. "Unless you think it's uncivilized to tell you again that this is bullshit."

"I don't think so." Smith held out his hand. Webster handed him a sheaf of papers and Smith sifted through it. "You've been asking for McMurphy all over the Barbary Coast, and then he turns up dead. That suggests to me that you found the object of your search, and did what you'd been paid to do."

Before Cade could answer, Webster spoke up, his voice dripping with disgust. "What kind of white man would debase himself by working for the God-damned Chinese?"

That one rocked Cade. How the hell did Webster know about that? He decided to bluff. "What the Sam Hill are you talking about?"

Webster advanced on the chair where Cade was shackled, towering over him. "You think we don't have informants in Chinatown? We know you're taking money from the Green Dragon Tong." He looked for a moment as if he was going to backhand Cade. He straightened up and looked down at his prisoner as if regarding some new breed of loathsome insect. "Do you deny it?"

Cade didn't see any point in trying to if they had informants. "Yeah. I lost my job with Hamrick. But the head of the tong still wanted McMurphy found." He looked back at Smith. "But more than that, he wanted to know who McMurphy was plotting with to make the Chinese look like they were attacking a white family."

Webster scoffed. "You want us to believe that nonsense? It was the Chinese who attacked the Hamricks. And they haven't yet begun to pay for that." He shook his head as if unable to believe Cade's stupidity. "These heathen scum are a plague on San Francisco, Cade. Literally. They bring disease. They corrupt God-fearing people, particularly females, with their vile drugs and potions. If I had my way, I'd put them all on ships back to China. Then I'd sink the ships."

Cade shrugged as best he could in the cuffs. "I get it. You got a burr up your ass about the Chinese. Truth is, I ain't totally pleased with 'em myself. But I wasn't hired to kill McMurphy. Just find him."

"And once found," Smith said, "what did you expect the tong to do? Invite McMurphy to tea?"

"I don't know. I just know I didn't kill him." A thought occurred to Cade. "What about his daddy? The crazy street preacher? He's still alive, ain't he?"

Smith nodded. "For now. But he's in the hospital. Unconscious. He was beaten so severely about the head that the doctors say he's bleeding inside his skull. It doesn't look good for him. Or for you."

"Shit." Cade slumped in his chair and stared at the table. The old man could clear him if he woke up, and if his brains hadn't been scrambled by the beating. But those were two huge ifs on which to be staking his life. He looked back up at Smith. "So, let me get this straight. You know I travel heeled. When I find McMurphy—who I wouldn't recognize by sight if he jumped up and bit me—you think I'd beat him to death, and his daddy, with my bare hands? All by my lonesome? That's the tale you're going to tell?" He shook his head. "Pretty damn thin, boys. Pretty damn thin." He leaned back in the chair. "I think we're done here. Either let me go, or I need a lawyer."

Smith and Webster looked at each other. Smith got up and went to the door of the interrogation room. "Sergeant Dunleavy," he called out. In a moment, the door opened and Dunleavy was standing there smiling that unpleasant smile.

"Take Mr. Cade to the cells," Smith said.

Dunleavy nodded and pulled his baton from his belt. "With pleasure, sir."

Cade shuffled ahead of Dunleavy down the dank, gloomy corridors that led to the cells. They'd shackled his ankles now as well as fastening his wrists behind him with the heavy iron cuffs, and Cade didn't much like his chances of surviving the beating he knew was coming if he was bound up like this. When he hesitated, Dunleavy prodded him in the back with the baton. "Move your ass, shit-kicker," he growled.

Cade picked up his shuffle. "I could get along a little faster if you'd take these damn chains off my legs."

Dunleavy poked him in the back again. "Oh, I don't think you're in much hurry to get where you're going."

They'd reached the cells. The tiny rooms were stuffed with wretched humanity, desperate faces looking out through the barred doors, filthy hands gripping the bars. Some were silent, some were shouting insults and demands in a Babel of languages. The smell of untended shit buckets and unwashed bodies nearly made Cade gag. It was hot as hell down there, and beads of sweat were beginning to run down Cade's face. One rolled to the end of his nose and hung there annoyingly. Cade shook his head like a dog to dislodge it. "What's the matter, Dunleavy? Afraid of what I'll do to you if I'm loose? Scared of a stand-up fight," he took a deep breath and took the plunge, "you ball-less, cousin-humping, Paddy son of a bitch?"

The ruse didn't work. Dunleavy just chuckled. "Keep talking, cowboy. You'll be singing a different tune in just a bit. You'll be begging to confess your sins, and more."

"I got plenty of sins, you cocksucker," Cade growled, "but none I'm going to confess to a yellow-livered, tater-eating bottom feeder like you."

They'd come to the end of the line of cells. An iron door with a small barred window set at eye level in the brick wall. Dunleavy opened it and stepped aside. The shouting from the cells grew louder and more intense. The men in the cells knew what went on in that room. Some were jeering Dunleavy, others taunting Cade. Dunleavy ignored them both, pushing Cade against the wall and reaching for the ring of keys on his belt. The movement caused him to take his eyes off Cade for a moment. Cade braced himself. *I may be about to get a whaling,* he thought, *but I'm damned if I'm going to just lay down for it and not get a lick in myself.* As Dunleavy swung the heavy iron door open and turned toward him, Cade leaped forward and smashed his forehead into the policeman's nose.

CHAPTER FORTY-EIGHT

Dunleavy screamed with pain, bright crimson blood erupting from his broken nose. He brought both hands up to his face, dropping his keys on the floor. He kept a grip on his baton, however, so Cade rammed into him again, hard, driving him back against the door of the last cell. Black and brown hands reached from between the bars to grab him and pull him backward. Shouts and curses from the other cells rose to a deafening cacophony. Dunleavy squealed and lifted the baton, but someone reached through and snatched it away. Dunleavy struggled against the clutching hands, crying out in a terrified, high-pitched voice. Cade dropped to his knees, looking for the keys Dunleavy had dropped. When he spotted them, he plopped down on his ass and felt for them with his bound fingers, picking them up and fumbling them into his palms. Dunleavy was still trying to break free from the hands that held him against the bars. Someone had brought the baton across the copper's throat and was pulling hard. *Jesus,* Cade thought, *if he dies, I'll hang for sure.*

"Don't kill him!" he cried out. "We can use him to get out of here." The advice was ignored. Cade swore and turned back to the people in the cell behind him. Four Chinese faces regarded him with expressions ranging from curiosity to terror. "Look." He turned and showed them the keys he held behind his back. "See if you can get these cuffs off my wrists." They looked at him blankly. "God damn it," Cade muttered. He looked back to where Dunleavy was beginning to turn blue. "Don't kill him, you damn fools," he yelled.

227

There was the clang of a door from the far end of the cellblock and a thunder of booted footsteps. What looked like a dozen officers had piled into the corridor and were pounding their way toward him.

"Ah, shit," Cade said disgustedly. He turned to the men in the cell who were still engaged in choking the life out of Dunleavy. "It's over!" He called out. "Let him go!" Then the officers were on him, fists flying. He took a punch to the head that knocked him cross-eyed, then another to the gut that doubled him over. He fell to his knees, then another punch knocked him over onto his side. Everything turned into a blur of fists and boots and pain until mercifully the red world turned black.

***

Cade awoke with the taste of blood in his mouth and every muscle screaming with pain. He slowly sat up, groaning as the motion hurt him in even more places.

He'd been lying on a rough wooden board fastened like a shelf to the wall. His hands and feet were free, but as he swung his legs over, he saw his boots were gone. He blinked in surprise and looked around.

He was in one of the barred cells, three walls surrounding him and the bars on the fourth. Boards like the one he'd been lying on were fastened to the other walls. Two other men sat on the makeshift beds, watching him. One, a big bruiser with an unshaven face and a walleye that wandered off to one side of its fellow was regarding him defiantly, his prominent jaw stuck out as if he was daring someone to punch him in it. He was wearing Cade's boots.

"God damn it," Cade muttered. He stood up, wavering a little. His head wasn't fully recovered from the last beating, and it looked like he was headed into either taking another one or handing one out. He wasn't thrilled with either idea, especially since, given his condition, the first possibility was the most likely one. But he knew if he just let someone take his boots, his life in that jail cell, what there was left of it, would turn into a living hell.

"Gonna need those boots back, fella," Cade said as reasonably as he could.

The walleyed man didn't move. "Don't know what you mean, friend."

Cade crossed the narrow cell in two steps, trying not to stagger. He stood over the thief. "I mean, *friend*, those are my fucking boots, and you're gonna give them back. I'm having a truly shitty goddamn day, and I'm not in any fucking mood for any of your bullshit. Take the boots off, and give them the fuck back to me."

The man started to rise. "Go to—" Before he could get the last word out, Cade grabbed him by the throat and slammed his head against the wall. The thief tried to throw a punch with one hand and grab the hand strangling him with the other. Cade pulled him forward, then slammed him into the wall again, the back of his head striking the brick with a sharp crack. Both eyes seemed to focus together for the first time before rolling back in his head. The man went limp and collapsed back onto the makeshift bunk. Cade let him fall, then bent over and pulled the boots off the unconscious man's feet. As he sat back on his own bed to pull them on, he glared at the other man in the cell, a skinny Mexican with a drooping moustache. The Mexican held up his hands to show he was no threat. Cade nodded and finished putting on his boots. He sighed and leaned back against the wall of the cell. "So, what time do they feed us down here?"

The Mexican shrugged without speaking.

"Hey," Cade said, "you *habla* the English?"

The man looked at him, blinking in confusion.

Cade sighed. "Guess that's my answer." He leaned back against the wall, closing his eyes. He probed with his tongue where a tooth had been knocked loose. He needed to lie down and let his bruises heal, but he didn't want to be asleep when the boot thief woke up.

If he did. A thought made him get up and check to see if the man was still breathing. He couldn't tell at first, and a feeling of dread ran through him until he saw the slow rise of the man's thick chest. He let out his own breath and took his seat back.

He didn't know how long it was before he heard the scrape of a key in the lock. The door swung open with a creak of metal on metal. Captain Smith stood in the doorway. "Cade. Come with me."

Cade stood up. "If you're takin' me to another beatin', thanks, but no, thanks. I kinda had my fill of those for the day."

"Shut up and get moving. You're going before the judge." Smith's mouth was set in an angry line. "Someone hired you a lawyer."

Cade blinked in surprise. "Well. That was mighty neighborly of someone. Who was it?"

"Like you don't know." Smith stepped back. "Get moving."

The other detective, Webster, was standing in the corridor. He looked even less happy than Smith. He held a pair of cuffs in his hands.

Cade sighed and held out his wrists. "I honestly don't know, fellas, who'd spring for a lawyer for me."

This time it was Webster's turn to snarl at him to shut up. So he did. He fell in between them, with Smith leading and Webster bringing up the rear.

They walked through a maze of narrow corridors, clanging iron doors, and steps, finally entering the courtroom from a side door. It was crowded and noisy, a hubbub of voices bouncing off the dark paneled walls. Cigar smoke hung in the air. A line of wretched defendants sat on a bench before the Bar, shackled together. Most of them appeared to be Chinese. The pair of rough-looking young white men on the bench were trying to shove themselves away from the stolid Chinese and not getting far. The spectator seats behind the Bar were packed as well. Cade saw someone stand up at the back of the room, leaning forward as if to get a better look. It was Mei. Cade suddenly realized with a sinking feeling who his benefactor was.

A group of well-dressed men who Cade assumed were lawyers was gathered to one side of the room, chatting and smoking. One noticed him and peeled away from the group, walking over to greet Cade with a big smile that made him instantly nervous. "You'd be Mr. Cade, then? Mr. L.D. Cade?"

Cade shifted uncomfortably. "I would. And you are?"

The lawyer's smile widened. "Jenkins, sir. Walter B. Jenkins, Esquire. At your service." He turned to Smith, who was glowering at Jenkins. "Captain Smith. So nice to see you again." He nodded at Webster, standing behind Cade. "And Lieutenant Webster." Webster muttered something under his breath that Cade couldn't fully hear, but it sounded like "shyster."

Jenkins went on as if he hadn't heard. "Gentlemen, may I have a moment to confer with my client? Alone?" He looked at Cade's wrists. "And out of those cuffs?"

"You can talk to him," Smith said through gritted teeth. He nodded to the jury box on the other side of the room. "Over there. Where we can see you. But the cuffs stay on."

Jenkins was still smiling. "Very well." He led Cade past the little knot of lawyers, who looked at him curiously. Jenkins held open the little gate to the raised area where the jurors were seated during trials and Cade stepped up. They took seats side by side. Jenkins leaned over and spoke to Cade in a low voice. "The judge will be in in a moment. Say nothing. Everything has been arranged."

Cade answered in the same low tone. "I might feel a smidge better if I knew what the arrangement is."

Jenkins chuckled. "All you need to know is you'll be released. On your own recognizance."

"I thought I was being charged with murder."

Jenkins shook his head, a disgusted expression on his face. "They have nothing to hold you on, and they know it."

"Glad we see eye to eye on that. But, ah, there's something you should probably know." He took a deep breath. "When they were takin' me to the cells, a sergeant named Dunleavy was gettin' ready to rough me up. I kind of pushed back, and, well…"

Jenkins just nodded. "I know. And a minor riot ensued." He patted Cade on the knee like a fond uncle. "As I said, Mr. Cade. Fear not. Everything is arranged."

Cade grimaced. "Sounds like the fix is in."

Jenkins smiled. "This is San Francisco, Mr. Cade. The fix is always in. Just be happy that this time, it's in your favor."

"That'll be a nice change," Cade muttered.

A door at the back of the courtroom opened. "ALL RISE!" an officer bellowed.

"Remember," Jenkins said. "Say nothing."

CHAPTER FORTY-NINE

"Oyez, Oyez, Oyez!" the bailiff called out in a deep, gravelly voice as everyone stood. "This Police Court for the county and city of San Francisco is now in session. The Honorable Sebastian K. Apple presiding. God save the State and this Honorable Court. Be seated."

Cade looked the judge over. He looked to be about sixty, with a fierce, craggy face and an impressive mane of dark hair, streaked with gray and brushed back. He looked like the kind of judge who'd sentence you to hang and charge you for the rope.

The previous noise of the courtroom had subsided, but there was still a rustle of people taking their seats and a low murmur of conversation. The judge picked up his gavel and banged it impatiently on the bench in front of him. "Come to order!" he barked in a voice that instantly silenced the room. In the stillness, he picked up a sheaf of papers in front of him. "Mr. Chalmette, call your first case."

A lawyer with red eyes that looked as if he'd spent the previous night and part of the morning in a saloon stepped up. "People versus Leviticus Deuteronomy Cade."

Cade winced a bit at the reading of his full name.

The judge looked up. "Impressive name." He wasn't smiling. "And what is this biblically named gentleman accused of doing?"

"Murder, your honor."

A gasp rippled through the courtroom, followed by a renewed

buzz of conversation. Cade noticed a smartly dressed man in the front row take a notebook out of his elaborately embroidered vest. *Hellfire*, he thought. *Now the damn newspapers are here.*

"Order!" the judge bellowed, pounding his gavel. The room settled down. Judge Apple looked at the papers in front of him, then looked back up, his brow furrowed in puzzlement. "Mr. Jenkins."

Jenkins stepped up and inclined his head respectfully. "Good morning, Your Honor."

Apple nodded back. "Good morning. What you've filed here appears to be a writ of *habeas corpus*. Not a motion for bail."

"Correct, Your Honor. We are here to address the validity of Mr. Cade's confinement. You see, my client is being held without even being charged yet. Held, Your Honor, on mere suspicion. And very thin suspicion at that."

Apple scowled. "This is neither the time nor the place to try the merits of this case, Mr. Jenkins."

"That's the problem, Your Honor. There is no case to try. The solicitor has not even deigned to file a formal indictment."

The judge turned to the prosecutor. "Is this true, Mr. Chalmette?"

Chalmette looked down at the papers in his hand, then back up. "It doesn't appear—I mean, no, sir. I don't have a copy of any charging documents."

Apple leaned back in his chair, his scowl deepening. "And does the solicitor intend to file any such document in the near future?"

Chalmette had the blank expression of a schoolboy enduring a dressing down. "I don't have any information on that, Your Honor."

"So, on whose authority is he being held?"

Jenkins pulled a sad face. "That would be Captain Smith, Your Honor."

Apple looked around the courtroom. His eyes lit on the detective, standing at the side of the room. "Captain Smith? Can you explain why Mr. Cade is locked in our jail?"

Smith stepped forward. "We are conducting inquiries. He's

being held for questioning, Your Honor."

Jenkins looked sadder. "And would those inquiries include what is commonly known as the 'third degree'?"

"Objection," Chalmette blurted.

"Overruled," Apple growled. "I was getting ready to ask about the bruises I can see from here on the prisoner's face."

Smith looked angry enough to chew nails. "The prisoner was injured while being subdued, after attacking Sergeant Dunleavy while being taken to custody. An attack which started a riot that nearly cost Sergeant Dunleavy his life."

Well, hell, Cade thought.

But Jenkins was shaking his head furiously. "Not so, Your Honor. There was a disturbance in the cells, to be sure. The prisoners were rightfully outraged over the abuse they saw being administered—with worse being promised, I might add—by Sergeant Dunleavy to my client, who was handcuffed and helpless at the time." Jenkins stepped back and indicated Cade with a sweep of his arm. "A man not only innocent, but an actual hero of the late conflict. A man who served the Union. Decorated for valor. A man who led the charge that broke the Rebel line at Chickamauga."

What the fuck? Cade thought. He stared at Jenkins incredulously. But the lawyer was just warming up. "In the years since, Mr. Cade has himself worn a deputy's badge, helping cleanse the frontier towns of lawless elements. He's guarded women and children on the long trek west. He's been a model citizen in all respects."

Apple was shaking his head. "All right, Mr. Jenkins."

Jenkins went on as if he hadn't heard. "And during this altercation, I believe the men who arrived on the scene will tell the court that he was pleading—*pleading*, I tell you—with the other prisoners resisting this outrage to spare Sergeant Dunleavy's life."

"I said that's *enough*, Mr. Jenkins." Apple turned back to Smith. "While I don't intend to conduct a full trial on this matter, can you tell me what the particulars of the crime are?"

"Yes, Your Honor. Mr. Patrick McMurphy was murdered, and his elderly father grievously assaulted, in his boarding house on Kearney Street."

"In the Barbary Coast," the judge said.

Smith nodded. "Yes, Your Honor. And Mr. Cade had been asking a number of people where Mr. McMurphy could be found."

The judge nodded. "And?"

"And…Mr. Cade had recently been employed by Mr. McMurphy's former business partner. Mr. John Hamrick."

Apple looked puzzled. "I believe I know the name. Is it your contention, Captain Smith, that Mr. Hamrick, a respectable businessman, employed Mr. Cade to assassinate Mr. McMurphy?"

Smith looked shocked. "No, sir. Nothing of the kind."

Apple went on. "I'd think not. Or I'd be inquiring why Mr. Hamrick isn't in custody as well."

Jenkins spoke up. "Especially since Mr. Cade was no longer in Mr. Hamrick's employment at the time of Mr. McMurphy's tragic murder by," he looked at Smith pointedly, "persons unknown."

"Thank you, Mr. Jenkins." Apple looked at Chalmette. "So, let me make sure I understand the People's contention for holding Mr. Cade in custody. A man is murdered in the Barbary Coast, an area infested with robbers, footpads, and the general scum of the Earth. And the sole evidence that Mr. Cade committed this atrocity is he was asking questions about the decedent's whereabouts. Does that about sum it up?"

Chalmette shot a poisonous look at Smith. "I believe that's a fair summation, Your Honor."

Apple shook his head. "Captain Smith, anything to add?"

"No, sir," Smith said through gritted teeth.

"All right then." Apple banged his gavel. "The prisoner's release is hereby ordered. Effective immediately." He looked at Smith. "Get those cuffs off him."

Smith didn't speak. From the way his jaw was clenched, Cade

didn't think he could speak right then. He crossed the still silent courtroom. Cade held out his hands. When Smith had unlocked the cuffs, Cade spoke for the first time. "Thank you kindly, Captain."

Smith didn't answer. He took the cuffs, turned on his heel, and walked away.

"Call your next case," the judge said.

CHAPTER FIFTY

"I don't know who this Cade fella is you were talking about in there," Cade said, "but I'd surely like to meet him sometime. He sounds like a hell of a man."

They were standing at the front desk of the jail. A fat and disgruntled sergeant had gone to fetch Cade's property.

Jenkins smiled. "I may have gilded the lily just a touch. But Judge Apple was a staunch Union man, whereas Mr. Chalmette served in the Louisiana Zouaves. It always helps to wave the Stars and Stripes when those two are in the courtroom." He slapped Cade on the shoulder. "Knowing the law is important, Mr. Cade. Knowing your judge, however, is priceless."

"I reckon." Cade sighed. "So how much do I owe Mr. Kwan for hiring you? And greasing whatever palms needed greasing? Not that I don't appreciate it, but I don't like being in any man's debt."

Jenkins's smile never wavered. "I'm sure I don't know what you mean about palms being greased. And as for your patron, they prefer to remain anonymous at this time."

The sergeant returned. He was carrying Cade's coat, hat, belt, and the Navy Revolver in its shoulder holster. He handed them across the table and Cade put them on. He touched the brim of his hat. "Thank you, Sergeant."

"You have to sign for them," was the only reply. The sergeant slid a piece of paper and a pen across the desk. Cade reviewed the list of his property and signed.

"And now," Jenkins said, "my work here is done, for the moment, at least. Mr. Cade, I wish you good fortune." He extended a hand.

Cade took it. "Likewise."

Outside on the busy street, Cade looked around. It was a long walk back to his hotel, and he still felt a little unsteady on his feet. He spotted a saloon a few doors down and headed for it. He still had a few coins jingling in his coat pocket, and while it was still early in the day, he could use a little straightener right now.

He'd only taken a few steps when a familiar voice called out to him. "Mr. Cade."

He sighed, stopped, and looked around. Mei was leaning out of the window of a black brougham. "Would you care for a ride back to your hotel, Mr. Cade?"

He thought it over. It looked like Kwan wasn't done with him yet. "Sure, Little Sis."

She looked startled. "What did you call me?"

"Just an expression." He opened the door and she slid over to let him in. Before he boarded, he looked up at the driver. Not the White Orchid this time. The Chinese man on the driver's seat was looking him up and down with a challenging expression as if sizing him up. *Boo How Doy*, Cade thought. He got in, taking the seat opposite Mei. "Hope I didn't offend you."

She regarded him curiously. "Not many white men would care if they offended a Chinese girl."

"Not many Chinese girls could have my throat cut if I pissed them off."

She looked shocked. "I would never do that."

"Good to know." Cade looked around. "So, where's your pal? The White Orchid, I think you called her."

"I don't know. She is on other business, I suppose."

"If you don't mind my saying so, you two are kind of an odd team. How'd you get mixed up with Kwan, anyway?"

Mei bit her lip, looking troubled. "I'm the one who told him about McMurphy and…and the other man. The one trying to blame the Chinese for attacking Mr. Hamrick. And now Mr. McMurphy…" She stopped. Cade could see her eyes glistening with tears.

"And now McMurphy's dead."

She nodded, looking miserable, then took a deep breath and regained her composure.

"Mr. Kwan wants to know," she said evenly, "if McMurphy told you anything before he died."

"He wouldn't have," Cade said, "because I didn't kill him."

She blinked in surprise. "You didn't?"

"No. So, thank Mr. Kwan for his help. Maybe it'll make him feel better to know he sprung an innocent man."

She frowned. "Sprung?"

"Got me out of that calaboose. I didn't kill McMurphy. Even though everyone seems to think I did."

She shook her head in confusion. "But if you didn't kill him, who did?"

"Good question. Could have been just a robbery gone bad. It was the Coast, after all. Or maybe," he leaned forward, "maybe it was the fellow he'd been talking to. Maybe he's trying to shut up everyone who can identify him. Which would include you, Little Sister."

The news didn't seem to frighten her. She just nodded. "I knew he was thinking it. I could see it in his face. He wanted to kill me the last time he saw me. That's why I went to Mr. Kwan." Her voice was still matter-of-fact.

Tough little mouse, Cade thought. He was liking her more and more. "There's something I've thought of since the last time we talked."

She nodded. "Go ahead."

"How come McMurphy never figured out he wasn't talking to a Chinam—I mean, a Chinese?"

"As I said. He sat behind a screen."

"Where?"

She looked away from him. "My grandparents' shop." When she looked back at him, he finally saw a tear rolling down her face. "The shop wasn't doing well. I took money from him to let him use the premises. I didn't know…" Her voice choked. "I didn't know what trouble this would cause."

He fished in his coat pocket for his handkerchief, took it out and handed it to her. She looked at it dubiously.

"It could use a wash, I admit," Cade said.

She took it, dabbed at her eyes, and handed it back. "Thank you," she said stiffly.

He stuffed it back in his pocket. "Don't blame yourself, Little Sis. Sometimes something just seems like a good idea, and later, well… let's say I've made some of the same kind of mistake lately."

She smiled. "You are a kind man."

"Thanks." The carriage was slowing. Cade pushed the curtain aside and looked out the window. They were pulling up to the steps of The Royal Hotel. Among the people coming and going, he saw a figure standing on the steps, looking impatiently at his pocket watch.

A tall man with a craggy face and chin whiskers. Cade blinked, then said "Mei. Look here."

She leaned over and put her face next to his.

"That guy there," he said. "Looking at his watch. Ever seen him before?"

There was a pause, then she drew in her breath quickly and muttered something in Chinese.

"That's the fellow? The one who came to your grandparents' shop?"

Her voice was a whisper. "Yes."

Things were falling into place for Cade. "Sit back."

Mei took the seat again, her eyes wide. All the blood had drained from her face.

"Get back to Kwan," Cade said. "Fast. I'll take care of this son of a bitch."

"But…you know him?"

"Yeah."

"You have to give me his name."

Cade did. Then he stepped out of the carriage and walked over to the steps. The man looked up. "Mr. Cade," he said, his face stiff.

Cade smiled as he heard the carriage rattle away. "What can I do for you, Mr. Tremblay?"

CHAPTER FIFTY-ONE

Hamrick's lawyer didn't return the smile. He reached for the pocket of his vest, and Cade had the Navy revolver out before he could recall thinking about it. Cade heard a woman passing by give a quick scream.

Tremblay stepped back, his face blanching with shock. "What are you doing?"

"You need to take your hand away from where it's going, Mr. Tremblay."

The bushy eyebrows drew together in anger. "I am an officer of the court, sir. Here to deliver legal process."

"That's nice. So reach in, real slow, and use two fingers to pull out whatever it is you have to deliver. And if it ain't paper, I'm going to blow a goddamn hole right through you."

Tremblay's eyes narrowed, looking Cade up and down. "You're as insane as she is."

Cade had an idea who he was talking about, and he didn't like it a bit. His voice was soft, but he took up the slack on the trigger. "Best get to it."

The lawyer slid his hand inside his coat and slid out a folded sheet of paper. He held it out to Cade. His hand didn't shake.

Cade reached out with his free hand and took it, never taking his eyes of Tremblay's. The paper was thick and heavy, of the finest quality. "Why don't you tell me what this is?"

Tremblay let his hand fall back to his side, his face filled with contempt. "That, Mr. Cade, is an injunction."

Cade still didn't look at it. "A what?"

"A legal order, issued by Judge Wheeler. You are hereby forbidden, under penalty of contempt, to enter on or near the premises of John Hamrick or Marjorie Townsend Hamrick, or any property or business owned by either or both of them. You are not to approach them or any of their agents, servants or employees."

Cade slid the paper into his pants pocket. "Uh-huh. And does Marjorie know about this?"

Tremblay shook his head in theatrical sadness. "Mrs. Hamrick is not well. Not in her right mind. Her recent...encounter with you is proof of her growing mental instability."

That rocked Cade for a second. His aim wavered slightly, then he raised the pistol again.

Tremblay went on, his smile becoming more condescending. "Arrangements are being made for her care. At a facility where she can rest."

"You cocksucker," Cade snarled. "Your plan to get her and her daughter killed fell through. So now you've come up with this bullshit?"

Tremblay was silent for a moment. A veil seemed to drop from his eyes, and the look of pure malevolence Cade could see there almost made him pull the trigger right then. But in a second, the veil was back again, and he was all puzzlement. "I have no idea what you're talking about."

Cade lowered the gun. He wanted to shoot the lying son of a bitch so bad, he could taste it. For that brief second, he'd seen the killing look in the man's eyes. But it was clear the lawyer wasn't going to draw on him. Not on the street. Killing him now would be in cold blood, in front of witnesses. That would be a short road to a quick drop. "Mei identified you. You're the one who was talking to McMurphy. Taking his money. I bet Hamrick loved that part. He got to fuck his old partner in the ass one more time, for old times' sake."

"You need to be careful of your next words, Mr. Cade."

Cade ignored the threat. "McMurphy thought he was paying the Chinese to kidnap Marjorie and Violet. Hold them for ransom. So he could get back some of what he thought Hamrick stole from him. But something was going to go wrong, wasn't it? They were going to end up dead. The Chinese were going to get blamed, which would be easy, because," he thought of Alton's words, "everyone here hates John Chinaman." He shook his head. "And Hamrick would get all her money to himself."

Tremblay was shaking his head in disbelief. "Do you have any idea how insane—?"

"What happened, Tremblay? The cutthroats you hired to do the deed turned up late? They were supposed to be done by the time we got back?"

"All right, Mr. Cade," the lawyer snapped. "I've heard quite enough slander from you." He looked around. A well-dressed couple who'd stopped to gawk looked away and moved off quickly. "I'm an officer of the court. A well-respected member of the community—"

"When Mr. Kwan finds out it was you who tried to put this crime off on him and his people, you're a fucking dead man. You might rather I be the one to plug you. I hear the Chinese can get plumb inventive when it comes to making a short life seem real long."

Tremblay sneered. "I don't concern myself with the Chinese."

Cade caught sight of the hotel's front desk man coming down the steps toward them with definite purpose. His usual graciousness was absent. Cade turned to him. "What?" he snapped.

The desk man gave him back glare for glare. "I wanted to inform you, sir, that your effects have been packed and are waiting for you. We request that you remove them, and yourself, immediately."

Cade turned back to Tremblay. "More of your fuckery? This was Marjorie's account."

Tremblay's smile was pure malicious glee. "Those accounts are now under court protection. Meaning mine. You won't be allowed to take advantage of that poor sick woman's frailties any longer."

"I want to talk to her."

Tremblay's smile grew wider. "I almost wish you would try. However, as that order in your pocket says, if you do try, you will be imprisoned and/or fined as provided by law in cases of contempt. Assuming, that is, that the Pinkertons I've persuaded Mr. Hamrick to employ as *actual* security don't deal with you first." He lifted his hat in an ironic salute. "Goodbye, Mr. Cade." He walked away, never looking back, confident in a way that only a man who knows that money and the law will keep him safe can be.

CHAPTER FIFTY-TWO

She hadn't wanted to sleep; she suspected without knowing for certain that John had the key to her bedroom, and she dreaded the thought of him coming upon her helpless. But she'd been up for hours, her anger as hot as a steamship boiler. With nothing happening, no sound on the other side of the door, no John upon whom to vent her rage, she soon found it flagging and dying, her energy going with it. That was the plan, she realized. It was a siege. And the key to a siege was to wait out the besieger. Her will was stronger than her husband's. She knew it. She wasn't going to sign his damned papers and give up her father's legacy. Still, as the hours dragged on, her eyes became heavy. Finally, she propped herself up on the bed, pillows at her back, and let her head fall back against the wall as she dozed lightly.

She dreamed of ships, the fast clippers that her father had commanded, then commissioned to be built, flying like birds before the strong Pacific wind, bringing tea, spices, and other goods from the Orient. Each of the great, sleek clippers bore their ornately carved figureheads, a strong, resolute feminine figure, jaw set, staring into the distance and daring the sea to do its worst. In her half-dreaming state, she became one of those figureheads, but alive, her sights set on the horizon, the wind blowing through her hair. Then the wind caressing her hair became hands, male hands, *his* hands, caressing her, making her feel things she hadn't felt in what seemed like forever...

A harsh rapping on the door jarred her out of her dream. "Marjorie."

John's voice. She had never hated a voice as much as she hated that one at that moment.

"Go away," she called out, her voice rusty with sleep.

"There's no need for this." John's voice was calm, reasonable, the voice of a parent speaking to a willful child. If she'd had her shotgun at that moment, she'd have picked it up and blown him in half.

"I agree," she said to the closed door. "Let me take my things and go. With Violet."

He chuckled. "Surely you don't think I'd let my child go off to who knows where with a madwoman."

She tried to keep her voice steady. If she gave voice to her rage, she'd just play into his hands. "I'm not mad, John. You know that." She couldn't resist the next jibe. "If there's anyone who needs to worry about losing his mind, John, it's you. Given what we know about the effects of the French pox." She sharpened her tone. "Have you caught it again, John? Have your visits to the Barbary Coast caught up with you again?"

There was silence from the other side of the door. Then, in a tight, high voice, he said, "Sign the goddamn papers, Marjorie."

"Go to hell," she answered.

"The action in lunacy has already been filed." His voice had regained its prior calm. "And an injunction against your cowboy. If he comes anywhere near you, or me, or this house again, he'll be thrown in jail. If my men don't kill him first. I suspect he knows that. He's gone from your life, dear. Forever. There'll be no rescue for you."

She was composing a retort when she heard John's footsteps moving off down the hallway.

No rescue, she thought. She felt the wound in her heart at his words about Cade. Then she took a deep breath. *Well, then. I'll just have to rescue myself.* She looked around the room. Her eye fell on the servant's door across the room. Bridget had occasionally brought her meals in her room up those stairs. She shook her head ruefully as she realized she'd never considered that those stairs ran both ways, that they could be used for more than bringing her whatever she desired.

The door opened with a slight creak, and Marjorie froze. There was no sound from below. She picked her way slowly down the stairs, wincing at every slight squeak of the old stair treads. She paused at the tiny second story landing, her hand on the door before she pulled it away. As much as she wanted to go to her daughter, she had to make sure there was a clear escape route. There wouldn't be much time to make their exit. *Down the stairs*, she thought. *Out the back door. To the stables...and then what?* She didn't know, and that realization made her want to sit down on the steps and weep. But she straightened her spine and crept down the steps to the first floor. At the bottom of the stairs was the door she assumed opened onto the kitchen. She put her ear against the rough wood and listened. What came through, muffled by the thickness of the door, was a rough male voice, one she didn't recognize. "Where the hell are those sandwiches?"

A familiar voice answered: Bridget's. "You just settle yourself, Mister. They'll be ready when they're ready."

There was a harsh scraping sound, like a chair being shoved backward, then a cry from Bridget.

"You watch your goddamn mouth, you Paddy bitch," the unfamiliar voice grated. "Or you'll get a lot worse than that."

Marjorie leaned her forehead against the door. The brutes John had hired from the notorious Pinkerton Detective Agency were guarding the back way and, she assumed, the front. There was no way out that she could see. She gritted her teeth. She wasn't going to give up. There had to be a way. In her mind, she heard her father's voice. *There's a way through, Margie*, he'd tell her whenever there were setbacks or reversals in the company's business. *Always a way past the rocks.* She slowly ascended the back stairs, her mind working, seeking the way through.

CHAPTER FIFTY-THREE

Cade ignored the contemptuous looks from the formerly respectful front desk man. "Hope you weren't expecting a tip," he said.

The man didn't answer, just pointed imperiously toward the door.

Cade picked up his trunk and hoofed it.

Outside, he stopped to get his bearings. He had a few dollars left in his pocket, so he wasn't going to be sleeping in the street. He'd already decided he was going to go to Marjorie, that slick lawyer and his papers be damned. He pulled the sheet of heavy stationery out of his pocket and examined it. The legal verbiage was thick and dense, and Cade could comprehend about every fourth word. He let the paper fall into the street. *First thing I need,* he thought, *is a place to lay up and figure the next move.* He thought of Captain Alton and the *Marjorie Ann.* He'd been told to stay away from Marjorie's property as well, but he had a feeling that if Alton knew what was going on, he'd have a thing or two to say about it. He was sweating a bit with the effort of hauling the trunk down to the livery he'd used earlier, but it didn't take long for him to hire a modest wagon to take him down to the wharf.

What he saw when he got there, however, made him draw up short. The wharf was being patrolled by a pair of characters whose store-bought suits and bowler hats couldn't cover up the air of thuggish menace they gave off. He reined in the horse and regarded the *Marjorie Ann* from down the street, trying to look like just another teamster come down to haul his cargo from the wharf to its buyer. He noticed that the well-dressed bruisers didn't venture up the narrow gangplank onto the ship. The big mute Russian he'd seen guarding that drawbridge stood at his post, arms across his chest, glaring down at them. They conspicuously took no notice.

"Pinkertons," a voice at Cade's left elbow said. He looked down. Alton was standing there, staring at the wharf and the guards set there. "On *my* wharf." He hocked and spat into the street, then took a long, angry pull on his pipe.

"But not on your ship, I notice."

"Pah!" Alton spat again. "Not while I command her." He seemed to sag a bit. "Which may not be long."

"So, what the hell's going on?"

Alton looked up at him. "I was hoping you could help explain that. Your colored fellah said you'd been arrested and that some sort of legal process was goin' on."

"Yeah. I think I might have some skinny you'd find useful."

Alton tapped the ashes of his pipe on the heel of his boot. "Well, you can explain it to me over a drink." He nodded to a long, low building near the wharf. "Tie up at the warehouse over there, and meet me at the foot of Meig's Wharf. At Cobweb Palace."

***

The Cobweb Palace was true to its name. The boxy, two-story wood-frame structure was nothing much to look at on the outside, but the inside was like something from a fever dream. Cade entered between a pair of intricately carved totem poles, grotesque yet strangely beautiful faces leering at him from either side. Inside the barroom, actual spiderwebs festooned the ceiling, draped like ragged lace across the expanse and drooping along the walls. Alongside the bar arced huge walrus tusks and whale teeth, delicately engraved with scrimshaw. A monkey shrieked at him from a cage next to the bar, and a parrot flew free inside the confines of the high ceiling. "Rum and Gum!" it called out. "Rum and Gum!" The place was largely empty this early, with only a few solitary drinkers at the bar and a trio at a table near the monkey cage, two of whom appeared to be face down asleep at the table.

Cade spotted Alton sitting at a table near the bar, a pitcher of beer and two full glasses sitting in front of him. He took a seat. "Lately I've started to wonder," he said, "if this place is a city or a goddamn lunatic asylum."

Alton smiled and began packing his pipe. "I allow as sometimes it's a bit hahd to tell." He struck a lucifer and lit the pipe, taking his time to do it properly. "Now," he said when he was satisfied, "tell me why I have ahmed brutes patrolling the wharf alongside my ship."

Cade had been steadily working at his beer while Alton lit up. He put the half-empty glass down. "Hamrick's making a move on Marjorie's property. He's got some slick lawyer filing papers."

"Hmmm." Alton took a drink and a draw on his pipe. "The word 'papers' can covah a lot of ground, Mr. Cade."

"For one thing, he's trying to have the court rule she's crazy. So he can take control of her business. Including this one. And it's not the first flim-flam he's tried."

"Go on."

"You remember that McMurphy fella?"

Alton nodded.

"It's like I told you before. This McMurphy had a scheme to kidnap Hamrick's wife and child. Hold them for ransom. He thought he was paying the Chinese to pull it off. But it was Hamrick's lawyer Tremblay who was the one hiding behind a screen. Pretending to be from the tongs. I think the deal was to kill Marjorie and her daughter. Blame the Chinese, and probably get rid of McMurphy afterward."

"Interesting." Alton didn't seem perturbed. Cade knew from

dealing with them in the Army that New Englanders could be a close-mouthed bunch, but Alton's lack of apparent concern was starting to annoy him. The Yankee captain peered at him through the cloud of smoke that was beginning to gather around him. "And you put a stop to that."

"Yeah."

"So now John's trying this legal dodge." He made a sour face at the word "legal." "Nevah cared much for this Tremblay fella, I must say. Tell me, what else has been filed?"

Cade hesitated, then blurted out, "An order for me to stay away from Hamrick and all his property."

"Ah. And, I suppose, his wife."

Cade looked away. "Yeah."

Alton nodded sagely. "Now we get to the core of the mattah, I think." He took another contemplative drag on the pipe, then sighed. "Marjorie was a willful child. It only got more pronounced as she got older. I tried to tell her father it would get her into trouble. Of course, he just laughed and told me that was what she was going to need to run the business." He looked at Cade. "I'm sorry you nevah got to meet Mistah Townsend. I believe the two of you would have liked each other immensely."

"That's nice to hear," Cade said, "but we've got a problem now. You said there wasn't much you wouldn't do for Marjorie. For her daddy's sake. Will you help her now?"

Alton looked mildly surprised. "Of course. Did you have any doubt?"

"I guess not."

"So," Alton drained his glass, poured another from the pitcher, "how do we go about this?"

CHAPTER FIFTY-FOUR

"Marjorie."

She was standing at the bedroom window, looking down on the courtyard behind the house, considering how she might best get her daughter and herself down from the third floor and not coming up with any ideas. The sound of her husband's voice made her teeth clench with rage. She decided not to answer. It didn't seem to make any difference. He went on.

"I've brought you something to eat." He paused. "I won't be accused of starving you out."

It was so like him. Looking at everything though the lens of how it would be regarded by their peers. Or those he wanted to be peers. She shook her head. There was no denying she was hungry. And thirsty. God, she wasn't just thirsty, she was absolutely parched. Still, she refused to answer.

"I'm just going to leave this outside the door. Don't worry. Bridget prepared it." Then she heard his steps moving away.

Marjorie stood by the window and stared at the door. She didn't know if it was her hungry imagination or if she was actually catching the scent of roast chicken. Legs shaking, she crossed the room and hesitated, her hand on the doorknob. She put her ear to the door. There was no sound on the other side. Slowly, she opened the door.

A silver tray sat on the floor. The aroma of food was stronger now, and she knew it wasn't her imagination. Her mouth watered, not just for the smell of the food, but at the sight of the two crystal carafes, one of water, one of a deep red wine, that sat beside the covered plate. She looked around, up and down the hallway, hating the way it made her feel furtive, like a hunted animal. She dragged the tray into the room, not picking it up until she'd locked the door securely again.

She picked up the tray and carried it to the table. The smell of food was overpowering, but the thirst was even more compelling. She poured water into the deep glass tumbler provided on the tray and drank deeply. She pulled the cover off the plate and saw the roast chicken she'd smelled earlier, flanked with a mound of mashed potatoes with a craterful of gravy in the center and a pile of green beans glistening from the slab of fatback nestled at their center. She poured the tumbler full of wine and fell on the meal with a will. It took almost no time for her to clean the plate, drain the carafe of water, and make a serious dent in the wine.

At first, she thought the drowsiness that fell over her was a result of how she'd gorged on the heavy meal. But the lethargy dragged and sucked at her like an undertow, until she realized what he'd done to her. She didn't know if it was the water or the wine he'd drugged. "You son of a bitch…" were her last slurred words, spoken to the empty room, before she passed out.

***

Cade sat in a second-floor window of the abandoned house behind the Hamrick mansion, surveying the place with the eye of a besieger. From time to time, his eyes strayed to the window of Marjorie's bedroom. There was no movement there. He caught glimpses of a stocky man walking back and forth across the back courtyard, carrying a rifle at port arms. One of the Pinkertons. His eyes never stopped moving around the narrow space. Cade had seen more than a few sentries in his time, and this one seemed to know his business.

Samuel came out the back door and headed for the stable. The Pinkerton man approached him, all swagger and aggression. Samuel drew to a halt, his head bowed submissively as the Pinkerton stood over him, hands on hips. He could see the black man's lips moving as he responded to the Pinkerton man's questions. Finally, the Pinkerton seemed to be satisfied and he let Samuel pass, but not without a shove in the direction he was going anyway. Another big man Cade didn't recognize appeared in the back door and called something to the one who'd been questioning Samuel. That one headed on in the house. And why not, Cade thought. It was daytime. Only a fool would attack a house in broad daylight.

Well, it looked like Cade was that fool.

Samuel had disappeared into the stable. Cade slipped out of the house and through the still unmended hole in the hedge the false Chinese had cut. With a glance toward the house, he entered the stable. He saw Samuel, standing before one of the stalls, patting one of the horses on the muzzle as he affixed a feed bag.

"Hey, partner," he called out softly.

***

Samuel was so startled, he almost dropped the feed bag. "Cade," he said, "what the hell are you doing here? I thought you were in jail."

"Seems I have friends in high places," Cade said. He turned and looked out of the stable door, checking for the Pinkertons' return. "I've come to get Marjorie out of here."

Samuel rubbed his chin. "Really?" He shook his head. "I mean, I could tell you had it bad for her, Cade, but—"

"Listen to me," Cade said urgently. "That attack by the Chinese? The one where they were supposed to kidnap Marjorie...Mrs. Hamrick?"

Samuel grimaced. "I don't think I'll ever forget that, Cade."

"Well, that wasn't the goddamn Chinese. It was set up by Hamrick's lawyer." Cade explained what he'd learned from Mei and how she'd identified Tremblay as the man trying to blame the kidnapping and eventual tragic death of Marjorie Hamrick and her daughter on the Chinese. When he was done, Samuel was shaking his head in disgust.

"White sons of bitches." He looked at Cade. "No offense."

"None taken."

"The little girl, too?"

Cade nodded grimly. "She's not really Hamrick's daughter."

"Still." Samuel snuck a look out the carriage house door toward the house. "So, what's the play?"

"You in?"

Samuel nodded. "I never liked this damn job anyway."

"You think you can get Bridget on board?"

Samuel frowned. "I don't know. She's not that fond of Missus, but she loves that little girl like it's her own. And she's got no reason to love these damn Pinkertons."

"Okay. You'll need to talk to her. Where's Hamrick?"

Samuel shrugged. "Inside. In his office."

"Okay." Cade explained what he had planned. When he was done, Samuel was smiling. "I definitely think Bridget will go for that."

"Okay, then."

CHAPTER FIFTY-FIVE

The two Pinkerton men had finished their luncheon and were back making their rounds. Samuel sat at the table, eating his own meal and speaking to Bridget in a low voice.

"That bastard," she hissed when he was done. "And now he's trying to pack Missus off to the madhouse." She gritted her teeth in rage. "And God alone knows what's to become of that sweet little girl."

Samuel nodded. "So. You in?"

Bridget nodded. "Oh, aye. I'm lookin' forward to this like Christmas."

***

Renfrew Boyle paced up and down in the narrow strip of grass in front of the mansion, rifle at the ready, his eyes on the street. He was bored, and full from the lunch the Irish cook had fixed for him, and what he really wanted to do was lie down under one of the trees on this street, pull his hat down over his eyes, and take a nap. Or better yet, have a quick roll in the hay inside this nice house with the red-haired cook, then a nap. Bridget, was it? No matter. She was a little skinny for his taste, but he'd liked the cowed look in her eyes when he'd smacked her. It was always better for him when they were at least a little afraid.

He sighed. This daydreaming was useless. Being found off his post would cost him his job, and he needed the work. He looked back at the house, wondering exactly what it is he was supposed to be guarding. As he regarded the front door, it swung open. Bridget was standing there, beckoning to him. He looked around, then mounted the steep steps.

"Mr. Boyle," the girl said, her eyes downcast, "I was wonderin' if you could help me with somethin'."

Boyle grinned. "And what would that be, darling?"

She giggled at the endearment. "I think there's a broken slat under me bed. Can you help me fix it?"

Boyle's prick stood to attention at the unmistakable invitation. He licked his lips and looked around again. The street was quiet. No one would notice if he took time for a quick poke. The head of the detail, Sears, was walking sentry out back, and hell, he'd understand, one man to another. Maybe he'd even share the little redhead. She seemed to like things rough. Why else would she extend such a blatant invitation after the wallop he'd given her? "Lead on, honey."

He followed her down the hallway, to a door next to the kitchen. She opened the door with a wink back at him.

The room was tiny, with a battered dresser, table, and washbasin the only furniture other than the bed. The bed was the only thing that interested him. She was leaning over, her hands on the mattress. "It's right here," she said, with a slight back and forth swaying of her backside.

"You don't have to ask me twice." He leaned his rifle against the wall and advanced, ready to lift that skirt, grab her by the hips, and go to town. But he'd only taken a step when she whirled around, an entirely different expression on her face, a short-barreled carriage gun she'd pulled from beneath the blanket in her hands.

"Then I won't have to tell ya twice to get on yer knees, ya feckin' prick."

Boyle's mouth opened and closed like a landed fish. This wasn't the way things were supposed to go at all. He briefly considered making a grab for the gun, but the blazing fury in her eyes told him she wouldn't just pull those double triggers and spread his brains across the walls of the narrow room, she'd enjoy it. He sank slowly to his knees.

She nodded, an expression of grim satisfaction on her face. "Good lad. Now turn around. Face the door."

Still numb with shock, he shuffled on his knees in the small space. He caught sight of the rifle propped against the far wall. He was calculating his chances of leaping to reach it when he heard her voice again.

"Now, little man, tell me again how yer goin' to give me another smack."

He opened his mouth to answer, but before he could, an incredible pain exploded in the back of his head and everything turned black.

***

Bridget stood over the unconscious Pinkerton man. "What's the matter, stud?" she taunted, "Cat got yer tongue?"

She'd nearly pulled the trigger on him. It was what he deserved after laying his hands on her, but she knew she'd swing for it. A poor girl never had any chance with the law, in her experience, so she'd had to satisfy herself with clouting him on the head. She bent over to make sure he was still breathing, then took a length of clothesline from beneath her bed and bound him tightly, hand and foot. She straightened up when she was done and regarded her handiwork. "Pinkertons," she scoffed. "Not much, from where I stand." Satisfied he wasn't going anywhere any time soon, she picked up the rifle he'd propped against the wall and put her ear to the door. She heard no footsteps in the hall, so she quietly slipped out. She made her way to the stairway, casting a glance at the library door. Mister had been in there all day, working on who knows what. Hopefully, he'd stay there. Moving as quietly as she could, she headed up the stairs to Violet's room.

CHAPTER FIFTY-SIX

It was a cool day, but Sears was starting to sweat in his woolen suit. The heavy meal he'd had wasn't helping. He considered taking off his coat, at least, but he had a feeling it wasn't something Mr. Pinkerton would approve of. He had never met the great man personally, but he knew that the professionalism of his operatives was something in which he set great store.

It was bad enough he was saddled with Boyle as a partner. The man was crude and slovenly in his habits, and Sears had had to reprimand him already for spending more time ogling the lady of the house and the skinny Irish cook than he gave to his duties. He left the coat on, bearing the discomfort with a rapidly growing irritability.

He noticed the black servant whose name he couldn't remember headed to the barn. "You there," he called out. "Boy."

The black man stopped and turned around, a dull and blank expression on his face.

"Where are you going?" Sears called out.

The servant ducked his head. "Stable, suh."

"I can see that!" the Pinkerton man snapped. He wondered if the black was simpleminded. "On what business? You already fed them."

The head stayed down. "Mendin' tack, suh."

"Fine," Sears growled. In truth, he didn't really care, he was just bored. "Go on, then."

"Yassuh." He turned and shuffled into the stable. Sears resumed his pacing.

In a moment, the black man came rushing out, eyes so wide Sears could see the whites. "Suh!" he whispered. "Suh! Come quick!"

Sears frowned. Something had disturbed the man. He hurried over. "What is it, boy?"

The black cast an eye back over his shoulder at the open door of the stable. "Someone's in there, suh! In the hay loft."

"What?" Sears looked at him skeptically. "Who would be in there?"

"I dunno, suh, but he's up there."

"Wait here." Sears raised the rifle and advanced into the stable, eyes and ears straining. He stopped just inside the door, allowing his eyes to accustom themselves to the dimness. He could smell hay, horse, leather, and the rich aroma of manure. The bulk of a black carriage loomed on his right side. A line of three stalls ran along the building, and he could sense rather than see the horses inside. At the end of the corridor was a ladder that led up to the hayloft. He leaned forward, straining his eyes in the weak light. He thought he could see something or someone moving in the darkness. "You!" he barked. "Who goes there?"

There was no answer. Sears brought the rifle to his shoulder and advanced down the hallway. A horse whickered and stamped in its stall, disturbed by the unfamiliar intruder. Sears' attention flickered that way for a second, then he kept going. "Come down!" he ordered. "Or I'll shoot."

He heard a click behind him, then felt the press of cold metal against the back of his neck. "Drop the rifle."

He started to turn. The metal pressed harder. "I said drop it, motherfucker."

He was stunned to recognize the voice as that of the black servant. All the earlier dullness and subservience was gone. "Nigger," Sears said, "what the fuck are you playing at?"

There was a rustle from the hayloft. A man Sears hadn't seen leaped down, holding a short-barreled shotgun in his hands. "I wouldn't call him that again, if I was you. He gets a little testy about it." The voice turned hard. "Drop the fucking rifle."

The rifle clattered to the ground. Sears looked at the man with pure hatred in his eyes. "So you're the one we're supposed to be keeping away from the house."

The man nodded. "Not doin' that crackin' a job, are you?" He looked over Sears' shoulder at the black man who'd gotten the drop on him. "Mr. Clayborne, would you be so kind as to tie this fella up?"

The voice was cool and sardonic. "With pleasure, Mr. Cade."

"No," Sears said.

Cade raised an eyebrow and the coach gun at the same time. "No?"

"You do it. I don't want…him," he jerked his head toward the black man behind him, "touching me."

"Well, I'm powerful sorry, Mr. Pinkerton," the man called Cade said, "but we're on a bit of a tight schedule here, so we don't have time to educate you about emancipation and the brotherhood of man. So put your hands behind your back." Sears didn't move. Cade raised the gun. "Do it."

Sears obeyed, teeth clenched, as he bore the indignity.

"Now the ankles," Cade said. "Have a seat."

When he was bound hand and foot, Sears was further humiliated to be dragged into one of the stalls. The black man led the big black gelding out as Cade propped him up against the back wall. He squatted down and looked at Sears. "Now. We need to keep you from raising a ruckus." He took a bandanna from a back pocket. "I can gag you, or I can knock you senseless. The second one might look better to your employer, but it's likely to give you a headache. All that said, I really don't give a damn. So what'll you have, Mr. Pinkerton?"

Sears closed his eyes. He could hear the sound of the carriage being moved out to the yard and the whinny of a horse. He swallowed. The thought of being knocked unconscious frightened him. He didn't want the risk of a busted skull. But maybe that way, he could explain that he'd been bushwhacked. Overcome by numbers. He wouldn't have to admit that a damned darkie had gotten the drop on him. He'd never work again if that got out, and he'd sure as hell never live it down.

"Knock me out," he said.

***

Samuel had one of the horses in harness and was getting the second one situated when Cade came out of the stable. He was holding the coach gun and the Pinkerton man's rifle, which he set in the back of the carriage. "Be ready to go," he said. "You remember where?"

Samuel nodded. "Gold Wharf. Like before."

"Ask for Captain Alton."

Samuel turned from his work and looked at Cade. "You're not coming?"

"Yeah. Yeah. Of course. But, you know, if something happens."

Samuel turned back to hitching the other horse. "Nothing's going to happen, Cade. Now go. And hurry up."

CHAPTER FIFTY-SEVEN

Hamrick entered the room, looking down at his wife sprawled limp on the floor. "Poor sweet dear," he said with ironic sweetness. "Poor mad Marjorie." Grunting with the effort, he hoisted her up onto the bed and laid her out. Reaching into his waistcoat pocket, he pulled out the vial of Harrison's Elixir. It was a common patent medicine, available at any druggist's, principally made of opium combined with wine and recommended for "female troubles." He had to laugh at that. He was certainly clearing up his own female trouble. He reached down, raised her head up slightly, and pulled the cork from the bottle with his teeth. "Drink up, dear," he whispered and put the bottle to her slack lips. He was about to tip it up and pour the fatal dose down his wife's throat when the heard the pounding of feet on the back steps, then a familiar voice from below. With a muttered curse, he stepped back. Cade was here. He had no doubt the saddle tramp was coming for his wife. And he'd be armed. Hamrick's gun was in his own bedchamber. He slipped down the hall as silently as he could to fetch it.

***

Cade took the servant's stairs two at a time, his need to see Marjorie overriding any consideration he might have for stealth. "Marjorie!" he called out. Then again, louder, "MARJORIE!"

There was no answer. His heart pounding, he drew the Navy revolver.

He reached the second-floor landing, then headed up to the third floor to where he thought the bedroom was. At the top of the stairs, the way was blocked by a wooden door. He tried the knob. Locked. He pointed the pistol at the lock, then hesitated. If he fired blindly through the door, he didn't know who he might hit on the other side. He reared back and kicked the door hard with his booted foot. The narrow stairwell and the steepness of the stairway made for a difficult angle. The door shivered in its frame, but held fast. He tried another kick, with identical results. With the third kick, the door gave way and he entered the room.

Marjorie lay on the four-poster bed on one side, her face as pale as the sheets on which she lay. Her eyes were shut. Cade couldn't tell for a moment if she was breathing. Then he saw her chest rise and fall, one deep breath, then stillness. Then another slow rise and fall.

Cade sat on the edge of the bed and grasped her by one shoulder. "Margie. Honey. Come on. Wake up." He shook her gingerly, then more firmly. "Come on, girl. We've got to go." He shook her again. "We're going to your daddy's boat. Sorry. Ship. To Captain Alton. Remember him? He's got a room all ready for you. On the *Marjorie Ann*." He knew he was starting to babble. He took a breath to steady himself and shook her again, this time hard enough that her head shook back and forth. "Come on. Wake up, Margie. Wake up, honey lamb."

There was no response. The world before Cade's eyes began to turn red around the edges. He didn't know what had happened, but he knew John Hamrick had something to do with it.

He gritted his teeth and got himself under control. He had to get Marjorie out of the house, which meant getting her down three flights of stairs. The narrow servant's stairs would make the task doubly difficult. The front stairs were the easier way, but he still didn't know if Hamrick was in the house or where he was.

Those questions were answered when he heard a voice behind him.

"Step away from my wife, Cade. And put that gun down."

CHAPTER FIFTY-EIGHT

Cade turned. Hamrick was standing there in his shirtsleeves and suspenders, a pistol held in his right hand.

Cade stood and turned toward Hamrick. He brought his own pistol up to point at the center of Hamrick's chest. "What did you give her?"

"I didn't give her anything, Cade. She took an overdose of laudanum." He smiled nastily. "In madness and remorse for her transgressions against her loving husband and family." He raised the pistol and turned slightly, like some dime novel picture of a duelist. "But now, another story presents itself. I've come upon an intruder in my home. Come to ravish the poor madwoman who mistook her own selfish lusts for romance. No court in this country would convict me for killing such a man."

"Pretty story," Cade said. "But you're not going to pull that trigger."

Hamrick sneered. "You seem very sure of that."

"As sure as I am about anything. You know why?" Without waiting for an answer, he went on. "It's like I told you when we first had that lunch together. I don't kill a man who don't have the killing look." He cast a quick glance at the woman on the bed, then looked back and steadied his pistol on Hamrick. "Oh, you can hire a murder out, or have that snake of a lawyer of yours do it. You can slip poison into someone's food or drink. But you don't have what it takes to look a man in the eye and pull the trigger. You don't have the balls to take a life face to face. And that's why I'm not going to kill you, either."

The gun in Hamrick's fist trembled a little, but he didn't lower it. "You're a fool."

Cade chuckled, the bitter laugh sounding like a man being strangled. "Oh, no doubt. No doubt about that at all. But this much I know. You won't die at my hand without that killing look. You'll die at the end of a rope after I let the law know you tried to kill your wife. Twice. I'm lookin' forward to being there for it. To watching you swing. And you know what I'm going to do then?"

Hamrick's voice was hoarse with fear. "What?"

Cade leaned forward, his voice a harsh whisper. "I'm going to go home and make love to your wife."

Cade's words struck Hamrick like a slap. The look of fear was suddenly gone, replaced by a consuming rage. His face turned crimson and he raised the pistol.

"*There* it is," Cade said as he saw the look. He shot Hamrick three times, twice in the chest, and, as Hamrick collapsed, the third bullet between his eyes.

"Sorry you had to hear that, sweetheart," he said to the unconscious woman on the bed, and holstered the pistol. He bent to sling her over his shoulder. "Let's go."

A scream from the doorway made him leap up, pistol in hand. Bridget was standing there, her face as white as a ghost's, her hand over her mouth. She was staring at Hamrick's body.

"What the hell are you doing up here?" Cade snapped. "You're supposed to be getting the little girl."

Bridget never took her eyes off the body. "I got her down there. She's with Samuel. I came back to see if Missus needed help. What… what's wrong with her?"

"The bastard tried to poison her. Laudanum, I think. Come on, help me carry her."

"Wait a second." Bridget went to the dressing table and opened a drawer. She came out with a glass bottle and pulled the stopper. "Hold her up."

Cade pulled Marjorie to a sitting position, her head lolling against his shoulder. Gently, Bridget raised up her chin with one hand and thrust the opened bottle up under her nose. There was no reaction at first, then Marjorie coughed explosively, her whole body seeming to convulse. She thrashed so violently that Cade nearly dropped her.

"Hold her tighter!" Bridget snapped, and shoved the smelling salts beneath Marjorie's nose again. This time, her eyes snapped open, wild and unseeing. She gagged and choked, and Bridget barely had time to step back before Marjorie leaned over and vomited on the floor. Cade nearly let go, but he held tight, steadying her with a strong arm around her shoulders as her stomach emptied. When she was finished, she groaned and raised her head. Her hair hung lank about her sweat-slicked face. She turned her head to look at him uncomprehendingly.

"Levi?" she whispered.

Before he could answer, Bridget was there with a water-soaked cloth. "Here now," she said in a gentle voice, as if soothing a sick child. "It's goin' ta be all right, pet. Let's get ye cleaned up." Still dazed, Marjorie let Bridget wipe her face clean and tidy her hair. Bridget patted her hand. "There ya go. We'll get ye changed into some clean clothes when we get where we're going." She looked down. "Cade," she said, her gentle tone vanished. "Ye'll clean yer own boots."

"Fine," Cade said.

"John?" Marjorie said, her voice rising. Cade saw her staring at the body on the floor. She turned to Cade, looking sick again. "Did you do this, Levi?"

He nodded grimly. "Yeah. He tried to kill you. Again. Then he—"

"Good," she interrupted.

"We need to go," Bridget spoke up.

Marjorie blinked. "Go? Why? This is *my* house."

"Tremblay," Cade said. "He helped John arrange the attack on the house. On you and Violet."

"Violet." Marjorie tried to stand, tottered unsteadily on her feet, then sat back down.

Bridget patted her shoulder. "She's fine, Missus. With Samuel. And we're going to go lay up on your nice big ship until Mr. Tremblay's...taken care of."

Marjorie's face twisted in disgust. "I'm not afraid of that snake."

"Afraid's not the point," Cade said. "He's got some bad people workin' for him. And he's still running around loose. I need to run him to ground. But I need to get you all somewhere safe."

Marjorie stared at him. "The *Marjorie Ann.*"

Cade nodded.

She stood up again, more steadily this time. "Well. Let's get going, then."

CHAPTER FIFTY-NINE

It was a wild, bumpy ride, with Samuel driving the team as hard as he dared. Cade sat up front with Samuel, the loaded coach gun across his lap. The women and the girl were in the back, Marjorie slumped against Bridget with an arm around her daughter on the other side. Violet clung to her mother as if she was drowning, whimpering with fear. Every now and then, Marjorie's head would droop and Bridget would give her a shake. "Missus," she said, "Missus." That would get her to raise her head and give Violet a reassuring squeeze.

"She needs a doctor," Bridget said to Cade.

"We'll get her one. When we get where we're going."

"Ya eejit," Bridget's voice rose. "She may be…" She stopped and put her hand to her mouth as Violet let out a sob.

"Cade," Samuel said in a low voice. "This may be a bad time to ask, but I'm pretty sure I heard shots from up there."

"Yeah. He drew on me. I did what I had to do."

Bridget crossed herself, then seemed to shrink back into the seat, looking away as the situation began to truly sink in.

The traffic was picking up, slowing the progress of the carriage. Samuel stood up behind the reins. "Make way!" he called out. "Emergency! Make way!" Some of the carts and carriages gave them the road. Others stubbornly maintained their paths, the drivers turning back to shake a fist or hurl a curse until they saw Cade raise the stubby coach gun. Then they wasted no time getting out of the way. Samuel weaved through the traffic, handling the carriage like a steamboat man navigating a treacherous stretch of river.

Finally, Cade spotted the forest of masts above the buildings. "Almost there," he told Samuel. "Right on East Street, then down about a quarter mile until you reach Gold's Wharf."

They made their way along the waterfront streets until Cade spotted the *Marjorie Ann*. But it was Marjorie who raised her hand to point it out. "That's the one."

Samuel pulled the carriage to a stop. Bridget craned her neck to see, then whistled as she regarded the ship. "She's a beauty."

"Yes," Marjorie said with obvious pride. "She is." Cade turned to look at her. She was deathly pale, but she had her head up, her chin raised defiantly in that way that captivated him all over again.

Cade spotted Sorokin, the huge Russian, standing his usual guard at the top of the gangplank. "Hey!" Cade jumped down ran toward the gangplank, one arm waving. "Sorokin!"

The big man didn't answer, just stood there with his massive arms across his chest, looking down impassively.

"Let us on board," Cade called up. "Mrs. Hamrick needs a doctor. She's been poisoned."

The big man didn't move. He just stood there looking at Cade as if he were a noisy drunk asking for a boat ride.

"Get the captain," Cade said. "Come on, man."

Marjorie stepped up beside him. The huge Russian blinked in surprise. He moved for the first time, but toward them, the wood of the gangplank creaking under his weight.

"Cade," Samuel said nervously as he walked up beside Marjorie, "what is he going to do?"

"I don't know." Cade could tell nothing from the look on the big man's face.

"Well, ask him."

"Won't do any good. He can't talk. But it's okay. He's on our side. I think."

Bridget had come up to stand behind them, a wide-eyed Violet clasping her hand. "Lord above," Bridget said in an awed voice. "That's a big'un."

Sorokin had reached them by now. He regarded the group expressionlessly.

Finally, it was Marjorie who spoke up. "Mr...Sorokin, is it? We haven't met yet. I'm Marjorie Hamrick. Marjorie Townsend Hamrick. I'm the owner of this vessel." She held out a hand.

Sorokin looked at the outstretched hand for a moment, then, before anyone could stop him, he took it in his own hand and bowed over it. When he straightened up, he stood to attention, clicked his heels together like a soldier, then executed a perfect military heel turn and headed for the ship. Marjorie followed behind, head held high. Samuel and Cade looked at each other and shrugged before falling in behind him.

"Wait," Bridget said. "Ye mean to go on board?" She shook her head. "Oh, no. I don't know what kind of ruffians are on board that scow. I could end up carried off. Sold to the Arabs. Or even the Chinese."

Cade stopped and looked back. "Suit yourself. But you'll be alone in all that." He gestured back toward the crowded and dirty streets of the waterfront.

She looked back, then at Cade. "Out of the frying pan, into the bleedin' fire," she muttered as she passed him.

On board, Sorokin was leading Marjorie toward the cabins at the stern of the ship when Alton appeared at the doorway. "Mrs. Hamrick," he said. "We didn't know..." He stopped as she stumbled, almost fell. Only Sorokin's arm around her shoulder kept her up. "Dear God!" Alton cried out. He rushed to her. "What happened?"

Cade walked up. "Her husband poisoned her. Laudanum, I think. Tried to make it look like she did herself in."

Alton shook his head, his face darkening with anger. "Sorokin. Please guide Mrs. Hamrick to my cabin," he ordered. "Keep an eye on her."

"I'm fine, Captain," Marjorie said, but her pale face and quavering voice were unconvincing.

"I'll send for a doctor, ma'am," Alton said. "Please let me know if there's anything we can do to make you more comfortable." He nodded to Sorokin, who nodded back and resumed his heavy tread toward the stern cabins, Marjorie held and protected by his huge arm.

"She needs that doctor," Cade said. "Pronto."

Alton nodded. "I said I'd send for one. But tell me what happened."

Cade decided on an abbreviated version. "I found her unconscious. Hamrick was trying to pour more laudanum down her throat. I objected. He pulled on me."

Alton's eyes bored into his. "And?"

Cade looked around to make sure Violet wasn't nearby. "And I killed the bastard."

Alton nodded in satisfaction. "Good." He looked at Samuel and Bridget. "And who are these folks?"

"I guess you know the little girl. The other two work...I guess you can say they worked for Hamrick. They're with us now."

Alton looked them up and down. "Is this true?"

Samuel nodded. Bridget hesitated a moment, then nodded as well. Alton's answering nod seemed to seal the deal.

"How many crew on board?" Cade asked.

Alton looked at him quizzically. "Four. Myself, Sorokin, Scarface Henry, and Mr. Peters."

Cade thought of the men he'd seen on his last visit. "I can figure which one is Henry. And the black fellow is Mr. Peters?"

Alton nodded. "Not his real name, of course. Mr. Peters is the common nickname for a black sailor in San Francisco. No one really knows why."

"Huh. Where's he hail from?"

Alton shrugged. "He hired on in Indonesia. Not sure where

he's from originally. I assume somewhere in Africa. I can't wrap my tongue around his given name, so Peters it is."

"Still. Only four?"

Alton grimaced. "When a ship comes into port, the crimps descend. Plying the men with liquor and dirty pictures, luring them off to the boardinghouses and brothels. I'll be lucky to get a quarter of my last crew back when we sail again. Have to hire and probably train up a whole new one." He nodded at the men watching them carefully. "These three are the core, though. Good men. Absolutely loyal to me."

Cade looked around. The dark-skinned man he'd seen on his previous visit was standing a few feet away, arms crossed across his chest, a hostile expression on his face. Cade looked up. The scar-faced man was seated on the crosstree of the nearest mast, looking down with an expression even less friendly.

"Meaning no disrespect to your fine crew, Captain," Cade said, his voice carefully neutral, "but can we count on them to be on our side once the ball opens?"

Alton's eyes narrowed. "You're expecting trouble?"

"Tremblay has a knack for getting other people to do his dirty work for him." Cade looked out over the waterfront. "We may get some trouble from him. I want to know if your boys will stick."

Alton smiled grimly. "They'll follow orders."

"But they don't seem happy about it."

Alton grimaced. "There's an old sailor's superstition that a woman on board brings bad luck. And now we have two, not to mention a child. But don't worry, Mr. Cade. These men are loyal." He smiled. "Have you noticed the lack of Pinkertons on the wharf?"

Cade had been too rattled to think about it. "Yeah. What happened to those two?"

"They went for a swim. And didn't come back." Alton looked back toward where Sorokin was coming out of the raised cabin area at the stern. "If you'll excuse me, I'm going to tend to Marjorie."

"I thought you were calling a doctor," Cade said, alarmed.

"I'll send Henry for one," Alton said. "But in the meantime, I'd be a poor captain indeed if I didn't have some physic for crew and passengers." He gestured to the man in the rigging, who clambered down, agile as a monkey. The two conferred for a moment, then Henry headed down the gangplank and Alton disappeared into the cabins at the stern.

Cade looked around at the crew who remained on the *Marjorie Ann*, at Sorokin and Mr. Peters. He'd caught a glimpse of the killing look in each of their eyes. He just didn't know who the look was going to be for.

Sorokin, the huge Russian, strode over to where Violet was pressed against Bridget. As Bridget pulled her closer, he knelt down to bring his ugly face closer to the little girl, who looked at him with wide eyes. He held out one hand, palm open and upward.

Violet stared in fascination. "Are you a giant?" she said.

Sorokin's face split in a crooked grin and he nodded. Slowly, as if approaching a strange dog, Violet extended her own small hand and placed it in Sorokin's. The hand seemed to disappear as the Russian closed his fingers gently over hers and gave a light squeeze before opening his hand again. He winked, and Violet giggled.

Peters beckoned. "You come," he said. "We get you cabin. Safe place."

Bridget looked dubious. She opened her mouth as if to say something, then looked over at Samuel and shut it. She turned back to Peters. "Thank you, sir, for the hospitality." Taking Violet's hand again, she followed the dark-skinned man toward the stern.

Cade followed. "There's a place down the way, one of Townsend's warehouses," he said over his shoulder to Samuel. "Put the horses up there."

Samuel nodded. "You want your scatter gun?"

"Yeah. Take the rifle. Get back as quick as you can. And look sharp. I have a feeling this ain't over yet."

CHAPTER SIXTY

Tremblay rode up to the Hamrick mansion in his one-horse buggy. He frowned as he saw the gate open to the rear courtyard. Carefully, he turned and steered down the narrow alley. In the back, the stable door was also open. There was no sign of anyone else around. His frown deepened. He needed to tell John that Cade had found them out and the two of them needed to decide what to do about the pesky saddle bum who'd caused them so much trouble. He'd warned Hamrick that it was a bad idea to bring someone else into the house at this delicate juncture, but John had laughed off his concerns. "The man's a buffoon. He'll never twig to what's going on. And what better way to establish that I was concerned about the Chinese than hiring a bodyguard to protect me from them?" Well, this Cade had more brains than Hamrick had given him credit for. And now, he was in the employ of the very Chinese they'd hoped to blame. He was going to have to be dealt with. Maybe by the Pinkertons, maybe by his own people, but dealt with by any means necessary. And soon.

Tremblay dismounted and looked around, his unease growing. He walked to the back door and tried the knob. The door swung open at his touch. He entered the silent kitchen, eyes and ears attuned for any sound. Suddenly, he heard a loud thump, then another, as if someone or something was being hurled against a door, over and over. He followed the noise into the narrow hallway that led from the kitchen to the dining room. There was another loud thud, coming from a door down the hall. Tremblay inched down the hall and listened at the door. He heard muffled rustling, as if something was moving inside. Heart pounding, he slowly opened the door.

It was clearly a servant's room, tiny and haphazardly furnished. A man lay on the floor next to the bed, bound hand and foot, a gag thrust into his mouth and held there by a strip of cloth. He glared up at Tremblay, the rage and frustration in his eyes causing the lawyer to step back. Then he recovered his composure. This must be one of the Pinkertons Hamrick had hired to guard the house after Cade's departure. He bent down, untied the cloth, and pulled the gag from the bound man's mouth. The man coughed and spit for a moment, working his jaw in circles as if to get it working again, then looked up at Tremblay. "Who the hell are you?"

"Not a burglar, lucky for you." He bent over and picked at the knots that bound the man's wrists behind him. "And who might you be?"

"My name's Boyle. I'm a Pinkerton."

"And a fine advertisement for the company you are." Tremblay straightened up. "You've got these knots pulled so tight I can't undo them. I'll be back in a moment." He went to the kitchen and came back with a sharp carving knife. Boyle had struggled to a sitting position, his back against the bed. Tremblay bent down and cut the ropes around his ankles, then the ones holding his wrists. Boyle stood, tottering unsteadily as the circulation came back in his feet, rubbing one wrist, then the other to get the blood flow back in those limbs.

"Where's Hamrick?" Tremblay said. "And his wife?"

Boyle couldn't meet his eyes. "I don't know. Last time I saw Hamrick, he was in the library. She was upstairs."

"You damned fool," Tremblay snapped. "You were supposed to be guarding them. How'd you end up tied up on the floor of the servant's room?"

"Bitch tricked me," Boyle mumbled. "Brought me in here for a roll in the hay, then pulled a gun on me." He touched the back of his head and winced. "But she didn't have to clout me in the damn head."

Tremblay shook his head in the disgust. "Idiot. Where's the other one? The other man that was with you?"

Boyle looked sulky. "I don't know. He was out back."

They found the other man in the stable. He was still out, bound just as Boyle had been. Boyle cut him loose and sat him up. His head drooped, a line of drool running from his mouth. The back of his head was matted with blood. "Shit," Boyle said. "We need to get him a doctor. Looks like he got hit a lot worse than I did."

Tremblay didn't answer. Both of the guards gone, the house empty. Where was John? He got up, leaving Boyle with his unconscious partner, and re-entered the house.

He found Hamrick lying in the doorway to the bedroom. There was no need to check the pulse or listen for breath. Half his head was blown away. Tremblay stood there for a moment, breathing hard, his mind racing. This had to be Cade's doing. He saw a pistol lying a few inches away and picked it up. A plan was coming to him.

He carried Hamrick's pistol downstairs. It would make a better scenario if John was unarmed when Cade shot him. And Tremblay intended to make sure that neither Cade nor Marjorie ever got a chance to tell a different story.

When he got back to the stable, the other man was awake, sitting up, his eyes looking vague and unfocused. There was a puddle of vomit on the stable floor next to him. Tremblay squatted down next to him. "What's your name?"

"Sears," the man mumbled.

"And were you the senior agent in this debacle?"

Sears blinked in confusion. "What?"

"Were you in charge here?"

"I...I guess." Sears shook his head, his immediate groan of pain indicating that the sudden motion was a mistake. "What…what happened?"

"I was hoping you could tell me," Tremblay said. "John Hamrick is dead. Murdered."

"Oh fuck," Boyle whispered.

"Yes. Oh fuck." Tremblay shook his head and stood up. "Hamrick dead, his wife and daughter gone, the house emptied. Was it Cade?"

Sears looked up at him, his expression that of a schoolboy asked to recite a lesson he hadn't learned. "Cade?"

"Yes, Cade. The one you were supposed to be guarding this place against."

"We heard the name," Boyle said. "We never met him."

Tremblay smiled thinly. "I think Mr. Sears did."

"There…there was two of them," Sears blurted. "No. Three. They bushwhacked me."

"Indeed," Tremblay said. He raised the pistol and shot Sears in the center of the forehead.

Boyle leaped up from where he'd been crouching beside his superior. "What the fuck—?" was all he had a chance to get out before Tremblay shot him between the eyes. The man fell like a tree, crashing to the floor of the stable on his back, his limbs twitching spastically.

Tremblay watched him with close interest. He brought his free hand up and felt of the vein in his own neck. His pulse was steady and strong, not seeming elevated at all. He found that curious and filed the information away in his mind for later. This kind of killing didn't have the erotic charge of his escapades, but there was a definite enjoyment to watching the men die.

When Boyle finally lay still, Tremblay retied his hands and feet, then did the same for Sears. When he was done, he stood over the bodies and shook his head. "Poor fellows," he said out loud, rolling the words around on his tongue. "Ambushed, bound, and foully murdered by the villain Cade and his Negro henchman as part of Cade's bloody-handed rampage against the husband of his lover." It was the kind of story the cheaper sort of newspaper would make into an overnight sensation. He could make sure of it with a few well-placed coins in the hands of some of the less scrupulous publishers. Now, all he had to do was make sure anyone who would tell a different story wasn't around to do so. But where would they go to hide out?

He sucked thoughtfully at his teeth. They wouldn't dare go back to The Royal Hotel. He'd made sure to close out that account. The answer came to him and he nodded, smiling with satisfaction. There was only one place she'd go. He'd make sure that was no refuge. If he could put the right words in the right ears, what was left of Marjorie Townsend Hamrick's world would burn to ashes, and she and her cowboy lover with it.

It was a shame, really, Tremblay thought. With him as executor and trustee of the Hamrick estate, the Townsend assets would make a fine addition to the portfolio and a rich vein to be mined. But she and Cade were loose cannons. They had to be disposed of. And besides, the assets were most likely insured.

Tremblay smiled to himself as he considered the possibilities. This city offered so many opportunities for a man with the right kind of mind to make his fortune. And Lionel Tremblay, Esq. was possessed of just that sort of mind.

CHAPTER SIXTY-ONE

The doctor Scarface Henry brought back was a thin, pale, consumptive-looking young man who looked as if he wasn't far from needing a doctor himself. Before entering Alton's cabin where they'd placed Marjorie, he was racked with a fit of coughing that left him leaning against the doorpost with one hand, pressing the other to his chest.

"Jesus," Cade muttered. He looked at Scarface Henry. "Where the hell did you find him?"

The sailor looked at him stonily and answered in an accent that Cade couldn't place. "You think you find one faster down here, big man, you welcome to try."

Cade shook his head as the doctor picked up the bag he'd brought with him, a huge, well-worn leather satchel that looked almost too heavy for the man to haul around. Cade followed as he entered the narrow passage in the raised stern. The doctor didn't seem to notice.

The captain's cabin was a far cry from the cozy place he'd shared a whiskey with Alton in a time that seemed a century ago. It was hot and close, the air stinking of vomit from the bucket that rested beside the bed. There was barely enough room for the people already inside—Captain Alton, the consumptive doctor, and Marjorie on the bed. Cade had to wait in the doorway. The sight of Marjorie made him draw in his breath. She was awake, but the ride to the ship had taken a lot out of her. She'd changed from her vomit-soiled dress into a man's denim pants and white shirt. Her face was almost as pale as the shirt, and a lock of her hair clung haphazardly across her bone-white forehead. He wanted to go over and brush it back into place, but there was no way to reach her in the crowded cabin.

The doctor was straightening up from where he'd been leaning over the bed. He took his stethoscope from his ears before speaking. "How much laudanum did you take, madam?"

Marjorie shook her head. "I'm not sure. It was given to me. In my food."

The doctor frowned. "In your food?"

Cade spoke up. "Her husband tried to poison her."

The doctor blinked in surprise. "Poison?"

"Yeah. And he was trying to give her more while she was out cold."

The doctor had quickly recovered his composure. "Do you know how much he gave her?"

"No. I don't know if he got any down her. I interrupted him."

"Interrupted?"

Alton broke in. "Best not inquire further."

The doctor stared at him for a moment, then shook his head. "I need to finish my examination." He looked at Cade. "If you have nothing more to add, you may go."

Cade gritted his teeth and went out onto the deck. He stood at the railing, looking out over the dark thicket of masts and smokestacks in the harbor. Lights twinkled here and there on decks, and over the water, he heard the lonesome call of a boat's horn. He couldn't tell if it was coming in or going out. This whole world of the waterfront was foreign to him, the most foreign place he'd been in a city full of strange places. The smell of the harbor filled his nostrils, a rich mix of salt water, dead fish, and coal smoke. He looked back to the waterfront, ablaze with light and noise. Behind it, the city rose, glittering and shimmering, like some fairyland come to life. He felt like it might take a lifetime to drink it all in.

In a few moments, Captain Alton joined him at the rail. "Dr. Jordan believes Mrs. Hamrick will make a full recovery."

Cade felt a loosening in his chest. "That's good." He frowned. "Assumin' this Jordan knows his business."

Alton looked back over the water. "He's a graduate of the Hahvahd Medical School. First in his class. Had a fine career ahead of him."

"That's nice," Cade said, "but what's his story now?"

Alton puffed on his pipe before answering. "He's dying. Stomach cancer. He doses the agony with opium." Alton upended the pipe and tapped it against the rail, spilling the ashes into the water. "So he understands more than a little about the effects of the poppy. He can calculate just the dose he needs to dull the pain, while keeping most of his wits about him."

"Most."

"Mr. Cade," Alton turned to face him, "he's a better doctor with a dose of opium in him that half the drunken pill-mongers in this city."

Cade sighed and leaned on the rail. "Guess I'll have to take your word for it."

As if summoned by the conversation, the doctor appeared at Alton's elbow. "I think the crisis is past," he said. "She needs to rest and let the drug work its way out of her system. Keep an eye on her and make sure her breathing is strong."

"Will do," Cade said. "And thanks, doc."

"You're welcome," the doctor said. He squinted into the darkness, looking out onto the wharf. "Who do you think that is?"

Alton joined him and looked over. "Some ruffian. Looking for an unwary sailor or some other easy pickings." He smiled grimly. "He'll find none here."

"Maybe," Cade said, "but it looks like he's bringing some friends."

In the darkness on the wharf, beyond the ship's lanterns, a crowd was beginning to gather.

CHAPTER SIXTY-TWO

After a while, Alton left. The doctor went back on shore. Cade stayed by the rail, unsettled by the dark figures he saw going to and fro on the wharf and appearing on the street at the head of it. There seemed to be an unusual amount of interest in the *Marjorie Ann*, and it made Cade uneasy. He glanced over at where Sorokin stood at the top of the gangplank, arms across his chest. He didn't seem disturbed by the increased traffic, but then, it was hard to tell if anything worried the giant Russian.

Cade paced the deck, casting occasional glances at the wharf, trying and failing to gauge whether the number of people was increasing or decreasing.

Eventually, Scarface Henry walked up, his rolling gait marking him as a seaman. "Come down," he said in that accent that Cade couldn't place. "Eat."

Cade's stomach had been growling for a while, but he'd been ignoring it because he had no idea how he was going to fill it, and he had other things on his mind. He cast a glance over at Sorokin at the top of the gangplank.

"Everything fine," Henry assured him. "You need to eat."

There wasn't any arguing with that. Cade followed Henry below.

The crew space beneath the main deck was as low-ceilinged as everywhere else he'd been on the ship, but wider, spanning the width from one side to the other—starboard to port, he remembered. The shoreside crew of the *Marjorie Ann*, missing Sorokin but augmented

287

by Samuel, sat around an iron pot set in the center of the floor on a dais of bricks. They were spooning some kind of stew into their mouths from a mismatched collection of ceramic bowls. Mr. Peters handed him a bowl, a toothy grin splitting his coal-black face.

"It's good," Scarface Henry assured him. "Mr. Peters' special recipe."

Cade glanced over at Samuel, who was spooning a dollop of the stew into his mouth.

Samuel caught the quizzical look and shrugged. "Tastes all right."

Cade accepted the bowl Peters handed him and took a bite. The stew was indeed delicious, a bit spicy with seasonings Cade wasn't completely familiar with, but tasty all the same. He also had trouble identifying the meat. He looked up to see Peters and Henry looking at him intently. "It's good," he reassured them.

"You okay with the meat?" Scarface Henry asked, his expression strangely anxious.

"Why wouldn't I be?"

"No reason," the scarred man said with a little too much nonchalance. "But...you remember the Pinkerton men?"

Cade looked down at his bowl. Suddenly the chunks of meat in the brown stew looked a little too greasy and fatty. He looked over at Samuel, who was staring into his own bowl in undisguised horror.

Cade smiled and looked up at Mr. Peters. "What's the sailor's version of the word 'tenderfoot'?"

It was Scarface Henry who answered, his expression confused. "Tender...foot?"

"Greenhorn. Rube. New fellow."

Henry said something to Peters in a language Cade didn't know, but thought might have been French. Peters burst out in a huge laugh that almost doubled him over. He turned to Cade. "Landlubber." He started laughing again, so hard Cade thought he might choke.

Scarface Henry nodded, smiling. "Lubber for short."

Cade turned to Henry. "Tell your shipmate here that me and my partner here may be green, but we ain't lubbers." He put down the bowl and stood up. "Listen, you two. I don't know what's about to happen. But I know that there's one cold-blooded son of a bitch out there who means Marjorie, the lady who pays your wages, harm. He wants her dead, I'm pretty sure, and he's gone to some pretty severe lengths to make it happen. And I'm willing to go to some pretty severe lengths to keep it from happening." He looked at the circle around him. "I can take a joke as well as the next fella. But I have a feeling things are about to get serious. Can I count on you?"

Peters and Henry looked at one another, then back at Cade. "To do what?"

"Help me look after Marjorie...Mrs. Hamrick." An inspiration occurred to him. "And defend your ship."

Scarface Henry smiled. "Now you talk our language, landlubber."

Peters gestured to the bowl in Cade's hand, then looked at Samuel. "Eat your goat stew. Make you strong. Strong for fight to come."

Cade looked down at the bowl. "Goat." He spooned up another mouthful. "Goat I can stomach."

***

The word had spread, passed through the saloons, music halls, brothels, and deadfalls by Butt Shaughnessy and his hoodlums. They'd been given an incentive to spread the rumor by liberal application of Tremblay's gold, and they set to their task with a will. By midnight, the word was all over the Barbary Coast, all the way down to the waterfront.

There was a ship in harbor at Gold's Wharf. The *Marjorie Ann*. Just in from China. And she carried the plague with her. The Black Death.

It was a story that took hold and spread because it played into the worst fears of the people of San Francisco. Fear of the unknown, fear of the Orient (a land known by all for poverty, corruption, and pestilence), and most of all, fear of contagion in a town where the majority of people were packed together side by side like matches in a box. Light one as it lay next to the others, and the whole box would go up like a firework. That was the image Shaughnessy's industrious messengers spread through the Coast. That quarter, always susceptible to rumor and sensation, lapped it up. Soon enough, they felt the reckless intoxication of the elixir they'd imbibed, a draught more powerful than whiskey when it came to clouding minds.

Rage, begotten of fear.

Small groups began to gather, talking among themselves in low voices. Those low voices were quickly augmented by the louder, more strident voices of Shaughnessy and Tremblay's paid provocateurs. Before long, handbills began to appear, "special editions" of the area's less ethical tabloid publications, asserting that not only was the decimation of the city imminent, but the city government was ignoring the risk as corrupt officials lined their pockets with graft from powerful interests that, while unidentified, were certainly foreign in nature. In a city where the concept of corrupt officials lining their pockets to the detriment of the people was not only widespread but widely accurate, the idea took hold. The small groups came together, fed off each other, eventually coalesced into a mob that began a march toward Gold's Wharf, their low grumble growing into a roar as they made their way to the threat on the waterfront. Along the way, weapons began to appear as if by magic among the crowd: the usual clubs and knives at first, then blackjacks, cleavers, and slung shots. Before long, firearms supplied and wielded by the hoodlums made their appearance. Handguns, mostly, but a few shotguns and long rifles as well. But the thing most commonly carried by the people headed for the *Marjorie Ann* was fire, in the form of torches and lanterns. Because while the rumor mongers and written broadsides usually just complained about some imagined ill or outrage, the ones that circulated among the crowd that night recommended a very specific remedy.

Burn the Plague Ship *Marjorie Ann*. Burn it to the waterline. And let none of the infected escape.

CHAPTER SIXTY-THREE

Cade was sitting by the bed, going through the laborious ritual of reloading the cap-and-ball revolver. He looked over at Marjorie every few seconds to make sure she was still breathing. He'd just snapped the cylinder on the pistol closed when he heard the shouting.

Marjorie's eyes opened slowly. "What's that?"

"Don't know," Cade said tersely. "I'm going to find out. Stay here."

He encountered Bridget in the short corridor, her eyes wide. "What's all that racket?"

Cade could hear the tumult increasing. "Stay here," he repeated.

Out on deck, he could see the skeleton crew of the *Marjorie Ann* lined up along the rail, looking down to the wharf. Samuel was with them, his arms folded across his chest. He was closest to Cade, and he turned as Cade came up beside him. "This looks bad."

Cade looked over the four-foot railing. On the wharf below, a group of people was gathered, stretching the length of the ship. They were a motley group, most of them raggedly dressed, with a few swells here and there. Cade noticed with a twist in his gut that those were the ones who appeared to be carrying rifles and handguns. He spotted about a dozen women who, judging from the dress and gaudy makeup, had come from the brothels and cribs. There must have been a hundred people in the group, and none of them looked happy. In the flickering light of the torches and lanterns carried by many, Cade could see expressions of rage and disgust. Quite a few looked terrified, eyes wide enough to see the whites from twenty feet away. Some were shaking their fists, and almost all were shouting. In the uproar, Cade couldn't make out what they were saying.

"What the hell are they so haired off about?" Cade asked.

Samuel shook his head, his face grim. "I heard someone yell something about plague."

"Plague? On this ship?" Cade looked down the railing. Sorokin and Mr. Peters were trying to pull the gangplank back on board the ship to keep anyone from boarding. A pair of tough-looking characters had taken hold of the other end and were trying to wrestle it away. Sorokin gave a mighty heave and yanked the wooden gangplank out of the hands of one. The other, refusing to let go, was pulled into the water between the ship and the wharf. The crowd nearest to him burst into laughter and jeers as the man spluttered and struggled in the water.

"This looks ugly," Cade muttered.

"Agreed." Samuel reached down and picked up the rifle they'd taken off one of the Pinkertons. The other was propped up against the railing. Cade realized he'd left his pistol and the coach gun in the cabin. "Back in a second."

In the cabin, Cade checked the pistol, made sure it was loaded. He grimaced. Six shots wasn't going to hold off that mob, and this damned cap and ball revolver took a damned eternity to reload. He didn't know how many shots the rifles they'd taken had in them, but he wished now they'd looked around for more ammunition. There were two shots in the double-barreled coach gun and a few shells. He hoped like hell there were more firearms on board, because if that flock of dingbats outside got out of hand, this was going to go very badly, very fast.

"What's happening?" Marjorie demanded. She was sitting up in the bed, fully awake now.

"There's a crowd outside," Cade said. "They've got it in their heads that there's plague on board."

"Plague?" she scoffed. "That's absurd."

Cade went to the door. "Tell them," he muttered.

"I will." She stood up, her face determined.

"I didn't mean it," Cade said. "You stay here."

"The hell I will," she snapped. "This is my ship."

There wasn't any use in arguing with her, Cade saw. "Just keep your head down."

When they got back on deck, Captain Alton was standing at the rail, attempting to address the crowd. "What's the meaning of all this?" he bellowed. "What do you people want?"

His vehemence seemed to quiet the crowd slightly. Some looked around at each other uncertainly. Then one of the better dressed men stepped forward and spoke loudly enough to be heard on deck. "You've just come in from China, right?"

"Aye," Alton called back. "We brought a hold full of tea and silks. What of it?"

"That's not all you brought back!" another voice called.

Alton scowled and addressed the speaker as if he was dressing down an unruly sailor. "What the devil are you babbling about?"

The tone didn't set well with the crowd. They began to stir and mutter restlessly. Cade grimaced. He'd seen mobs in action before, and talking down to them never worked.

"We're talking about plague!" the first man shouted. "You know what it could do if that pestilence took hold in this city?"

For once, Captain Alton was speechless. He shook his head, clearly not believing what he was hearing. After a moment, he regained his voice. "There's no plague on this ship. None."

"Liar!" a voice called. Another voice joined in. "Liar!" The crowd took up the chant. "Liar! Liar!" The crowd was in full voice again, and Cade saw the chance of getting out of this without violence slipping away. Then the chant began to change. "Liar! Liar!" began to be replaced with, "Burn it! Burn it!"

CHAPTER SIXTY-FOUR

"Shit," Cade said. He ran down to where the captain was standing just as the first lantern shattered against the side of the ship. It didn't catch, but fell hissing into the water. But soon the air was full of flung torches and lanterns, arcing over the water, their flames reflected below. Most of them fell short, a few burst against the side of the ship, but one lantern made it over the rail, bursting at the foot of one of the masts. Flames began to spread.

"FIRE ON DECK!" Alton called out. There was the crack of a rifle, and the captain pitched forward, falling to his knees before going over onto his face. Cade skidded to a stop in front of him just as another rifle shot zipped past him, so close he could feel the wind of the bullet. The single shots became a ragged volley. Bullets buzzed like angry bees by Cade's head. He dropped to the deck and belly-crawled to the rail.

He looked over to where Samuel was crouched down to avoid the fusillade aimed at the ship. When the shots slowed a bit, he popped up and returned fire, shouting something that Cade couldn't make out. Someone in the crowd screamed in pain and rage, and the wood of the railing splintered in front of Samuel as the armed members of the crowd all turned their aim on him.

Cade took the opportunity to come to one knee, the Navy revolver drawn. He saw a man running toward the edge of the dock, his right hand swinging back with a lantern gripped tightly, ready to toss. Cade braced the heavy pistol on the wood of the deck, took aim, and fired. He'd been aiming for the man's chest, but the shot took him in the forehead. He staggered as the top of his head disappeared, but momentum carried him forward, pitching him into the dark water as the lantern fell from his slack hand. It burst on the wharf and the crowd parted around it. Their cries and shouts of rage rose to a howling roar like a hurricane.

Cade took aim at another man he saw in the crowd who was kneeling and pointing a rifle at the ship. The shot caught the rifleman in the throat and knocked him back on his ass, clutching vainly at his throat for a moment before toppling over on his side. Someone leaned over to pick up the rifle and Cade shot him too. He thought he heard two rifles now, firing from the deck, and looked down the rail. Marjorie had picked up the other rifle and was firing into the crowd, her face as calm and intent as if she was at a shooting range.

"Marjorie!" he yelled. "Get down!" She ignored him.

Another torch made it over the rail and landed a few feet away. The planks of the deck began to catch. Bullets singing overhead, Cade tried to crawl toward the fire, shucking off his coat with the idea of using it to smother the flames. He heard the sound of running footsteps, then Mr. Peters leaped over his prone form. The bucket of water he was carrying sloshed onto him, soaking his clothing. Peters threw the remaining water from the bucket onto the smoldering torch, then threw himself flat on the deck as the riflemen on the dock turned their attention to him. He rolled to one side and looked at Cade reproachfully. *You brought this on us*, his look said as clearly as if he'd said it in the King's English.

"I know, man," Cade muttered. "I know. Sorry."

Peters shook his head and rose to a crouch, heading for the rail opposite the mob. He went over it without stopping, and Cade heard a splash as he went into the water.

"Can't say as I blame you, son," Cade muttered. He rolled to the rail and stuck his head up. Samuel was firing steadily now, taking a shot, then ducking down and heading to another firing point.

Judging from the way the crowd was beginning to waver, moving this way and that, his shots were taking a toll. Some of them, particularly the more raggedy men and the painted whores, started running down the wharf, unnerved by resistance. This wasn't what they'd signed up for. But the ones who remained, twenty-five or so, were the ones with rifles and torches, and they didn't look like they were going anywhere. Cade sensed this was the hard core, and he had a feeling he knew who was backing them.

"Cade!" Samuel called over to him. "I'm running dry!"

"Shit," Cade muttered. Samuel was nearly out of ammunition and he was down to his last three rounds. He looked around. Sorokin was standing upright by the mast that had been the first to catch fire, carrying a good-sized bucket in each hand. He set the left-hand one down and threw water over the steadily growing fire from the one he carried in his right. Steam rose from the flickering blaze licking up the mast. As the huge Russian bent for the other bucket, he staggered slightly, letting out a loud grunt. Cade saw the blood starting from his side where a bullet had struck home. Sorokin shook his head like a bull in the ring shaking off the pain of the spears and hoisted the second bucket. Cade got up, head and shoulders over the rail, and spent his last three shots on trying to keep the mob's heads down to give Sorokin a chance. As he turned back and slumped down, fishing out his silver powder horn, he saw the big man dump the second bucket over the flames, then stagger as another shot hit him in the back. The flames hissed and sputtered, but didn't go completely out. Sorokin began to crawl away.

Cade looked toward the stern. He and Samuel could follow Peters over the rail, but he didn't know how to swim, and he doubted Samuel had had the chance to learn. Further, there was still Marjorie to worry about, not to mention her daughter and Bridget. He cursed to himself as he began the laborious loading process on the cap-and-ball revolver. He shook the powder from the horn into one cylinder, fitted a brass projectile over it, then pushed it into place with the loading lever. *This is going to take too long,* he thought as he fished in his pocket for the small case of percussion caps that fit over the nipple at the back of the cylinder. As he did, he looked up and saw the longboats on their wooden cradles. If he could get one in the water, putting the ship between them and the mob, maybe they could get away. But each boat was a good ten feet long, solidly built. There was no way one man could get one into the water by himself, and then get everyone into them, including a child and a woman still sick from being poisoned. He looked around for Scarface Henry, but he was gone. Probably over the rail with his shipmate. Alton had said they were loyal, but that was apparently to him, and whatever loyalty they had to the ship died with him.

He spotted Sorokin, who'd made it to the raised lip of a hatchway where he slumped in a sitting position, his head down. He'd taken two shots but he was still breathing. Cade shook him by one shoulder. The Cossack raised his head groggily, his eyes bleary and unfocused. "Sorokin," Cade said again, pointing behind him at the longboats. "We need to get one of those boats in the water." Sorokin stared for a moment, then raised his own finger to point silently. Cade looked. He realized that Samuel had stopped firing. With nothing to keep them at bay, the mob pitched more lanterns and torches onto the deck and the starboard boat was burning. "Well, there's one left," Cade muttered. He looked over at Sorokin. The man's eyes were wide open and staring. He was gone.

CHAPTER SIXTY-FIVE

Cade shook his head. "God damn it," he muttered.

He couldn't see through the smoke and flames where Samuel was, couldn't tell if he'd ceased firing because he was shot or just out of bullets. He saw a figure between the boats, obscured by the smoke but moving toward him. "Clayborne!" he called out. But it was Bridget who emerged from the choking cloud, running at a crouch, carrying something in one hand. As she reached Cade, he saw she was carrying the stubby carriage gun in one hand and a bandolier of shells in the other. Well, that was something. The shotgun wasn't much good at range, but maybe he could discourage the bastards. Not that he could do it for long.

"Where's Samuel?" he asked, taking the shotgun from her hand.

She looked at him, wide eyed, her hair wild and disheveled around her pale face. "I don't know. I saw him throw the gun down, then everything was all smoke. And flames." He could see the tears running down her face and knew that it wasn't just her eyes watering from the smoke. "I'm afraid."

"You're fine, girl. Keep yourself together." The flames from the boats were rising, and Cade could see that before too long, he'd be cut off from the stern of the ship. "Come on," he said. He headed toward the port side, as yet untouched by flame.

Bridget stopped him with a hand on his arm. "Cade."

He stopped, looking at her impatiently. "Come on, Bridget. We've got to move."

"Please, Cade." Her eyes were panicked. "Don't let me burn. I'm afraid. Don't let me burn."

"I won't." He tried to pull his arm away.

She gripped it tighter. "Shoot me. Please."

He succeeded in pulling his arm free. "I'm not going to shoot you, you crazy—"

"PLEASE!" she shrieked. "It's better than that." She gestured toward the flames getting closer.

"Come ON, damn you!" Cade roared. "Or stay here and burn." He turned and ran down the port rail, not looking back to see if she followed.

The heat felt more intense as he reached the door to the stern house. "MARJORIE!" he shouted. Before he could open the door, it swung wide.

Samuel was there, carrying the other shotgun. Marjorie was behind him, holding Violet's hand. "We're all right, Levi."

"Good," Cade said. He looked at Samuel. "You good to help me with one of those boats?"

Samuel nodded. "Lead the way."

Cade turned to Bridget. "Get them ready. And see if you can find some rope. Once we get that boat in the water, we're going to need to start lowering people down."

Bridget didn't move. She was still trembling and looking at the flames.

"MOVE, damn it!" Cade used his cavalry voice, the one he'd used while applying a boot to the ass of a slacking trooper. "You don't want to burn, this is how we go."

"Okay," the terrified girl whispered, and pushed past them into the cabin. Cade could hear Violet crying.

"Come on," Cade said to Samuel. "Let's see if we can figure out how to get this damn boat from up here to down there."

As Samuel nodded, another volley of shots rang out. Samuel staggered to the left, crying out in pain. He slumped to the deck, clutching at his arm.

Cade crouched beside him. "Easy, partner," he said with a calm he didn't feel. "Where are you hit?"

"My arm," Samuel groaned. "I think it's broken."

Cade's frustration boiled over. "God damn it," Cade snarled. "That is *enough*." He ran to the rail, dropped behind it, and propped the coach gun on the splintered wood. He spotted the hoodlum who'd addressed the captain earlier and drew a bead on him. Some instinct seemed to warn the man, and he turned to face Cade. He saw the shotgun leveled at him and began backpedaling frantically. Cade fired. The shot missed. Cade took aim again, fired, missed again. He dropped down, broke the shotgun open, and reloaded. As he did, he looked behind him and saw that the second longboat was on fire. There was no way off the ship now. As if sensing their final victory, the flames roared higher.

"I'm sorry," he said softly. He was talking to Marjorie, to Bridget, to Samuel. He'd led them to this place that had become a deathtrap. He looked back up, teeth clenched. If they were going to die, he was going to take some of the bastards responsible with them. He snapped the gun closed, raised himself to look over the rail again, and took aim. The hoodlum who was clearly the leader of the group was calling out something to his soldiers. He turned back toward the ship, a smug look his broad face. He was enjoying the prospect of burning a shipful of helpless people alive. He was also presenting a target that Cade couldn't possibly miss. Cade tightened his finger on the trigger, then stopped.

The hoodlum was looking down at his own chest, a puzzled look on his face. An unfamiliar object seemed to be protruding from his body, shiny and glistening wet in the flickering torchlight. He reached up with both hands to grip the unexpected growth, but it disappeared as if it was something from a dream. Blood stained the front of the hoodlum's white shirt. He fell forward bonelessly, falling to the wharf on his face. Behind him stood a diminutive figure, dressed all in black, a hood over their face. With a careless snap of the wrist, the figure flicked the hoodlum's blood off a gleaming foot-long blade. The figure held an identical blade in the other hand. Cade couldn't see a face beneath the black hood, but there was no doubt in his mind who it was holding those blades.

The White Orchid had come.

CHAPTER SIXTY-SIX

For years afterward, Cade tried and failed to describe what he saw next. The black-clad figure moved through the crowd of hoodlums as if they were made of smoke, bobbing and weaving, sliding between and around the larger figures on the wharf, the blades in constant graceful motion. Sometimes it looked almost like a ballet, other times like a snake's mating dance. But wherever the dancer went, blood arced from slashed arteries and opened throats. Men screamed in agony or sprayed their life's blood from windpipes severed by one or another of those wicked blades.

At first, the crowd of hoodlums was shocked into immobility by the storm of bloodletting that had descended on them. Then they began to react. One raised his rifle to fire at the killer wraith moving among them. Cade staggered him with a double-barreled blast from the coach gun, then the man went down as the black-clad figure thrust a blade home into his throat. Another who'd heard Cade's shot turned his gun back toward the ship. A sudden leap forward, the flash of crossed blades, and that man fell to the planking of the wharf, his head rolling free of his body. At that terrible sight, the few hoodlums remaining broke and ran. The black figure stood for a moment, watching them run, as if deciding whether to give chase. They didn't see the wounded man behind them rising to one knee, a pistol held in one shaking hand. As he raised his hand to fire at the back of the figure in black, Cade called out a warning, the cry merging with the roar of a shotgun from beside him. The figure whirled and leaped, blades flashing, and took the man's pistol arm off at the elbow, but he was already falling, chest shattered by the shells from the coach gun in Marjorie's hand.

The figure pulled her hood back, shaking out her long hair from beneath it. She looked up at Cade, then at Marjorie standing beside him. Flicking the blades clean again, she re-sheathed them in a hidden scabbard on her back. The White Orchid's face was as lovely as Cade remembered as she stared up at the ship, her face illuminated by the glow of the fires that burned behind Cade. But there was none of the mischievousness or playfulness she'd seen before. She was as pale and lovely as a marble statue, and as cold.

More than anyone Cade had ever met, she had the killing look.

As Cade watched in amazement, The White Orchid stepped backward, crouched, then began running at full speed toward the side of the ship. As she reached the edge of the wharf, she gave a huge leap. Just as it looked to Cade as if she was about to fall into the water, she grabbed at one of the lines holding the ship to the wharf. She caught it with one hand, then the other, and began making her way hand over hand toward the rear deck.

"Who in the world *is* that?" Marjorie said from beside him.

"She works for Kwan," Cade said. "They call her The White Orchid." He ran to the spot where the line joined the vessel to lend a hand of his own, but she'd already swung aboard. They stared at each other, then Cade said, "Ah, thanks."

She didn't smile back. She was looking at Marjorie. She gave a quick bow. "Thank you. Good shot."

Marjorie nodded back. "You're welcome."

"So," Cade said, "you can talk English."

She didn't smile. "How many?" she said. "On ship."

"Five." He held up five fingers to illustrate. She nodded and strode past him. Cade followed. When she reached Samuel, she knelt down and examined his arm intently. Samuel's face was sweaty, his skin looking grayish. "Who...?" he croaked. "Where...?"

"Shhhh." The woman gently tried to lift the arm. Samuel cried out. She just as gently set it back and stood up. "He needs doctor."

"You got one handy?" Cade said. He gestured at the flames, then began coughing as a slight shift in the wind blew a choking cloud of smoke over them. "I think this is our biggest worry." The heat was so close, Cade was feeling as if his skin would blister at any second.

She shook her head. "No worry. You go soon." She went to the rail, stuck two fingers in her mouth, and gave a piercing whistle. Someone answered from the water, shouting in Chinese. She called back in a commanding voice. Cade walked to the rail and stood beside her.

On the waters of the bay, coming toward the *Marjorie Ann*, was a flotilla of small, flat-bottomed boats, each piloted by a Chinese man at the rear with a long sweep. At the front of the lead boat sat a familiar figure, a slender girl in a long gray skirt and a white blouse. Mei waved at Cade. Her face was illuminated by the flames, and Cade could make out her usual grave expression.

He waved back, then turned to say something to The White Orchid, but the woman was gone.

"That," Marjorie said, "is a very unusual young woman."

Cade nodded. "Honey, you don't know the half of it."

"I think I like her."

"Good to know. But we've got to get out of here." Cade bent over Samuel. "Come on, partner. Time to go." Samuel just groaned in pain. Cade was squatting down to try and get under him to lift him up, but he was stopped by Bridget's scream.

"Highbinders!"

CHAPTER SIXTY-SEVEN

Cade turned to look at where she was pointing. A half dozen grapnels had caught on the railing, and men in black were clambering over the rail, like pirates bent on plunder. There were seven of them, and they were as rough-looking a crew as Cade had ever seen, many with scarred faces and one with a missing eye. Cade could see hatchets and short clubs dangling from their belts, but no one drew. If Mei was with them, they must be Kwan's men. The *Boo How Doy* began shouting to each other in Chinese and quickly organized themselves into an impromptu fire brigade with buckets hauled up from the boats. Bucket after bucket was poured onto the flaming longboats, but all they could accomplish was to hold the line for the moment.

"Mr. Cade?" Mei had come aboard, hauled up by one of the *Boo How Doy*. She was breathing hard and a little damp from her crossing, but her eyes were bright with excitement.

"Little Sister," Cade said fervently, "you are a sight for sore eyes."

She nodded. "Mr. Kwan sends his regards."

"I hope to thank him personally," Cade said. "Right now, though, we need to get off this damn ship." He gestured to the group huddled on the port side of the stern house. "But we've got a child with us. And a sick woman and a man with a broken arm, and both of 'em need a doctor pronto."

Mei frowned. "What is 'pronto'?"

"Now. Right away."

"Ah." Mei raised her voice and called out to the group of *Boo How Doy* fighting the fire. A pair of them detached themselves from the bucket brigade and ran over. One was a hulking brute with a nasty scar above his brows and the other a smaller man with an eyepatch. She spoke to them quickly, gesturing at Cade and his people. There was a brief, querulous exchange which ended with Mei speaking a few sharp words. Cade thought he heard the name Kwan mentioned. Eyepatch shrugged, went to the rail, and hauled up a rope. In a twinkling, he'd fastened a makeshift lasso. He gestured at Cade.

"They will lower you down," Mei explained. "One by one."

Cade grimaced. He didn't like the idea of trusting his life and the lives of the others to this crew, but there wasn't much choice. "Okay. But get the women and the child off first."

Mei nodded and spoke to the man with the lasso. He looked surprised, but shrugged.

The operation didn't take as long as Cade had imagined. Marjorie went down first, followed by Violet. Bridget went down to another one of the boats, then Samuel, limp and unconscious but still breathing, was lowered gently into the boat with her. Cade looked over the rail to make sure everyone was situated, then turned to Mei. "Okay, Little Sister. Your turn."

As Eyepatch was fitting the lasso under her arms, the young Chinese girl regarded Cade gravely. "Mr. Cade, I must ask that you not call me that."

Cade blinked, taken aback by the request. "What? Little Sister?" He shrugged. "Okay. I don't mean anything by it."

"I know," she said. "That is why I'm asking you not to use it."

Cade shook his head. "Jesus. Okay."

When Mei was lowered down, Eyepatch hauled up the lasso and held it out. Cade shook his head. "No thanks. I'll let myself down."

The man looked puzzled, then held the lasso out again. Cade shook his head again. "I got it."

As he put one leg over the rail, reaching for one of the lines that dangled from the grapnels, Cade began to reconsider. But the amused look in the highbinder's one eye made up his mind. Awkwardly, he got into position, both hands on the rope, his feet braced against the hull. As soon as he tried to let go with one hand, he began to slide down, losing his footing and slamming against the hull. The rope began to slide between his hands, burning his palms. Cade grunted in pain and let go, falling ten feet to crash into the front of the boat just below him. The boatman looked down at him without expression as he lay stunned by the fall.

"Well?" Cade said, the words coming out as a groan of pain. "Let's get goin."

***

Tremblay looked around the crowded, noisy saloon and sipped at his whiskey. It was a fine single-malt Scotch, and very expensive, but he barely tasted it. He took out his pocket watch and looked at it, frowning. He'd expected to hear something back from Shaughnessy and his people by now. He didn't know how much longer he could stand here alone in this crowd, among the noise, the smoke, and the stink, for the sole purpose of establishing his alibi.

A buxom whore sidled up to him, breasts straining at the laces of her too-tight bodice. Her face was heavily painted, but he could still see the lines beneath. "Buy me a drink, honey?" she whispered in a voice which he supposed was meant to be alluring, but whiskey and tobacco had turned her voice into a mannish rasp.

He briefly indulged himself by imagining her as a player in one of his escapades, his hands around her throat, her eyes bulging in panic, then the knives... Something in his look made her smile fray a bit and she stepped back.

"Some other time," he said pleasantly.

"Sure, hon," she said, and moved off quickly.

Tremblay sighed. He'd done what he came here to do. A couple of rounds for the house had ensured that the bartender would remember him. He stepped out into the cool of the evening. The street here was broad and well-lit. Groups of men and a few couples strolled her and there. He spotted a cab and raised his hand. The horse plodded slowly over to him. "Take me to 128 Montgomery," he barked up to the driver without looking as he opened the door and entered. The driver, hooded and cloaked against the evening chill, just nodded. As the carriage pulled away, the driver threw back the hood, revealing the face of a strikingly beautiful Chinese woman.

The White Orchid twitched the reins to speed the horses up to a canter, shook out her long black hair, and smiled. The night was young, and it was going to be very, very long for a particular *gwai loh*.

***

"Well," Cade said, "here we are again."

Mei didn't translate. She sat off to one side of Kwan's desk, hands folded in her lap, looking down.

"Thank you kindly for all the help," Cade went on. "But I'd like to know where my friends are."

Mei didn't translate that, either. She answered on her own. "The black man—"

"Mr. Clayborne," Cade interrupted.

She looked annoyed, but corrected herself. "Mr. Clayborne is having his arm set and the rifle bullet removed."

"By a Chinese doctor?" Cade said.

Mei raised her chin and looked at him. "Does that matter?"

Cade sighed. "I guess not."

Kwan said something in Chinese. There was a brief exchange

before Mei spoke to Cade again. "The doctor says it will not be necessary to amputate the arm." She smiled thinly. "Which is more than an American doctor might say."

"You ain't wrong," Cade admitted. He grimaced as he recalled a pile of severed arms and legs piled behind a house commandeered for a field hospital after Cold Harbor. "What about Marjorie?"

"She is resting," Mei said. "She will be fine. Her daughter is with her. Everything is being done to make her comfortable, and soon Mr. Kwan will arrange for her to return home."

"Home." Cade shook his head. "That might be a problem."

Another brief conversation between Kwan and Mei ensued. "Not for very much longer."

"What do you mean? There's a dead body upstairs. I know because I killed him."

Kwan spoke. Mei listened. Then she said, "Mr. Kwan does not know what you mean. Mr. Hamrick was shot dead tonight in a brothel in the Barbary Coast."

"A…what?"

Mei went on. "Mr. Kwan extends his deepest condolences to the widow and child. As a gesture of sympathy, he has arranged for the house to be cleaned, top to bottom, knowing Mrs. Hamrick and the household would need the rest and the time to comfort one another in this difficult period of bereavement."

Cade stared across the desk at Kwan. "You son of a bitch," he said with grudging admiration.

Mei frowned. "I do not think you want me to translate that."

"No." Cade shook his head. He thought for a moment, then turned to Mei. "Tell Mr. Kwan I will be forever in his debt."

They spoke back and forth, then Mei nodded. "He says, this is true. But perhaps not forever."

"Only until he wants something from me."

She didn't speak to Kwan. "Mr. Kwan is happy to work for better relations between our people."

"I'll bet." Cade stood up. "Okay. I get it." He looked at Kwan. "But I just want you to know one thing. I won't kill for you."

Mei hesitated, then spoke. Kwan looked amused. "That will not be necessary."

"Right. He's already got someone for that."

Mei smiled. "As you say."

CHAPTER SIXTY-EIGHT

They stood side by side on the sidewalk in front of a building that had once housed a bakery. The sign painter was putting the last touches on the new sign: CADE AND CLAYBORNE. INVESTIGATIONS. PERSONAL PROTECTION.

"Sure you don't want your name first?" Cade asked. "I kinda think Clayborne and Cade rolls off the tongue a little better."

"Little late for that now," Samuel said. He grimaced as he adjusted his arm in the sling that cradled it.

"Arm still paining you?" Cade asked.

"Some. But I'm trying to stay off the laudanum."

"Good plan," Marjorie spoke up from behind them. She walked up to stand beside them as the painter began putting the brushes away. She was veiled, dressed head to toe in black. "It looks prosperous already."

"Well, we can hope," Cade said. He wanted more than anything in the world to lift that veil, see her face, kiss those lips. But she was in mourning. Officially. She'd do nothing but observe the proprieties.

"I'm not saying never, Levi," she'd told him. "But just…not right now. Not so soon after all that's happened."

And that's how they'd left it. Cade sometimes wondered if she'd been playing him, if she'd just come to him to seal his allegiance and make sure he was fully committed to her protection. But he couldn't be sure either way.

"Thanks for the loan, Missus." Samuel was saying.

"I think Mrs. Hamrick will do in future, Mr. Clayborne," she said lightly. "You're a man of business now, not a servant."

He smiled. "Then thank you, Mrs. Hamrick."

"You're quite welcome. I needed to diversify my holdings after… the recent setback. And I have a feeling about you two." She turned toward where a small black one-horse buggy waited by the curb. "By the way, Mr. Cade, I have a gift for you."

"Thank you, ma'am," he said, "but you've already done a lot for us."

She returned with a large wooden box and handed it to him. It felt heavy. "Open it."

Cade fumbled a moment with the latch, then opened the box. He stared for a moment in surprise. "This looks like…"

"It's the same make and model as your revolver. But chambered for the new cartridges. Mr. Simonson says if you drop your pistol by his establishment, he can have it converted to use the same ammunition." She smiled. "You never know when you're going to need to reload quickly."

He closed the box. "Thank you, ma'am. But hopefully, that day won't be soon."

"Yes. Hopefully. You gentlemen have a pleasant day."

Cade tipped his hat. "You too, ma'am." As she drove off, Cade turned to his partner. "Well, let's get to work."

THE END

About the Author

Born and raised in North Carolina, J.D. Rhoades has worked as a radio news reporter, club DJ, television cameraman, ad salesman, waiter, attorney, and newspaper columnist. His weekly column in North Carolina's *The Pilot* was twice named best column of the year in its division. He is the author of six novels in his acclaimed Jack Keller series: *The Devil's Right Hand*, *Good Day in Hell*, *Safe and Sound*, *Devils and Dust*, *Hellhound on My Trail*, and *Won't Back Down*, as well as *Ice Chest*, *Breaking Cover*, *Broken Shield*, and *Fortunate Son*. He lives, writes, and practices law in Carthage, NC.

Acknowledgements:

Any work dealing with 1870s San Francisco —its societal divisions, racial tension, roller-coaster economy, and decadence— is going to rely heavily on classic works such as Herbert Asbury's The Barbary Coast and Benjamin Estelle Lloyd's Lights and Shade in San Francisco, and this book is no exception. The website Sfgate.com also provided innumerable tidbits of information about Gilded Age San Francisco, as did foundsf.org and kqed.org.

The Red Boat Opera companies were an actual phenomenon, and in the 19th century they were indeed centers of the resistance to the declining and corrupt Qing dynasty. Whether or not they were also secret schools for teaching the martial art of Wing Chun is, like a lot of the history of the martial arts, a matter of dispute, legend, and occasionally total balderdash.. When there was conflict between sources, I went with the one that was most fun. I am indebted to the work of Lorretta Siuling Yeung and her MA thesis paper "Red Boat Troupes and Chinese Opera" found online at https://getd.libs.uga.edu/pdfs/yeung_loretta_s_201005_ma.pdf, as well as Ben Judkin's article "Understanding the Red Boats of the Cantonese Opera: Economics, Social Structure and Violence 1850-1950." found at https://chinesemartialstudies.com/2013/11/15/ understanding-the-red-boats-of-the-cantonese-opera-economics-social-structure-and-violence-1850-1950/

Finally, special thanks to Alexandra Sokoloff, Carolyn Ritchie and John Lovell for reading and advice on the early drafts.